1
THE FLOAT

I was floating, peaceful and weightless. Arms and legs outstretched, a human pinwheel. All I wanted to do was float forever. It felt right. This was where I was meant to be, everything was going to be okay. I was just me, without a past or a future. Even as I rose slowly towards the light, everything made sense. I didn't have a care in the world, there was nothing that I couldn't solve, no problem I couldn't handle, as I continued to rise effortlessly towards the blurry, indistinct hand that reached for me.

Breaking the surface, I spat out my mouthpiece and pulled down my mask before kicking leisurely towards the boat and the oustretched arm of my mate Dave, sunnies on, green zinc stripe down his nose. I'm not sure what he thought he was protecting as that schnozz required its own beach umbrella to escape sunburn. I guess it did save him having to sunblock the lower part of his face.

'How many you got, Lach?' he asked as he leaned down to take my string dive bag. Inside were eleven abalone of various sizes and none of them legal.

'Not enough yet,' I said as I reached for the ladder with one hand and tossed my flippers into the boat with the other. It was time for a break, to take the scuba gear off, to drag myself free of the water. As much as I love diving, being immersed and breathing air through a respirator takes a toll. Having spent most of the morning in the water after a pretty crummy night's sleep, I was bushed.

I dropped onto the deck next to my flippers and pulled off my neoprene bonnet. My body weight had returned, making my movements awkward. Getting free was a herculean task. Exhausted, I wiped my hair off my forehead and watched Dave tip my latest contribution into our secret storage tanks under the bench seats. We'd installed those compartments ourselves. The tanks would keep the abalone happy and wet until we got them back onto dry land. Mind you, I've never seen an unhappy abalone.

As Dave screwed the false bottom back in place, I munched on a banana and looked to the shore. There was a momentary glint of light from the bush but then it was gone. I watched the eucalypts for a while to be sure but there was nothing more. Probably just an empty beer bottle catching the sun. Looking back to Dave sitting on the bench seats that guarded the morning's poaching efforts, I knew that if we were ever boarded by Fishery Officers, those seats would be the first place they looked. Then again, we'd never been boarded. I looked for some wood to tap to maintain our good luck but couldn't see a splinter. Fibreglass would have to do.

We were on the ocean side of Shark Island near Port Stephens. Every time I come here to dive, I can't get over the clear waters, the great fishing, beautiful beaches and the ancient concrete toilet blocks. It's a place that few people other than retired locals and grey nomads seemed to know about. Which was fine for us, as catching a camouflaged creature that barely moves is a lot harder than it sounds. In a country where it's hard to make an honest living, a dishonest one isn't much easier.

'How many more, you reckon? Last count has it about seventy in the tank.' Dave handed me an iced coffee from the esky.

SOMETHING FOR NOTHING

ANDY MUIR

AFFIRM
press

Published by Affirm Press in 2017
28 Thistlethwaite Street, South Melbourne, VIC 3205.
www.affirmpress.com.au

National Library of Australia Cataloguing-in-Publication entry available
for this title at www.nla.gov.au.
Title: Something for Nothing / Andy Muir, author.
ISBN: 9781925344936 (paperback)

Cover design by Christa Moffitt, Christabella Designs
Typeset in Bembo 12.5/17.75 by J&M Typesetting
Proudly printed in Australia by Griffin Press

The paper this book is printed on is certified against the Forest Stewardship
Council® Standards. Griffin Press holds FSC chain of custody certification
SGS-COC-005088. FSC promotes environmentally responsible, socially
beneficial and economically viable management of the world's forests.

'Few more. An even hundred would be good,' I said as I looked at the shoreline of Tomaree National Park again. Had that flash just been sunlight glinting from a broken bottle or was it a pair of binoculars? Surveying the edges of Fingal Bay, I heard Dave smacking his lips before declaring iced coffee to be the nectar of the gods.

If anyone was on shore looking at us, all they'd see would be two blokes in a boat out for a spot of fishing. There'd be me: average build, average height, lean like a toned whippet, clambering in and out of the water in my scuba gear. Then there'd be the lanky Dave, sporting the extra weight of a retired footballer. While I was in the water, he'd spend time with rod and line over the side, hoping for something more than a march fly to bite as he applied another layer of zinc to his nose.

Dave took another long pull from his drink. 'I like the sound of an even hundred, Lachie-oh. Time for a new locale?'

When we had a huge ocean of possible places to find abalone, why stay in the one spot? I shifted my dive belt and leaned back onto my dive tanks, letting the sun warm my salty skin as Dave opened the throttles on his Mercruiser engines. On such a pearler of a day, with the roaring high-horsepower engines ripping through the water and leaving a white funnel of foaming tail behind us, life was good.

Lying on the deck, eyes shut, I drifted off into that place somewhere between sleep and waking, enjoying the prickle of salt drying on my skin. After the time spent underwater, my body thawed as the sun's warmth crept into my limbs and chest. I know sunbaking is now a capital offence unless you're slathered in sunscreen but the simple pleasure is as hard to quit as smoking. Lying there, eyes closed, I felt my muscle memory take control, convincing my mind that I was still underwater, neutrally buoyant once more.

Which was when we heard the thud.

'What the hell was that? You knock your tanks over?' Dave called, slamming the throttles into neutral and ducking into the small forward cabin to see if we'd been holed.

Lifting myself from the deck, I peered over the side to look for something in the wake or, heaven forbid, sticking half-in, half-out of the fibreglass hull. I couldn't see anything. Dave emerged from the small cabin looking just as puzzled.

'You see anything, captain?'

He shook his head and pointed a thumb at the water. 'Can you *tsck-tsck*, over the side? Take a squizz?'

Donning my mask and snorkel, I rolled my eyes before dropping backwards into the briny blue. Now that I'd dried out in the sunshine, the water felt much colder. I rose to the surface, blowing air through the snorkel whale-like to clear the pipe of water. Breathing the slow, rhythmical, in-out of the ocean swimmer, I swam around the boat looking for any damage and what might have caused it.

Except there wasn't any damage, only a few large fish Dave would have loved to drop a line on. When I drifted around to the back of the boat, I noticed something just below the water surface a short distance behind us. It was a rectangle – maybe a suitcase? Except suitcases don't normally come with a long weighted anchor hanging straight down beneath them. Whatever it was, it was not natural. Surfacing, I spat the snorkel from my mouth and looked up at Dave now hanging over the back of the boat, a sun halo silhouette.

'Anything?'

When I assured him there was nothing wrong with the boat he clutched his chest and breathed a thank you to the heavens.

'But I think I saw what we hit. Gonna go take a look.'

Forcing the snorkel back into my mouth, I gave a salute and duck-dived towards the shape still hanging there in the blue. Judging by the tiny barnacles and small growths of weed that had decided the object was a great place to call home, this thing had been in the water for some time. In all my years underwater, I'd never seen anything like it.

I grabbed the rope hanging below the black plastic-wrapped rectangle. There was some sort of weight wrapped in duct tape at the end of it. As I made my way back to the boat, my trophy followed diligently, a fat kid on a fun run – somewhat of a drag but not giving up.

I held up the weird anchor for Dave to hook the gaff into. Hefting the package up out of the water into the boat was tough, but we managed it. Then I hauled myself up, colder and even more tired than the first time.

'What the bejabbers is that?' asked Dave, hands on hips, looking at the encrusted rectangle dripping on the deck.

'Whatever it is, I don't think the person who lost it is gonna be happy about it,' I said, tapping a knuckle on the shrink-wrapped plastic. It wasn't hollow.

'Open it, ya big girl. Ever heard of salvage? Finders keepers.' Dave was very insistent, as excited at the discovery as I was alarmed.

Pulling my dive knife out, I cut into the package and struck a thin skin of aluminium. I cleared more of the plastic away and pressed the point of my knife against the aluminium, feeling the metal resist before it gave way. Twisting the knife slightly, I pushed the blade further in. It came back up covered in a slightly dirty brown powder that, if found anywhere else, you'd think was wholemeal flour.

Dave leaned on my shoulder for a closer look at the powder. 'What is it? Drugs? Is it drugs?'

'Course it's drugs. What else floats in the ocean like this?'

'Drugs,' he said, pausing to contemplate what that meant before going on. 'Coke? You reckon it's coke?'

Shaking my head, I looked at the tip of my blade from every angle. 'Nope. Wrong colour.'

Dave was not keeping up.

'It's heroin,' I said.

'How do you know?'

'I'm guessing. Only two things are gonna be packed up like this and it's the wrong colour for one of them.'

'From where? Afghanistan? Asia?'

'How am I supposed to know?'

'You seem to be a walking Wikipedia on something I wasn't expecting you to know anything about.'

But neither of us needed the internet to know that if the case was full as a goog of this tan powder, then what we had in front of us was a fortune.

Dave grinned. 'Guess that means no more poaching abalone?'

'We're tipping it over the side,' I said.

'What?'

The more I looked at it, the more I wanted no part of it. Where Dave saw dollar signs, all I could think of was how much someone who lost something like this was going to want it back. Neptune wasn't going to come hunting for two blokes who'd pinched a bag of undersized shellfish from his watery depths, but a drug dealer missing several kilos of imported powder? This was a package full of trouble.

'Mate,' Dave said, 'that is a lot of money. Money we could both use.'

Looking from Dave and his zinc-striped schnozz to the dripping package, I knew that bundle was going over the side. As I began to hoist it up onto the gunwale, Dave grabbed my arm.

'Please, Lach. Come on. Think of me boys. This, it's like we've won the lotto without buying a ticket.'

That was a new one. As I looked at the package perched on the gunwale, ready to head back to a watery grave, Dave's fever began to catch.

'That is a lot of money,' I said, thinking about the gambling debt I was struggling to pay with our abalone hauls.

Dave lowered his sunglasses and looked over the rims.

'But I'm not selling it. You want it, you deal with it.' Even as I said it, I knew that wasn't how it would play out. Dave knew nothing about the world he wanted a part of.

'Sweet. And we'll split it. We found it together, so fifty-fifty, down the line. Fair's fair,' Dave said.

Letting the bundle drop back to the deck, I shook Dave's hand, setting him off on a little happy dance back to the wheel. I wanted to share his enthusiasm. I wanted to feel all happy and clappy, ecstatic and *yes, I'm a winner.* Except I came to Newcastle to stay under the radar. Anonymity is tricky to pull off. Shopping around a trunk of drugs was going to draw the kind of attention I'd worked so hard to avoid. Even with the Las Vegas-sized dollar signs flashing in my mind, I wondered if they were going to be enough to risk all that.

Dave's dancing at the wheel like he was auditioning for the lead in *A Chorus Line* seemed to say it was. Looking back to the national park shoreline, I hoped he was right.

2
THE SENSIBLE COURSE OF ACTION

We travelled back from Port Stephens to Dave's place in silence.

Every once in a while Dave would attempt to say something but the words would trail off before a proper sentence formed. As for me, I didn't feel like talking. So we sat, thinking our own private thoughts, confident the other was also preoccupied with what was hidden under a blanket in the boat bouncing on the trailer behind us.

Hanging on to the drugs was a risk. Trying to get rid of them could be an even bigger one. In the past I'd been willing to take risks and push things as far as I could. I'd slipped occasionally and let situations get out of hand, but that was the exception, not the rule. It was one of those slip-ups that saw me start poaching abalone. I lost big and then broke the number one rule by accepting a loan from the house to try to win back my losses. That debt was crippling.

Agonising over what to do about it, I'd developed a phantom toothache that sent me to the dentist. While flicking through one of the old mags that every waiting room collects, I came across an article about a poacher who had racked up some serious coin and led the authorities on a merry dance. Like all good crooks he got pinched in the end, but he managed to keep a lot of his earnings, which was fairly incredible – especially as he was raking in seven figures from the slimy shellfish. Not only did my teeth get a clean bill of health that day but I'd also found a way to help clear my debt. I even knew a buyer for the slimy, leathery, cleverly camouflaged abalone. I was pretty sure he'd be keen to get his hands on any I could find. So, the moral? Lose big and you, too, could be taking a dip over the side, looking to fill a bag with abalone.

Dave's involvement in our little illegal fishing operation was simpler: he was the one with a boat. That was about all Dave did have. Once upon a time, he'd been a primary school teacher, then his marriage collapsed for all those reasons that marriages do. Lost like so many are after a breakup, Dave opted to join the mining escapade that had taken the nation by storm. Signing on to drive big trucks on big twelve-hour shifts, up and down the big open-cut valleys, he earned big bucks that went on big toys and big fun as he sorted himself out. Once all the short-term girlfriends and casual flings were out of his system, his big pay packet started heading to his kids and the plans for their futures. Thankfully, he kept a couple of his toys, including his Bertram 20: the boat he'd lovingly refurbished, which was perfect for what we were doing. I also enjoyed how the boat reminded me of *Gilligan's Island*. So with the assistance of Dave and his Bertram 20, I had started to whittle away my debt. For me, it was necessity. For Dave, though, it was simple greed.

Now, with the package laid out on Dave's kitchen table, neither of us said a thing as we slowly set about unwrapping it properly.

The outer layer was black plastic, heat-sealed, while the layer under that was a thin piece of aluminium sheeting. Strapped onto the package were several simple buoyancy tanks made of two-litre plastic bottles, the kind you get engine oil in. Whoever had dumped this had a plan, and that plan was serious – even if they were yet to realise that it had gone pear-shaped.

Cracking open the aluminium revealed three layers of bricks, individually wrapped in plastic before being entombed in brown packing tape. Each was about the size of a large book, a fat James A. Michener type or Stephen King hardcover that exhausts your arms when you try to read it late at night. Apart from the one I'd stabbed earlier, the bricks were identical, right down to the dragon logo stamped on the front.

Dave opened another beer and drained it without taking his eyes from the haul. 'Jesus,' was his only comment.

Taking a deep breath to think, I picked up the end of the anchor that had been attached to the case and started to pull at the waterproofing. Cutting into it revealed a plastic object that looked like a bulky mobile phone and was roughly the same size.

'That a distress beacon?' asked Dave.

I dropped it like a hot coal. If it was a beacon, the owners of the package could be driving up the street to Dave's right now.

Dave took a different approach, picking the object up to study it closely. 'Yeah. That's a locator. But it's on the fritz. Must've rooted it setting it to a different frequency.'

'Why?'

'Why? Cos if they didn't, every rescue boat and aircraft on the east coast would have zeroed in on this the minute it was activated, thinking it was some backyard sailor gone overboard. That's why. But better safe than sorry.' Picking up the knife and a hammer he had pulled out earlier to help with the unpacking, he tapped the knife tip into the unit, splitting it wide open. He dropped the pieces onto his slate floor before slamming the hammer into each part. There was no way it was going to be sending a signal to anyone now.

'So what do we do with it now, Lachie?'

As I shrugged, Dave picked up his empty beer can and waggled it in my direction. Dutifully, I went to the fridge and pulled out another two beers.

'Thanketh you very much, good sir. And?'

Gulping my drink, I gave Dave a look that said, 'And what?'

'What do we do with this now? It's sure as fuck not staying here.'

I might have given the impression I was the brains of this operation but at this point I was all out of ideas. The normal response would be to hand it in to the cops but, as I said, having to explain how I found it could be a problem. As would why we'd unwrapped it.

Destroying it still seemed like a possible solution. Not sure how you get rid of narcotics. If you bury it in the ground, does it disappear? Or will every living thing that passes the spot run the risk of an overdose? I couldn't speak for Dave, but putting all the fidos, cats and kittens – not to mention the birds – in Newcastle at risk was not something I wanted on my conscience. Which left one option, and Dave was the one to voice it.

'It's the only choice, Lach. There's no other thing for it.'

I stood blankly, not wanting to admit that I knew what he was saying.

'Lach? Y'know anyone who'd be interested?'

'How do we sell it, Dave? It's not like you just look drug dealers up in the Yellow Pages! And I told you I didn't want anything to do with this. So how does that make me the one selling it?'

Dave looked horrified. 'Lachie Munro, you selfish prick. I'm a primary school teacher. I drive mining trucks. I don't know how to sell drugs.'

'You *were* a primary school teacher. *Were*, Dave! You're not a primary teacher anymore. You drive mining trucks. You're a truck driver.'

'But if I want to go back to the teaching profession when the mining boom ends – and it will end – how can I do that if I've been selling drugs? I don't know how to sell drugs.'

'Y'think I do?'

Unfortunately, I actually do know how to sell drugs. Dave didn't know that though. I'd never shared with him my little high school run-in with the law for selling some weed. Nothing major, just a little bit to a friend whose mum found it and hauled him before the principal, who called in the cops and yada yada yada. Long story short, I escaped a recorded conviction with a good behaviour bond. My mother would never let me forget it, making me promise not to turn out like my father. My surname, Munro, is her maiden name – her idea to help keep away my old man's reputation. I'd slipped a few times and gotten in trouble but that promise I made to her was serious. It was the reason I was now living in Newcastle.

So yes, I have form, but that in no way makes me a criminal, and it certainly doesn't make a drug dealer. Besides which, international drug cartels and distribution networks are on a whole other level to selling a bit of weed to schoolmates.

'So we what?' asked Dave. 'Burn it? Bury it? Flush it? Leave it on the nature strip with a sign – free to a good home? That is a lot of money to wave goodbye to.'

I didn't know what to say. Laid out on that kitchen table were enough bundles to set me up for at least this life. The idea of just walking away was rapidly fading.

'Dave, we sleep on it. We stash it in one of the cupboards, hide it until you make a decision.'

'Me? What happened to "we", partner?'

'You not hear me earlier? I'm not selling this. You want it, you deal with it.'

'But I might fuck it up.' Dave sucked on his beer, letting that reality sink in with the alcohol.

He had a point. It didn't matter who did the deal, we were in this together. If one of us went down, the other was going to follow.

'So, ah, if I'm the one carrying the most risk here,' Dave said, thinking aloud, 'the whole fifty-fifty, I think we need to take another look.'

'No. Deal's a deal. Equal pay. Equal risk.'

'Yeah, but –'

'No buts, Dave. We shook on it.'

'Yeah, but the stuff is here …'

I told him to get over it. We were going to sleep on it and come to the problem fresh in a day or so. Begrudgingly, Dave agreed, and we set about packing the bricks in an empty VB carton. The carton got stashed in the bottom of a wardrobe in the second bedroom. A few old blankets on top for good measure and any burglar worth their salt would know straightaway that something valuable was hidden there.

'Just forget they're even there until we work something out, mate,' I said, not sure why I was sounding so confident.

'I know. I trust you. You always come good. Just, me kids are coming in a couple of days. Don't want them in the same place as ...' He pointed a knobbly thumb at the VB carton.

I left Dave to mull over his future as he washed down his boat and flushed the engine in an old bin full of fresh water. Sometimes the best distraction is a mindless chore. Catching a glimpse of him sucking on another stubby, hose in hand spraying the hull, I suddenly craved a bit of mindless distraction of my own.

Knowing the next ferry to Newcastle was leaving soon, I hurried to Stockton Wharf, marvelling at how quickly a day could change. If the tide had been slightly different. If we'd been delayed at any point. If I hadn't been quite so keen to see what we'd hit. The ifs kept on coming as I boarded the ferry and found a seat for the three-minute journey across the shipping channel to the rest of Newcastle. Sitting there, the golden sunlight bathing the buildings plastered over the hills, I realised that somehow, despite my intentions, Dave had managed to handball the problem hidden in the VB carton to me.

By the time I stepped off the ferry on my side of the waterfront, I was miffed. I knew it was the most sensible course of action, but trusting Dave was trouble. We should have dumped the stuff back over the side. Now we actually had to do something about it. It's one thing to say, yep, we'll sell it, and a completely different bag to actually do it. Was it too late to get rid of the drugs? Sell or destroy? Drugs killed people. It was also making other people rich. I wasn't the one who imported it. It wasn't like I'd set out to get involved.

For better or worse, it was now too late to back out. Couldn't even surrender it to the local coppers: 'Hello, constables, I found this while poaching abalone and I ...'

The abalone! I'd forgotten the suckers and left them sitting in the tanks on Dave's boat.

Pulling out my mobile to call Dave, all I got was his stupid message bank. Probably face-down in the boat or snoring in front of the television. I left a message and then decided I'd better pay a visit to Billy Wong and tell him I had some abs that I could deliver tomorrow. What's a day for a bag of abalone, anyway?

And then an idea tickled the back of my brain. I might already have the right man, one who would let me kill two birds with one abalone.

3
BILLY WONG

'Lachie, long time, buddy.'

Billy wiped his hands on a tea towel that hung from his belt as I stepped into the kitchen from the staff entrance. Despite my reservations, I shook his hand. Around Billy you never really relax – you just do as you're told.

'Usual? Or you want a drink?' he asked, ushering me through to the dining room.

'Tea would be good. Been a big arvo.' I blew out my cheeks as I patted my stomach for emphasis.

Wong's Chinese Restaurant is completely old-school, serving the brightest fluorescent sweet and sour sauce you've ever seen – bright enough to distract you from the faux Chinese pictures on the walls, and the keyhole-shaped doorways and windows, all painted with layer upon layer of red paint. I know because I painted them. When not poaching abalone, I'm a house painter.

Despite the décor, the food at Wong's was good, popular and cheap. Nothing better after a few beers than a serve of their famous fried rice and a plate of the best spring rolls in Newcastle. In the fancy neighbourhoods, it was all Thai, Vietnamese and whatever else was fashionable that year, but Billy Wong's just kept on going. Although, like the Phantom in the deepest jungles of Africa, there had been many Billy Wongs. The current Billy Wong – who in an odd quirk was actually named Billy Wong, unlike the previous owner, Charlie Ho – took over the place and decided the restaurant needed a lick of paint to freshen things up. Which is how we met. I don't ask too many questions but I have a strong feeling that Billy actually won the place in a bet. Gambling is where Billy really makes his money. Upstairs in the function rooms, the lazy Susans in the middle of the tables turn for games of Mahjong that have no end under the guise of the Newcastle Chinese Social Club.

The social club was where I met my downfall. The thing about trades is that there is still a lot of black money: you get paid a bit on the side, or maybe you do a discount job for cash. That money can't go in the bank, and you have to be very careful how you spend it. So it becomes play money. Following one such job, after eating my fill and having far too many beers, I found myself drawn upstairs, lured with some gently encouraging words from Billy himself and a wad of cash that burned in my pocket.

I had a good couple of games and got hooked. It seemed so easy. Then I started to lose large sums. With cash in my pocket that needed to be spent, this wasn't much of a problem. It was Billy's kindly offer to spot me in the early hours of the morning as I attempted to win back what I'd lost that gave me my gambling debt. Once you've been hustled by someone using their pongs and kongs and Heavenly Winds, you know you've been hustled by the best.

'Fried rice and jasmine tea. Food of champions.' Billy had returned with my food and was about to sit down when I changed my mind.

'Maybe a beer wouldn't be a bad thing,' I said as I started to eat.

Rolling his eyes, Billy said something in Mandarin that

I'm positive was not polite. Returning with two bottles of Vietnamese beer, he smiled when he saw how much had already left the plate.

'So things good, Billy?' Even if they weren't, Billy wouldn't tell me. 'Interested in some seafood?'

Billy cocked an eyebrow at me. Seafood was our code. Not a very clever one, but then again, we were hardly high-end crooks being listened to by police monitors. In fact, the only other person in the restaurant was an old guy who looked like he'd escaped from his retirement home and was about to fall asleep in his beef and black bean. Most of the customers at Billy Wong's were takeaways or there for the upstairs Dragons.

Grinning, Billy clapped a hand on my forearm and gave it a shake that was anything but friendly. 'Mate, 'bout bloody time you got back in the water. Stocks are low, y'know.'

Not only was Billy the cause of my debt, he was also my saviour. He was the guy who bought my abalone. Legally, you can collect two of the regulation size in abalone season. When I went, I was collecting a lot more, generally about fifty times more, and most of them smaller than legal. A day's work on the seafloor earned me thirty to fifty bucks a kilo. Once you knew where to look, catching the things was relatively easy, just a matter of swimming along and collecting them. Especially in a marine reserve like the one north of Newie. It's a shame that abalone like cold water though. The best abalone comes from Tassie. The suckers love that cold, clean water, two things the ocean around Newcastle loses points on.

All that stuff, abalone, lobsters, oysters, they used to be poor man's food; the poor would go to the beach and fish up a feed. Now, they were seen as rich man's tucker, only for special occasions in a fancy restaurant. The fishing rights were harder to get so poachers like me picked up the slack. And I was just a small operator. I'd heard of a guy in Victoria making huge amounts shipping the stuff overseas to Singapore and Hong Kong. To make that kind of cash, the guy must have been one permanently waterlogged wrinkle.

In the restaurant, there was a lightly aerated tank that held some large abalone grazing on a field of green. These were just for show. What the customers got when they ordered were the undersized ones I collected. My smaller abalone would go into a secret tank before heading into the kitchen when a customer placed an order. The dish wasn't that popular with anyone but the gamblers upstairs, who sometimes ordered a plate for stamina or luck. Why else would you eat the rubbery things?

'Lachie, a delivery would be appreciated.'

As we clinked cups of jasmine tea to seal the deal, Billy's mobile rang. Taking the call, he left me to my meal and to work out how to ask him my next question – if he might know someone interested in purchasing some Class A narcotics. Gambling tends to bring out the worst in people; maybe someone he knew was in that line of work. But then how do you drop that bombshell into someone's lap? Which is worse: that they'll dob you in or that they'll take offence at being seen as a potential drug dealer? How do you put it? Is it, 'Billy, know any heroin dealers looking for a cheap couple of kilos?' It's not really a polite conversation opener. For a start, you're making some very big assumptions about the company they like to keep.

When my plate was clean and the teapot and bottle of beer empty, I still wasn't sure how I was going to ask Billy.

Stretching to see if there was a kink in my belly that could squeeze in a little more fried rice, I headed for the bathroom.

Standing at the urinal, I could see out into the delivery space where Billy was pacing with his mobile and a cigarette. I couldn't hear what he was saying, but from his wild arm movements he didn't look happy. It summed up my experience of Newcastle – all smiles on the outside but something dark underneath that you only catch a glimpse of every now and again. Looking at the basin and empty soap dispenser, I decided skipping the wash was the more hygienic option.

By the time I was back in the restaurant, Billy had returned. He was still agitated. Something was bothering him, despite the beaming smile. It was a bit odd but, then again, if you worried about everyone who was on edge and anxious, well, you could lose a whole day.

'You right, Billy?' I asked, not sitting down.

'Bit of a hiccup last week. One of my new cooks went missing.'

'Missing? Like *missing* missing? Or just missing?'

'Like fifty bucks in the gutter. Gone. No note, nothing. I was busy before, real busy with him gone. When you think you make a delivery?'

I told him I'd be back the next day. We walked through the kitchen, the cooks and staff ignoring us. Billy held the door open for me. As I passed him, he lit another cigarette and inhaled deeply. He looked at the burning end and then flicked the barely started ciggie past my shoulder into the stained concrete backyard. It could have been intimidation; it could have just been Billy.

'Tomorrow.'

'Yeah, yeah, tomorrow.'

'Sure you not want a ...' He pointed a thumb upwards, a big grin on his dial. 'Quick game?'

'Another time, Billy.' There was no way I was getting near those Mahjong tables again and Billy knew it. Didn't mean he was ever going to let up trying. He pulled the kitchen door closed behind me with a chuckle.

Maybe when I dropped off the abalone I'd be able to ask him about the drugs. Unlike the abalone, those packages weren't going to go off. There was plenty of time to work out the best way to ask if he knew any drug dealers or was looking to branch out himself.

Besides which, the night air was growing cool, and tomorrow I had to go to work.

4
AMBERGRIS

Monday. No one likes Mondays.

At least the job was painting Nobbys Surf Life Saving Pavilion. The pavilion, situated just under Fort Scratchley on the edge of Nobbys Beach, has been around since the 1920s. Who Nobby was I've no idea, but the old-style French windows all around his pavilion were a bugger to paint. I have no idea how my boss, Muzz, got the contract. But it made a change from the boxy apartments we usually did.

In Newcastle, painting apartments is the bread and butter, the easy money. You paint them once before they go on the market, then paint them again for the new owners. Often in the very same colours – maybe a shade darker or lighter, but off-white is still off-white. So the yellowy cream and sea-green highlights we were slapping about the pavilion were a colour holiday. As was working right on the beach. Being outside by the sand and water as you prep and paint, the wind blowing the smell of oil, acrylic and the dust away as you catch some sun? Pure bonus. The sea breeze seemed to clear years of paint and gunk I'd inhaled or splattered about my face holes while making tired apartments look schmick. Bliss.

I'd spent the morning prepping gutters and painting fascia boards. Those tasks gave me a prime view over the beach and surf. I think all of us working on the building were going slow. We'd tried to make this job last as long as possible but we all knew it was on the home straight. Who wanted to go back to boring old apartments?

Out along the breakwater towards the lighthouse I could see a growing flock of seagulls pestering something near the water's edge. Watching those birds flying up and down was like seeing ambulance lights as you drive along the freeway. You have to look, if only to kill the curiosity. So come morning tea, I took my burnt and bitter takeaway coffee along with a ham, cheese and tomato white-bread sandwich and headed for the birds.

'Where you goin'?' asked Maxie, the pint-sized apprentice.

'Walk,' I said.

'I'll come too.'

'You finished that sanding?' I said loud enough for Muzz to hear.

'You not finished? Jesus! What I bloody pay you skips for?' Muzz marched over to check Maxie's work. Our boss, Muzz – Mustafa, a Turk whose real name was Tom (a long story for another time) – always sounded gruff, but he was solid. Maxie's sanding was all fine, but razzin' on the apprentice allowed me to head off on my own as another lesson in surface prep was delivered.

A few minutes' walk along the breakwater had me close enough to hit the beach to see what the sea had vomited up. The seagulls were still wheeling and diving as I stepped off the gravel path onto the soft sand. Whatever it was had to be good to keep them there.

Drawing closer, my nostrils detected something that was far from good. I'd recently listened to a podcast about strange things in nature and was secretly hoping that what I was smelling was ambergris. That's the fancy name for whale vomit. The list of things whale spew goes into is amazing.

That lingering scent of expensive French perfume? You can thank the whale who ate a few million or so dodgy krill last month. Finding some ambergris would entitle me to a nice lump sum. Not that I'd ever heard of anyone in Newcastle picking up a chunk of ambergris, even though the whole coast is one giant whale mecca.

Still gripping my sandwich, I took one last swig of horrible coffee before tipping it out and crushing the cup to shove it into my white overalls. With the dry sand swallowing my feet before I hit the wet stuff, I was thinking that maybe this was my lucky day – that I was going to score a lump of whale vomit. A find like that was worth some sand in my work boots and a bombing of seagull poo as I shooed them caw-cawing back into the air.

The odd pasty shape on the wet sand could have been ambergris. Certainly looked like it'd been thrown up. So, thinking how big my pay cheque would be, I picked up a waterlogged stick from the sand as I came closer to the object. Something in the back of my mind was saying turn around. Never one to listen to what anyone tells me to do, especially my own subconscious, I kept on. Curiosity killed the cat like video killed the radio star.

If someone had told me to picture a torso with legs, arms and head removed, this slab would not have been what I imagined. I blame television. It's shown us so many bodies and injuries, and all of them bloody and fleshy. To see an actual dead body – it just didn't look real. We all forget that humans, when cut, are no different from the contents of a butcher's display fridge: for the most part they're red and bloody, often gristly with a chance of bone. This one had no red in sight though. Just a bloodless haunch of pork, more Christmas ham than rump steak, although still impossible to confuse with ambergris.

We don't normally have a heave at the butcher's. Not that I heaved. I was transfixed, unable to understand what was before me. How does this happen? How does someone leave a torso on Nobbys Beach? It's not like a pair of goggles or a towel. If you've ever been to the beach and spotted a dead fish on the high-water mark, or the body of a sea lion bloated and smelling like an overflowing rubbish bin on a summer's day, this was nothing like that.

I crouched down and used my stick to poke at the lump, but all my prodding did was shove the thing closer to the water. As the sea water foamed about the pale lump's edges, I tried and failed to convince myself that I was staring at an old sea lion or shark-gnawed dolphin. This was definitely the remains of a human torso. The flesh was pale, bloodless, and the nipples pointed skywards, two battery terminals waiting to be connected to zap life into the large dragon tattoo inked into the skin. A tiny crab scuttled for freedom from what had been the neck.

Which had me wondering – where the bloody hell was the rest of him?

The sound of Maxie vomiting his breakfast onto the sand behind me stopped any further ponderings.

'Jesus. That's a –' He vomited again.

'You okay, Maxie?' I didn't look to check, unable to take my eyes from the horror barely a stick's poke away from me.

Maxie put a hand on my shoulder for support as his other smeared his mouth clean on his sleeve. He was now unable to stop looking, too, his squeamishness giving way to horrified curiosity.

Finding a dead body on your morning smoko was not part of any normal day for a house painter.

'Guess you better call it in, Maxie. Got your phone?'

Still without looking away, Maxie had his mobile out and ready to call. 'Who do you call about a body?'

He had me there. But seeing it was clearly not natural causes, I guessed that the police might be interested.

'Yeah, right. Sure thing, Lach. Jesus. Duh!'

As he dialled, I stood up, leaving my stick in the sand, one end still touching the dead flesh. I went to brush the sand from my hands and realised I was still holding the remains of my sandwich. My appetite very much diminished, I tossed it to the water's edge where the seagulls dived and squawked until one greedy guts carried the whole thing off for himself. Watching the bird struggle into the air with his bounty, I noticed the dark clouds of a summer storm gathering on the horizon.

I looked back to the lump of human flesh and wondered who it was. This was a sick crime, intended as a serious warning or an extreme punishment. Either way, chopping up a body is not your run-of-the-mill crime of passion. This lump of what could pass for pork had done something bad either personally or through association. My mind spun with possibilities.

'Cops are coming. Said not to leave.' Maxie took another long look at the thing on the sand. Over his shoulder I saw another problem heading our way: Muzz striding down from the breakwater.

'What is it? Dead sea lion? Stop playing with it, you poofters. Get back to work!'

I kicked at the stick, watching sand spill off the large flayed stumps. Odd pieces of flesh wriggled with the feasting of tiny critters, reminding me of bonito flakes waving on top of agedashi tofu.

Now standing beside Maxie, Muzz was horrified to realise it was no sea lion. And I'm pretty sure he's never had agedashi tofu either.

'Bloody Jesus. Why you have to go find that? We got work to do. Christ, we gonna be stuck here for ages.'

He already had his mobile out as he turned and walked back towards the pavilion, arms waving to express his frustrations with the development. I understood the feeling. In the space of twenty-four hours, after five years without even a speeding ticket, I now knew of a cupboard full of drugs and was about to talk to the police about finding a dismembered body.

Stay low, stay out of trouble and keep my past to myself. That was the under-the-radar existence I'd worked hard to cultivate. No one in Newcastle knew my past. But once the coppers started asking questions and worked out who my father was, the jacks would never let up. Which also meant the package now really had to find a buyer. That cash might be the only chance I'd have at escape, if it came to it. If I needed to start again.

'Maxie?'

He looked at me and then quickly averted his eyes to the heavens to avoid looking at the body.

'Help out a mate and tell the cops you found this, okay?'

Seeing him agree, I looked out to sea, past the torso to the developing storm on the horizon. I really hoped that storm wasn't some omen.

5
RIGHT CROSS

'So you found it?'

Glaring at Maxie, who was sheepishly avoiding looking at me as he headed for Muzz up on the breakwater, I looked back at the detective. He was writing in his police-issued notebook with a green pen, covering the pages with a scrawl I'm not sure even he'd be able to decipher when he went to the notes again. He'd introduced himself as Detective Sergeant Jon Baxter. He was a little shorter than me, wearing an unpressed shirt under a cheap dark suit. He smelled of coffee and ambition.

'I found the ...' The word 'torso' stuck in my throat. Just didn't seem right to refer to it that way.

The detective took the hesitation to mean I was about to throw up. 'You good? Need a minute?'

'No. Just struggling to work out the right words. Y'know, for what to call it.'

He glanced at the torso lying under a black tarpaulin, surrounded by police tape and the swarming forensics team, before looking back at me in silent agreement. 'It's easier to refer to them as the deceased. It's a distance thing. Helps.'

Seems cops speak in real life just like they do on the news.

'Anyways, sooner we get this filled in, sooner you can get out of here. Lachlan, was it?'

So we continued asking and answering each other's questions while I watched the deceased being documented in minute detail. All the while the storm clouds built on the horizon and blew themselves out to return just that little bit blacker. Occasionally lightning would illuminate the clouds, adding to the electricity in the air as a second detective joined us from where she had been supervising the forensics. Baxter introduced her as his partner, Detective Shannae O'Keefe. I was stuck on how unusually tall she was as Baxter continued talking.

'Any plans to leave town, best cancel them. Need you to stay contactable for a few days. We might have some more questions to ask. Usual drill. If you have to leave, just let us know down at the station.'

'Sounds like bail.'

'Except you're not under arrest. So quite different.' He said it with a smile but, like all cops, it had that edge that came with the blue suit of truth, the power of the badge.

'I'll let you know then, Detective Baxter.'

'Detective Sergeant.'

'Sorry?'

'I'm Detective *Sergeant* Baxter. Ask at the station for Detective Baxter, no one'll know who you want.'

'There more than one Baxter? Staff room fridge must be confusing.'

'No. Only him,' said O'Keefe wearily.

Baxter couldn't help himself. That flash of power again as he grinned at me before walking back down the beach to his colleagues.

I headed for the breakwater pathway to where Muzz and Maxie were waiting. Muzz had smoked through a pouch of tobacco, the remnants of which were squashed into the gravel about his feet. Maxie, on the other hand, seemed close to wearing out the soles of his work boots, carving into the gravel what could pass for a bowler's run-up at a Test match.

'Guess that's the day done, Muzz,' I said.

Muzz nodded, resigned but in full agreement. 'Look at my hands. Day's a write-off. You imagine me cutting in with these hands. Might as well ask Maxie to do it. I'm toast for the rest of the day, so we pack up, find a bar quick split.'

Sure enough, his hands were shaking ever so slightly. Could have been the ciggies and the strong coffees he drank as much as the shock. But a drink and an early mark were always a good option.

'Give us a break,' Maxie arced up. 'I saw a dead man today. I'm never going to the beach again. I'm scarred for life. I'll probably need therapy. Bet that's not covered by worker's comp.'

He did look shaken up. Normally joking and full of weird stories about his adventures backpacking, he was looking mighty pale.

'You right, Maxie?' Without waiting for his answer, I held out some chewing gum. 'Here, chew this. Might help.'

Accepting the gum with a solemn nod, Maxie took a deep breath. 'Death gets me down,' was his profound declaration.

On the other side of the beach, a woman approached the forensic officers Baxter and O'Keefe were talking to. She wasn't a cop but she walked with the impatience of someone with better things to be doing. I watched her shake Baxter's hand before approaching the tarpaulin hiding the torso. Another man wearing the same uniform stayed back, grinning. Baxter seemed confused. I was captivated.

What is it that makes you notice someone? She was too far away to see anything other than she was short like her dark hair, which was cut into a bob. Even from a distance, her plain khaki utility pants and jumper couldn't hide how fit she was. From what I could see, I liked the view.

As I watched her bend down and lift the edge of the tarp, she gave a loud exclamation that sent her back on her heels. Then she was straight back up, heading for her guffawing colleague. Clearly, she had been the butt of a joke and that made me want to rush to her defence. But from the look of it, she didn't need anyone's assistance, as she got right in the joker's face. He seemed the sort who liked telling women that chicks can't take a joke, peppering his sentences with 'love', 'darling' and maybe a pat on the arse for emphasis. She got in first and decked him with a cobra strike of a right cross.

'Booyah! Smack down,' said Maxie. 'What d'you reckon that was about?'

'No idea,' I said, watching Baxter's attempt to pull the woman back from looming over her colleague on the sand. She was giving the joker a right bollocking, stabbing an angry finger at his chest like a one-fingered typist. When Baxter finally separated them, the target dusted himself off. He must have been a slow learner. As he started to say something else, Detective O'Keefe stepped in and gave him his second dressing-down.

'Great Northern?' asked Maxie. None of us had any objections as the argument on the beach continued, the woman flicking her right hand as if the pain from the punch would fly off onto the sand.

6
THE GREAT NORTHERN

It was a short trip to the Great Northern, a proud old pub standing sentinel on the intersection of Watt and Scott streets. All up, dealing with the cops and the body had killed just over half the day so we arrived at the pub on the tail end of lunch. Place was just about empty.

'So what are we drinking, gents?' I said. I was already parking myself on a barstool at the big U-shaped table in the front window, anticipating a cool beer tickling my lips to help wash away the aftertaste of the dead. Maxie got in first.

'Whisky. For the shock. I'm buying. Need to keep moving.'

I realised he was serious and looking even more ashen than before. For someone who wanted to keep moving, he wasn't.

'Maxie?'

'I just realised. Spirits.'

Neither Muzz nor myself could follow what he was saying.

'Whisky. Spirits. Ghosts.'

I wasn't in the mood. Truth be told, I wasn't feeling too crash hot after the day either. Not sure if it was the lack of lunch, the discovery or just the thoughts of my own mortality.

Coming back into the moment, I saw Maxie at the bar ordering whisky with beer chasers. Sadly, with him ordering, the beer was going to be mainstream. Not my first choice, but then anything with alcohol and a frosty temperature was going to be good. And Maxie's drink selection would allow for some much needed distraction in the form of complaining about his choice.

When the drinks arrived, we raised our whiskies in a silent toast before Muzz decided to add some words.

'To the departed.'

Those words didn't feel right. For all we knew, that torso could have been some psycho killer who got his just deserts, like in that TV show about the nice serial killer who goes around killing bad serial killers. I didn't want to be a part of that.

'Who do you think it is? Was?' asked Maxie.

We sat in silence, searching for an answer, before Maxie stunned us with a conversational left turn.

'I think after today I'm gonna take up the Art of the Hobo,' he declared.

When Maxie joined the crew, Muzz wasn't so sure he'd be a keeper. Maxie's slanted view of the world, the way he saw the positive in the negative, and had a knack for coming out with a weird phrase or idea and making it sound perfectly normal, meant life for the young apprentice was pure adventure. If he wasn't selling weed to backpackers, he was telling them stories about drop bears and all the things that can kill you Down Under. But very soon, Maxie started proving his worth. Despite his odd utterances, Maxie was a court jester with a work ethic, which was all that counted for Muzz. Life on the worksite was just more entertaining with Maxie around. If Maxie had been a fool, he would not have survived as a member of Muzz's team.

I realised suddenly that Maxie might know someone interested in my sea-retrieved package. Could I ask him? Did I *want* to ask him?

'Art of the Hobo? What is this bullshit?' As crew boss, Muzz gave off a belligerent air, but really he was a pushover.

His wife and five daughters had him wrapped around their little fingers.

'Hobo. A bum. I'm gonna hitch me a lift on one of them coal trains, take it to the end of the line. See the heart of the country.' Maxie extended an arm out away from the horizon, inland, his mouth pursed with a follow-through whistle.

'You're bloody useless. You'd end up on the wrong train, go twenty minutes that ways and drop into a bloody ship. End up in China, ya dickhead.' Muzz drained his whisky to mark the end of the discussion and wiped his moustache with a sweep of his palm. But Maxie disagreed.

'Days like today show you what life's really about. Living. Doing what we need to do to be human,' he said.

Muzz wasn't having a bar of it. He shook his head. Life wasn't about being a bum, doing what you wanted. It was about looking after your family. Responsibility. That was what life was all about.

I let them carry on. Having been solid on the beach and during the police interrogation, I was starting to find the day weighing heavily on me. Maybe it was a form of delayed shock or something. Worse, the feelings and thoughts running through my head were making me crave some alone time. I didn't want to hear about theories of life, hobos or hitching rides on coal trains.

'What you reckon, Lachie? What do you think about life?'

For me, life was about keeping your head above water and getting on with it. Doing what you could to stay off anyone's radar and out of any trouble. That was the bit I've always found difficult – the staying out of trouble part. Not that my crew wanted to hear any of that. Did I have a purpose to my life? If

I did, I wasn't going to be sharing it with Maxie. They wanted a joke and something to smile at.

With a sip of beer, I gave them the best I could on short notice. 'Life? No idea. I'm too busy just trying to get through the day.'

'But you got to have a purpose, man. You got to have a reason to get up in the morning and get out into it.' This from the man proposing to live the life of a hobo.

A flash of lightning to the north caught everyone's eyes through the thin leadlight windows. The interruption allowed Maxie's train of thought to evaporate as quickly as our beers. Seeing it was my turn to shout, I grabbed the chance to escape.

Standing at the bar, I ordered three of the boutique beers they had on offer. Seems these days every pub in the country had some micro brewer on tap. Some were good, some were bad, each had a different personality that I was happy to be introduced to. Maxie's escape plan lingered annoyingly. Only someone who knew Mum and Dad would pick up the tab when they got into trouble could seriously ponder just upping and leaving to live life as a hobo. Being homeless wasn't a status symbol. It was about not having any choices, and choices came down to having money.

I needed to get my abalone to Billy Wong and talk to him about my other package. If Maxie wanted to know the real reason why I got up in the morning, this was it: trying to stay one step ahead of the rapidly shifting equations of how much money I owed, what someone else owed me and what I planned to do about it.

Being short of money was nothing new. I don't know a single soul who hasn't participated in the black economy or the much loved Australian search for a freebie. If there were any cash jobs going, I hadn't heard about them. Jobs on the side were always welcome for a bit of extra moolah. My problem was I'd spent both my honest dollars and the not so honest.

Delivering the beers back to the boys, I was glad to see the conversation had shifted from the purpose of life to more important topics.

'So, Lach, weekend? What're your plans?'

'Maxie, it's only Monday.' I looked from Maxie to Muzz, who simply shook his head while rolling a cigarette, carefully licking it under his walrus moustache. So I took a swig of my beer and turned to look once again out the window.

'C'mon, tell us what you're doing and I'll get the next round.'

I took the pint-sized apprentice up on his offer and shared my plans. 'I dunno. Sleep in. Clean the house. Do some washing. It's forty-eight hours of pure party with me.'

Unimpressed, Maxie gave a '*pffft*' sound before sipping his beer as both Muzz and I stared at him with narrowed eyes.

'What?'

Like synchronised drinkers, our right hands slowly lifted to point to the bar, indicating he now needed to make good on his offer.

'Come on. Seriously? You haven't even finished them ones,' he protested. 'That wasn't an answer, that was bullshit. I'm not buying a round –'

'Rack 'em up, short stuff. We know you. You'll talk some more bulldust and then puff! Magic. Maxie has skipped buying rounds,' Muzz said, chuckling, as he finished smoothing out his cigarette.

Beaten, Maxie hulked off towards the bar, grizzling about getting the round but happy to use the chance to flirt shamelessly with the barmaids.

'Stupid dickhead. But I like him, heh. He's working out good. He remind me of you, the biggest dickhead on my crew!'

Being called a dickhead by Muzz was a sign of affection. The more he said it, the higher his esteem.

'You're not gonna light that thing in here are you?'

He was already heading for the street with his cigarette between his lips and lighter *chk-chking* for a flame. 'What they gonna do about it?'

He had a point.

By the time Maxie returned, grinning, thanks to a perve at the barmaid, I was quite enjoying the nice little beer buzz tingling my fingertips. I lined up my new beer next to the empty glass. As Maxie prattled about the friendly barmaid he was sure he had a chance with, I just about emptied my glass and was ready to go. Clapping him on the shoulder mid-sentence, I stood to finish my last mouthful of beer. It was rude of me but I was heading off.

'What? Already?'

'Yeah, Maxie. Got to go trim my pubes for your mother.'

He pushed me away, telling me to get fucked as I headed for the door.

'Hey, Lach? You reckon those cops are gonna want to speak to us again?'

A shrug was all I could manage. I didn't want to admit my fear that today wouldn't be the last time the cops spoke to us about that body. Better not to think about it. Let the future deal with itself.

'Dunno, mate. But I'll tell you what. I'd maybe hold off jumping on that coal train for a bit. Might make you appear guilty of something.'

Wide-eyed, Maxie nodded, accepting this as sage advice.

'Want me to tell your mum you'll be late home tonight?'

Maxie pulled a face and gave me the finger as I headed for the front door.

Outside, my boss was on the phone, speaking in a manner that suggested his wife. Smoke jetted angrily from his nostrils, so I guessed she was giving him a list of instructions for the drive home. I held up a hand and waved.

Muzz clamped a hand over the phone. 'You leaving? Soft, you's going soft. See you tomorrow, dickhead. We'll start late. Ten.' He turned back to his call.

I was all set to head off when I remembered I needed to visit the ATM. We might live in a cashless society but there are times when a couple of notes in the back pocket are still required.

The ATM at the Great Northern was located in the corridor by the grand old entrance. Waiting for the machine to be free, I looked about the space, marvelling at how a once grand building could be reduced to tackiness simply through neglect and poor additions that looked out of place next to the original Art Deco details.

Money withdrawn, the unmissable single-digit balance indicated Muzz hadn't done last week's pays yet. So I headed back through the bar for a chance encounter with the boss to tell him to do the payroll. The risk of another Maxie conversation, as enjoyable as it would be, was a delay I didn't want but was sure I could avoid. I had a date with some abalone.

I scoped the bar, but both Maxie and Muzz were nowhere to be seen.

'Excuse me.'

Turning, I saw a face that looked familiar. The woman from the beach was trying to get to the bar. She paused as if she recognised me. So I smiled but she looked away. Which I took as encouragement. I'm sure the abalone would forgive me.

'You were on the beach today,' I said.

Puzzled, she tilted her head ever so slightly to look at me again, trying to place me. Her eyes were green, the kind that could be blue in a different light, just like the ocean. I offered her my hand, which she took. By twisting my palm ever so slightly, I looked at her red knuckles.

'Your colleague is gonna have a nice shiner tomorrow.'

'Serve him right,' she said, pulling her hand free.

'Can I buy you a drink then? Or are you meeting someone?'

She wasn't in her uniform anymore but a pair of jeans and T-shirt that revealed my suspicions from the beach. 'Going to the gym' was not just slang for a night on the couch with takeaway for her. Even her tan was natural.

She curled a stray piece of hair behind her ear. 'A drink would be nice. My friend is late.'

'They say you should never drink alone.'

'Why's that?' she said, pausing as I offered her a bar stool.

'No one else's there to buy a round.'

She gave a soft laugh, then sat and smiled as I grabbed another stool for myself.

'Lachie. Lachie Munro. What'll you have?'

'White wine, pinot gris?'

Signalling to the barmaid, I asked what her name was as the drinks were poured. 'It's only fair. You know mine.'

'Karen.' She held out her hand again and I shook, a more formal joke. Those knuckles really needed some ice.

'Come on. I'll ask the bar staff. Help the bruising.'

She thought about it as she flexed her fingers. Much as I'd enjoyed seeing her on the beach, up close she was even more enjoyable. As I took in her beautiful face and caught the tiny upturn of her mouth, I could see a hint of sadness. Not waiting for her answer, I leaned over the bar, grabbed a handful of ice from the sink and dropped it into several paper napkins. I could feel Karen watching me the whole time. As I placed the ice on her knuckles, she broke eye contact to sip her wine. She looked quickly over my painter's whites.

'So Mr Lachie, Lachie Munro, house painter. I was on the beach because someone thought it would be funny. What were you doing there?'

'Searching for ambergris but found a body instead. Well, part of one.'

Talking about dead people and body parts was definitely a mood killer, as Karen shifted on her bar stool and we both tried to work out the next thing to say. She won.

'How you coping? Seeing that ... thing?'

A shrug said I was fine. A deep breath was the gear change for me to switch the subject before I thought too long and hard about that lump of meat again.

'Really?'

It'd been a while since someone had asked how I was feeling. Not something you talk about with your mates. Not something I really wanted to share but for some reason I did, telling her that despite the gruesome discovery, I was okay. But I didn't want to talk about my day.

'So you're not a cop.'

'Nope.'

'Gonna give me a hint?'

'Where's the fun in that?' She drank, smiling, not looking away from me.

I gave up. I had no idea what she did. So I ordered hot chips and another round.

'That's it? Not even a guess?'

'I prefer a mystery.'

When the chips arrived we polished them off quickly, leaving only salt and smears of tomato sauce that had us looking at the menu, contemplating dinner. I realised it had also been a while since I'd talked with someone who wasn't Dave or from a worksite. Even longer since I'd sat talking with a woman, seriously talking and laughing. I was enjoying myself. I tried to explain but clearly I was out of practice.

'Don't you have friends?' she asked.

'Course I do. But we get stuck in our tribes and routines. Don't say much more than hello to a stranger, if that. How long has it been since you met someone new?'

'Can't say,' she said.

I realised I was getting too heavy and needed to flip back to something a little less intrusive. She beat me to it.

'You look worried.'

'Me, nah. That's just my face,' I said, earning a laugh.

'You're funny. So don't worry. We're just talking,' she said, briefly placing her hand on my forearm, telling me there was no way we were just talking.

'So that friend …'

'I lied.' She smiled as our meals arrived.

She'd ordered a burger with the lot, I'd ordered the fish tacos. We continued talking. Sharing. My tacos went cold as we discovered we both loved diving.

'Please don't tell me you did a course on holidays in Asia,' I said.

'Oh, no. Wasn't anything like that. I hated swimming. Then someone suggested putting on some air tanks and it was a completely different experience. I was hooked. Now I'm a Divemaster. Trained in rescue. Search.'

'Yeah, right.' It was hard to hide how impressed I was. Karen had training that required serious hours underwater.

'Actually I wanted to be a marine biologist but didn't get the grades,' she added.

'Me too!'

'You wanted to be a marine biologist too?' Her eyebrows were trying to join her hairline.

'No. I didn't get the grades.'

'What about here? What are your favourite dive spots?' she asked.

'Heaps. Depends on what you're interested in seeing. So where's the craziest place you've dived?'

'Not really crazy, but freezing. Bottom of Tasmania, but I want to go even further.'

'There's further than the bottom of Tasmania?'

'Antarctica.' She made it sound like a wizard's incantation. Under her spell, I'd have gladly followed.

Somehow, the bar staff were calling last drinks, and security were collecting empty glasses and reminding everyone the Great Northern was closing. The night was done.

'Wow! How'd that happen?' Karen asked as we headed for the street.

'You're easy to talk to,' I said, too loudly.

She giggled. We were both drunk, but positive no one could tell as I nearly crashed into a telegraph pole and tripped into the gutter. Standing there, I was almost her height.

'You don't look so tall in the moonlight.' She laughed.

'There's a bar, that way … No, that way. If you're up to one more?'

She scrunched her nose and shook her head. We gazed at each other, not sure what to do. Then I slowly leaned in and kissed her. Breaking away, she smiled and took a deep breath.

'One-time offer. I have a great place. It is a great place,' she said confidently, nodding. 'We can go back there and … keep talking. Or not. I think, I mean … we've had a nice night?' Her confidence eroded.

My arm was already waving for a taxi.

The trip was short, the kind that pisses every cabbie off, and we pulled up on one of the notoriously steep streets Newcastle is plagued with. Unsure if I was to get out, I sat for a moment as Karen squinted at me, trying to focus.

'So you a Leo?' she asked.

Puzzling for a moment, I tried to remember my star sign and caught a glimpse of the cabbie watching in the rear-vision mirror.

'Pisces. I think.'

She held out her hand. Between the thumb and forefinger

was a business card. 'Been a good night, Pisces. Next step is yours,' she slurred as I again got a glimpse of that smile.

With my cheeks reddening in a blush that I doubt she noticed, I shoved the business card in my pocket without even looking and threw the money at the cabbie before I clambered after her onto the hilly street.

'Bloody hill.'

'Good thing this'd be me then.' She blinked with the heavy lids of the wasted as she pointed to one of the houses, a two-up two-down terrace, door on the street, a window either side just like a kid's drawing. I don't think a kid would draw the street on a forty-five-degree angle though. And down the lane beside her place, I reckon they'd probably stick a Tyrannosaurus rex.

As she rummaged in her backpack for a set of keys, I hung back, pretending I was simply there to make sure she would make it through her front door safely, just in case the situation had changed.

As she opened the door she turned and looked at me. 'Been pretty out-there tonight. Don't invite guys back here. Weird day.'

'Want me to go?'

'Just a nightcap and some more talk, but if you want to go ...'

Standing on that street was cold. I didn't want to go.

Her place betrayed the old roots of the city as the settlers from the old country tried to recreate something familiar in the new land, although the pokiness of the rooms had given way to a homeliness, a couple of walls knocked out to reveal raw bricks and polished floorboards. The sagging couch was inviting, as was the warmth and slight stuffiness of a house shut up all day.

'This do?' She held up a bottle of whisky and two glasses pinched between her fingers. With an offer like that, how could I refuse?

7
KNUCKLEDRAGGERS

My eyes felt the weight of the world attached to each lid as I slowly woke up. I squinted about the space as the sun started to push itself through the wooden Venetians, trying to remember where I was, who I was and what I had been doing. Glimmers came back to me. The bottle of single malt and two glasses on the bedside table helped remind my brain why it was not functioning and why my mouth was dry and tacky.

I'd slept like the dead, passed out on top of the soft cloud of a double bed. Trying not to wake the still sleeping Karen, I stood quietly, stretching out the stiff creakiness in an attempt to remind my body which bits were supposed to bend and which weren't. I was still wearing my clothes, and noted that Karen was still in hers too. Snatches of the night before dribbled into my consciousness, random frames from a lost movie.

Doing a very good impression of the zombie shuffle, I pulled the cover up over her and left her to her dreams. Despite the alcoholic pollution solidifying in my system, I needed to get to work. It was lucky I was still in my whites.

I crept as quietly as I could to where I imagined the kitchen to be, in a desperate search for water. Unable to find a glass, I gave up and drank from the tap. The hooting and juddering of the water pipes was enough to wake the dead.

Sure enough, Karen slipped into the kitchen, eyes squinting, hugging herself tightly as if trying to stop her body flying apart.

Croaking a hello, even I could smell the plumes of alcohol my mouth was emitting. I was surprised the indoor plants didn't shrivel and die on the spot. Despite this, I politely declined the offer of a shower and made my excuses to leave. She didn't protest.

'I don't normally do that,' she said, clutching the kitchen door to stay upright.

'Drink whisky with a stranger?'

She nodded. 'You probably shouldn't have stayed the night,' she said with a shy smile. 'Feel like I should be making you breakfast, ah … ?'

'Lachie Munro, and no breakfast required,' I said, smiling back at her as I made my way to the front door. 'If it helps, last night was out of character for me too. I guess neither of us felt like being alone.'

She smiled briefly before rushing for the bathroom.

'You okay?' I asked, starting to follow, but the idea of holding her hair back seemed wildly inappropriate. From inside the bathroom, she squeaked that she was all good.

As I let myself out, I felt her business card in my pocket. In crisp black it stated her name – Karen Miller – and the logo of the Department of Primary Industries. Below her name was her title: Fisheries Officer. A fisho. I had to laugh.

I went to throw it away but something made me slip it back in my pocket. Karen Miller. Even if it was sleeping with the enemy, there was something about her I really liked. The hangover proved it.

Even with Muzz giving us a late start, I needed to get a wriggle on as I found where I'd left my car the afternoon before. The Beast was a boring 1992 Nissan Hilux with covered tray, silver where it wasn't covered in drips and scratches. I treated the Beast mean, like a working dog, and it behaved well most of the time – apart from early mornings when it was a reluctant starter, like most of us. Parking on a slight hill was a treat to help the Beast get going, something I tried to do whenever I stopped.

Sitting in the driver's seat, my eyes took in the tip of rubbish that littered the interior. Archaeologists could trace my entire working career as a painter from the layers in the footwell. Across the dashboard was an array of gap sealer and fingerprints immortalised in paint. Like the tailgate covered in dribbles, drips and paint roller smears, every colour related to a different job and I could remember them all, despite most of the colours being hog bristle, seed pearl or quarter-eighth off-white satin. Alright, maybe there were a couple of bright-coloured memories, but feature walls were so last decade.

As I approached Fort Scratchley and Nobbys Surf Life Saving pavilion, I headed for a favourite café that makes great coffee and where everyone is served with a smile.

'Slick, sleep in? Double-shot takeaway?'

'Late start today, Roxy. Better bring us a menu with that coffee.'

Sitting down at one of the outside tables, I watched as Roxy made me my regular coffee before she came back out with the menu. Roxy is a great girl with a total rockabilly vibe. We had a thing a while back before she developed a taste for surfers. When I say 'thing', it was casual to borderline comatose. But that was her choice. Me, I could have gone a bit

49

deeper than late-night booty calls, and while I'm pretty sure she's not the one that got away, she'd be close.

'Know what you having today, Slick?'

Never knew where she got the name Slick from. Normally, hearing her say it made me gooey on the inside. Today, it just gave me a weird, totally unusual awkward feeling that took me a while to work out. Roxy calling me Slick made me feel like I was cheating on Karen.

'What's good today, Rox? How's your fella?'

Didn't that open the floodgates. Roxy had just been dumped by her latest board herder after a tumultuous three months, nearly a record for her and close to true love. Sadly, it was her now ex-boyfriend I had been looking to get a bead on. I didn't know why I hadn't thought of him sooner as a solution to finding a buyer for my little problem.

'So what happened?' What else are you expected to say? Honestly, I didn't give a rat's arse about her boyfriend other than as someone who might be interested in what I had to sell.

'Mum told me if it was a fight, he'll come back. Tail between his legs, but he'll be back.'

'You had a fight? Your mum's probably onto something. So, Damo still around? Maybe I could go have a word?'

Dabbing an eye with a napkin, Roxy shook her head while looking skywards, as chicks do when avoiding mascara smears. Her boyfriend wasn't coming back.

'The bikie told Damo if he ever set foot in Newcastle, he'd kill him. And not in a good way.'

I nodded sympathetically as I pondered what this guy must have been doing to upset a bikie. Generally it didn't take much to upset a member of an outlaw bikie club, but to get a threat like that, he hadn't just been making eyes at one of their girlfriends in a bar. Especially when Roxy tended to date dealers. It's no secret drugs are a dangerous line of work. Upset someone and you get threatened, cop a beating or end up chopped into little pieces. That thought suddenly loomed large in my mind but there was no way I was going to share it with Roxy. She was already traumatised enough without adding the image of a chopped-up torso to her head.

Roxy checked to see if anyone was close enough to hear then leaned a little closer. 'Where am I gonna get my weed now, Slick? He had the best hydro ever.'

I had no answer for Roxy as she stood there, trying to hold it together, but I made a mental note to tell Maxie to pay a visit to Roxy with a sample of his wares.

'You got any idea where Damo went, Rox?'

Seemed she did. Damo had come home looking white as a ghost before grabbing the few possessions he had and throwing them all in the back of his car. If you ever suspect someone of earning a bit extra on the side, look at what toys they have, it's a dead giveaway. From memory, Damo had a very nice Subaru Forester hotted up with every gadget and accessory you can think of and then some. Clearly surfing and full-time study paid well.

'That's the one. God, I loved that car.' Judging from the sly smile creeping across her face, Roxy had some fond memories of the car. She was still smiling as she finished the rest of her story. Damo had told her he was heading south. He promised he'd send her an address for emergencies but his plan was to hook up with some uni mates in Sydney.

Tale told, Roxy went off to fetch me some breakfast.

Sitting there, leaning back with my sunnies on while I got a healthy dose of vitamin D, I wondered which clan of bikies the surfer had tangled with. Newcastle, like everywhere, has some dangerous fringes. Someone on those fringes was going to be interested in my powder packages. Trick was making the right connection for an introduction.

As I mulled over my own problems, I missed Roxy's return.

'You lost there?' she asked, one hand shielding her eyes from the sun, the other on her cocked hip, having placed the eggs, bacon, hash brown, mushrooms and grilled tomato in front of me. She didn't break my heart but she came close.

'Just thinking about Damo. What club did he have the problem with?'

Roxy watched a seagull float by on an updraft. 'Stinky Finks?'

'That's not a real club, Rox.'

Bikie culture is an odd society, full of lost men who find themselves in large groups who like to fight, drink and root, not necessarily in that order. I can sort of understand that side of things but the alpha male raping and pillaging is a bit harder to get a grip on. And with the big four – the Hells Angels, the Rebels, Bandidos and Comancheros – the old ideas of two wheels and the open road has added the third wheel of organised crime. When you have clubhouses up and down the country, you have a handy distribution network for all kinds of things. If there's a dollar in it, they'll be interested.

'The Knuckledraggers,' Roxy said.

That surprised me. The Knuckledraggers were not in

the big league, not by a long shot. They were a tiny feeder club for a feeder club for one of the big four. From memory, they only had three clubhouses: one in Newcastle, one in Port Macquarie and one in Dubbo. But if they were muscling in on some poor surfer with a bitchin' hydro setup, maybe they were muscling in for bigger things, stepping up, as it were. It was a possible solution.

'You want any sauce?'

'Barbecue. And another coffee?'

Watching Roxy's shapely rear as she headed back in to get my sauce, I had a thought. 'Hey, Rox, Damo have any Asian mates?'

Roxy turned and looked back at me with one side of her beautiful lips curled up. 'Nup. You ever see an Asian surf?'

I had actually. There were heaps on the pro-am surfing circuit. Guess Roxy's interest in surfing didn't spring that far. As she disappeared inside, I went back to trying to nut out what was going on, because coincidences only exist in bad movies.

The Knuckledraggers. It was a big step up for those guys. Any other time, this bit of news would be a joke. If it was true, the world order was changing. I had no idea how I was going to be involved but as sure as night follows day, I knew somewhere soon my world was going to collide with all this. If nothing else, my instinct was excellent at sizing up the state of play. Trust it, my old man used to say, it's the only thing in the world that won't lie to you. Too bad he didn't listen to his gut about his own career.

My mobile started ringing and buzzing its way across the table.

'Dave?'

'Whereareyou? Needyoutocomehereandgiveusahand. Yeah,needsomehelp. Bitofhelpbegood.'

'Mate, slow down. What's up? I'm about to go to work.'

'Lachie,notaskingmuchjustcomeherefirst?'

'Can I come after work?'

That wasn't going to fly for Dave. He wanted me as soon as possible. Looking at my watch, I told him I'd be there in an hour. Whatever was going on, I didn't get a chance to ask, as the bozo hung up.

Left staring at my screen, I realised that sorting out Dave would make me very late for work. With the hangover still kicking in the back of my head, I did what anyone would do. I rang Muzz and pulled a sickie.

'What? You's fine yesterday. How you sick now?'

'Dodgy kebab, Muzz. After the drinks on the way home. Up all night, both ends.'

Grumbling, Muzz accepted my excuse before telling me he expected to see me the next day.

Never really happy to pull a sickie, I promised I'd be fine by tomorrow and would see him at the new job. That done, I now had the day free to deal with whatever had got up Dave's nose and sent him into a tizzy. It had better be good.

8
PANiC

There are two ways to get to Dave's place. One is a longish curving drive around the docks to Stockton, the other involves a short ferry ride across the shipping channel.

Erring on the side of caution, I opted to take the ferry rather than drive all the way around to Dave's. If I got pulled over, I would still be way over the legal limit. Losing my licence was not an option.

There was a coal carrier with a tax-dodging Panamanian registration headed for the horizon as I arrived at the ferry wharf. Why was it big business always found some shonky way of doing things, leaving the rest of us to get screwed? You don't have to look far for the dark and dodgy world. Or you can turn a blind eye and only see a large boat slowly making its way out to sea. Reality or romance, take your pick. It's always your choice.

The ferry chugged across the channel towards me. Most of the world's ferry trips are substantial. Not so the Stockton Ferry. All up, it takes about three minutes to cross the channel and twenty minutes each end to get on and off. Even though the stretch of water is so narrow you can clearly see the passengers board from the other side, it's a long wait if you miss it.

Turning my attention back to the massive bulk carrier, Maxie's comment about slipping away bobbed up in my mind. Maybe it was the hangover but suddenly the idea of escaping Newcastle felt pretty good. One day I might escape, see the world from a working boat, but that was not going to happen until I sold the package. So today the horizon was simply a line. My mission was to sort out Dave's problem, then collect the abalone and drop them off at Billy's. All things going to plan, I would have a quiet word with Billy about the other thing we'd pulled out of the ocean. It was going to be one of those days where I went through the motions, ticking items off my to-do list as I slowly sobered up.

Despite being so close to the city proper, the deep water channel the ferry had to cross kept Stockton perpetually stuck in low gear. Just about every other part of the city had been touched by the gentrification wand – places snatched up for a song and flipped for a fortune. Not Stockton. It has clung doggedly to its status as a happy little retirement hamlet by the sea. Speculators marvelled at why this was so until they saw Dave's. His place was pure asbestos sheeting, run down and tired. Anyone who bought it would be paying even more to remove it. Which suited Dave. He got to sit and watch as the oldies who lived around him kept their places neat and tidy, disapproving of the overgrown jungle of kikuyu grass turning his yard into a paddock. To stir them up, he would often talk loudly about trading in his lawn mower for some sheep or goats to keep the front lawn down. But as the old women tut-tutted and worried about snakes in the grass attacking the grandkiddies or their Jack Russells, not necessarily in that order, their husbands were looking at Dave's boat sitting neatly in his drive, all clean and in proper working order, dreaming of rocking in the swell with a line in the water and a fresh tinny in their hand, far from the grandkids and wife. Dave was the secret envy of his neighbourhood.

It took a while before he answered my knock on the door. He peeked out of the small window beside the front door, a wide-eyed mess. He wore an old cricket helmet and held his cricket bat, ready to strike.

'Jesus! What's up with you?' I asked.

Dave unlocked the door and pulled me through with his free hand, the cricket bat hanging by his side.

'Dave? You okay?' I said slowly, trying not to betray how spooked he was making me feel.

'Haven't slept.'

From the small pile of caffeinated energy drink cans in the hallway, it was easy to see what had helped him with this feat.

'Why haven't you slept? You eaten? Want me to make some toast? Scrambled eggs?'

Dave had other ideas as he fidgeted and popped the ring pull on yet another can of energy drink.

'Thought I was having a heart attack about an hour ago. Then realised it was just these.'

Apparently, Dave's remedy for energy-drink heart palpitations was to drink more and push through to the other side.

'You know how much is in the cupboard? How much money? Every noise outside the house sounded like someone coming to get it. That somehow they'd followed us. At 2am I tried to work out where I could get a gun and by three I'd dug out this.' He held up the cricket bat then tapped it on the side of his helmet before going on. 'Then I just sat up. With my bat, waiting for the fuckers.'

'Dave, it's been two days.'

'That's why I had to keep drinking those things. Stay awake.'

I took the cricket bat off him and made him sit down. As he carefully backed himself into a kitchen chair, I used the distraction to swipe his energy drink and pour it down the sink. People are worrying about kids and drugs? They should be more worried about those caffeine drinks. If they don't give you a heart attack, they give you instant onset diabetes. If only they weren't so tasty.

I poured Dave a large glass of water and watched him relax more with every swallow. I didn't know if the water would help flush the caffeine and sugar from his system but it couldn't hurt. Just having me there was letting him lower his guard.

As I filled his glass with more water, he gave me his best puppy-dog look. 'You gotta take it.'

'What? The …?' I nodded in the direction of the second bedroom, unwilling to give the contraband a name.

Excitedly, Dave nodded. I'd never seen him so wired.

'That's not the deal, Dave. It's safer here.'

The nodding turned to furious shaking. He wasn't having a bar of it. 'No. It's gotta go. Gotta get out of here. I need my sleep. Me kids are coming. They'll sleep in the same room as that stuff. And I've got a job. If I'm not top of my game, I could lose my job. If there's any issue, lives could be at stake. You seen the size of those trucks? If you're not thinking, you can crash, run something over, nothing good can come of it …'

Seeing him like he was, rambling on the border of incomprehensible, I knew – as I had known since not tipping the packages over the side – that I had no choice. But how was I going to carry several kilos of heroin home with me? I looked about the kitchen and the answer came to me in a flash of inspiration.

'Okay, mate. I'll get rid of it but I'll need to borrow a few things.'

The relief on his face was priceless. 'Really? You'll take it? Like, now?'

'I'll take it. But you got to get some rest.'

Dave nodded and drank another glass of water. Watching him, I ran my options through my head. At least the drugs would be under my protection, hidden somewhere of my choosing. Seeing Dave's eyes roll back into his head made me panic momentarily until I heard the soft snuffle of snores. He clearly wasn't going to be helping me move the package back to my place.

9
THE RAID

I carried two green shopping bags back to the ferry. Anyone giving me half a glance would see a bloke and his groceries. The borrowed tins of baked beans and frozen chips sitting on top of the bags helped.

Taking my seat on the ferry, I looked at the 'shopping' between my legs and remembered. The fucking abalone! Mind like a sieve.

This time when I called Dave, he answered sleepily on the second or third ring. He assured me he had it under control. He already had the catch in the shed in a drum covered with an old hessian sack and an old fish tank filter bubbling away. Living like that, the abalone could keep for a couple of days, maybe longer. I felt as relieved as Dave had when I agreed to walk off with the 'shopping'. Dave even had a plan to give the abalone a bit of food. Apparently they loved chook pellets. I didn't ask where or how he'd found that out. Probably wasn't even true.

Walking the streets of Newcastle CBD, I looked like many others returning to their car with their shopping. Even entering Billy Wong's through the kitchen with the bags didn't raise an eyebrow. A cook was attacking a chicken with a cleaver. Seeing the pink flesh and white bone lying on the large wooden butcher's block suddenly made me freeze. The second chop was enough to break the spell and I slipped into the restaurant to head for my usual table.

When Billy saw me sitting down, he headed over to join me. Didn't take a genius to see something had upset him.

'Mate, I am very upset. Upset indeed. Fried rice?'

I nodded, waiting for Billy to go on.

'That kitchen hand that disappeared? He's only gone and got himself bloody chopped up! They found him on the beach yesterday.'

'I thought he was a cook.'

'Cook, kitchen hand, he also helped with security up ...' He pointed to the ceiling.

'So how'd they work out it was him?'

'Tattoo,' he said. 'Bloody hell, mate. I am shitting bricks.'

'Why?'

'His tattoo. Was a dragon!'

I still didn't get the connection.

'Bloody Asian gang, Triads, Yakuza bullshit. No one is saying which one, but. Tattoo like that ... And he was in my kitchen with ...' He looked to the ceiling and I understood why he was so worried.

If his new kitchen hand was mixed up in some Asian gang and had said anything about what was going on upstairs, Billy might be about to get some visitors. If you took that thought to its logical yet paranoid conclusion, you might even think that same gang had installed the hapless cook–kitchen hand–security bouncer as a way to keep tabs on things as they planned a hit. Not that the game was really secret – those in the know knew about it. But a new gang in the area might have a point to prove. Gangs that carry machetes like to remove little fingers. Little fingers are very useful appendages. How else do you clean your ears?

My mind was already trying to make a connection to the Knuckledraggers. If they were the same operation, so be it. If not, was there some sort of turf war going on in Newcastle that had yet to make the headlines?

'I might have to leave town. You know? Maybe, quickly. Any hint of trouble, I'm gone, Lachie.'

He started to head for the kitchen then stopped. Came back. 'How will you know if I leave or ...'

He had a point. How would I know? My shrug wasn't really noticed as Billy's mind raced in its own loop.

'I ... I'll think of something.' He paused. 'Nah. Fuck that potato. I'm gonna get some security. Real security. Call a mate in.' Billy walked into the kitchen mumbling about how he hadn't had to worry about any of this stuff for years.

I couldn't recall ever seeing Billy so shaken. The flip side was that his preoccupations meant I didn't have to explain his late abalone. Win-win. The bags between my legs were another matter. Probably not a good time to bring them up.

Sadly, when he returned with my order, it seemed the abalone gave Billy Wong a chance to focus on something other than his now-dead kitchen hand.

'Where my abalone? How you forget the bloody abalone again?'

'Look, I'm sorry, Billy. I've just had a couple of those days.'

'You having a rough time?'

Nodding, I took the chance to scoop up some of the special fried rice.

'I'm so sorry, Lachie, that you having a rough time. You lost a kitchen hand too? No? Or had the police coming in asking you questions about gangs and shit? No?'

'Well, actually –'

'No! You haven't. That is my life since yesterday. So you

tell me a story that is better than that, okay?'

I went to start telling him about how I'd found the body but Billy's request had clearly been rhetorical, dismissing my story before I got a word out.

'I don't care. I want my abalone. Delays mean I get a discount. So you go and –'

A commotion at the front of the restaurant had Billy craning his neck to see what was going on. Into the dining room walked Department of Primary Industries Fisheries Officer Karen Miller, followed by Detective Sergeant Jon Baxter and his partner, Shennae O'Keefe.

I don't know who was more surprised to see who.

Karen looked at me for a moment then at my plate before turning back to Billy.

'Mr Wong, I'm here to inspect these premises for illegally sourced shellfish, check your permits for the shellfish in your restaurant – you know the drill. I want to see your purchase receipts and logs.'

Her words magically switched Billy into the consummate host.

'Officers, sit, please. I get you some green tea while I get the books. Feel free to look over the tanks. See anything undersize or underfed, feel free to point them out to me. And that goes for anything in the fish tanks as well.'

Nothing like a joke to cut through a bit of tension, although that one hung like a fart in Billy's wake as he disappeared to get all that had been asked of him.

'Good fried rice?' Detective Sergeant Baxter asked. I could see his investigator's mind clunking into gear. Not only was I the one to find the body but I was now in the place where the deceased had worked, talking to the guy's boss. Not a good look in front of someone whose line of work prevented them from believing in coincidence.

'Bit early for lunch, isn't it?' asked O'Keefe from somewhere near the ceiling.

Across the room, Karen ignored me completely. Detective Sergeant Baxter squinted at me, and not in a friendly way. O'Keefe just looked bored. I wanted to flee.

'Recommend the spring rolls as well,' I said, quickly adding, 'detectives.'

How fast can you finish a meal without looking suspicious? I didn't know, I just kept shovelling, praying I didn't trip over something on the way out and spill my shopping.

As Billy returned with the books and harsh words for one of the waitresses, who scurried back with a fresh pot of tea, I left a twenty under my plate and stole a quick glance at Karen before hotfooting it out of there.

Outside under the clear blue sky, I breathed a sigh of relief. If I had made the delivery of abalone – or worse – Billy would have had a load of black market abalone and a commercial quantity of narcotics somewhere in his restaurant that would have got him, and me, in a world of trouble. Hopefully, this would be how Billy saw it too. I walked in the direction of the Beast, weighed down by my two bags of 'groceries' and the equally weighty problem of what to do with them.

10
COUSIN LLOYD

I wasn't quick enough.

If you've never had a panic attack you won't know how terrifying they are. You can't breathe and you break out into a sweat as your heart races, trying to punch out of your chest. People mock them but you feel like you are going to die, that this is the one, the big H, the heart attack with your name on it. Completely terrifying.

By the time I got to the Beast, I was full blown. Driving home to Merewether, I came close to crashing thanks to my hyperventilating. The forced concentration it took to park calmed me enough that I was able to walk down the drive with my two bags of 'shopping'. But I only just made it to the couch before tunnel vision yet again shrank the world.

After sitting, hand clamped to my chest, for what felt like an hour as my heart danced the flamenco inside my rib cage, it all disappeared. I could breathe again, knowing it hadn't been a heart attack. I swear, it's scary. I now understood something of what Dave had been feeling when he disturbed my breakfast.

My place is a granny flat out the back of an old worker's cottage in Merewether, the land of young couples and families. Developers would love to get their hands on the worker's cottage, rip out its guts and extend it into a mansion with an outdoor entertaining area. The owner is Harry Kinniburgh, though, a man more than content to sit and watch the world change around him. He put in the granny flat about thirty years ago and that was the sum total of his renovations. I'd been living here for four years and it suited me. Simple, plain and with good neighbours, all of whom would be shocked and ashamed to find out what I'd brought home.

Like a caged beast, I paced the edges of the place, looking at the walls, trying to think of where I could keep the bricks safe. Finding a suitable spot was never going to be easy in my one-bedder granny flat. In the cupboards? Under the kitchen sink? Under the bathroom taps? Could I pull free the vent beside the bath or the ceiling fans? How much space was there under the bath?

Keeping my eggs in one basket was never the sensible option. I had to spread the risk like a merchant banker, divide the bricks up. Some could go under the sink with a bit of duct tape. Some could go in the exhaust vents in the ceiling and another lot could go in the back of the cupboard. Spreading it around would help keep it safe from any prowlers.

Popping an air vent off, I laid the bricks out between the ceiling joists. Taping the bricks under the sink was much harder. The stainless steel surface had years of grime and grot that the tape refused to stick to. After nearly an entire roll of duct tape, the bricks stayed put, shoved up the back under the taps.

Collapsing on the couch for a breather, I checked my chest and wrist for a steady pulse, the rhythm reassuring. As I sat, finger on wrist, counting the beats — three, four, five — it dawned on me that my idea to offload the contraband on Billy Wong was not going to be possible. A man who has just been raided was going to want to lay low, keep things on the straight and narrow. There was no way I was going to be able to ask Billy to find a buyer.

I needed to find someone else with the right connections. Roxy's ex-boyfriend Damo had been a blow out. Maxie was a possible but did I want to involve him? He shifted to the bottom of my list, my in-case-of-emergency option. Which is when I got all excited again.

Dialling Dave's number, I hoped the big lug wasn't still sleeping off his energy-drink hangover.

'Lacha-lene. To what do I owe the good pleasure?'

'Mate? You still got a cousin in the bikie scene?' I asked.

'Yebida yebida. Why, my precious Goldie-Lach?'

'Reckon he might feel like a beer?'

'A bloke who isn't up for a beer is a bloke that can't be trusted, good sir.' Clearly, Dave was starting to feel a bit more normal now his house was free of opiates.

'You set up a meeting?'

'Reckon he might know someone for the ...' Dave whistled a kind of *twee-dee* sound. Thank the gods he had the sense not to say the actual words.

'Worth a question. Sooner the better be good. Okay?'

He promised he'd get back to me but he thought something might even be possible for later that day. Even better. Almost made me feel okay about the prison sentence I had stashed around my flat. A quiet chat with someone on the periphery of the bikie scene to get the lay of the land was a good place to start. If it turned out that some bikie club was interested in stepping up, who was I to stand in the way of their ambition?

Relief laid me back on the couch with equal parts exhaustion and a sense of progress that shut my eyes before the next inhale.

When the doorbell buzzed, my pulse soared once again as I rose into wakefulness. A quick twenty minutes horizontal and I was a new man.

Opening the door revealed Dave looking the shiftiest I'd ever seen him thanks to a pair of polycarbonate sunglasses with mirror tints and far too many angles, the kind sported by cricketers or killer robots from the future.

'You ready? I left you a message,' he said.

Looking down at my mobile, I saw there was a missed call and a message from him.

'Fell asleep,' I said, listening to the message as I talked. He had set up a meet and greet with his cousin that afternoon. 'What's with the glasses?'

The question seemed as alien to Dave as being asked for directions to the local branch office of the Newcastle Feminist Society. He pulled them off his face to peer at them. 'What's wrong with them?'

'You look dodgy. They're distinctive, flashy, draw attention. If you were aiming for incognito for this meet and greet, those glasses will be remembered by every Tom Dick you run into. That's what's wrong with them.'

From the expression on his face, Dave was struggling to work out if I was joking or not. 'So you don't like me sunnies?'

'Who's driving? You or me?'

Knowing my opinion made no difference to his choice of eyewear, I stepped outside and waited for Dave to follow. Except now Dave was staring at me.

'You right?' he asked.

I had no idea what he was talking about, so I shrugged and pulled a face.

'You just look pale. Like you seen a ghost or something.'

'Too much coffee.' Who knows, maybe it was true.

'You good now?'

I pulled the door firmly shut and pushed back on it to make sure. Then I set off towards his green Holden HSV ute, another of Dave's failures at being inconspicuous, making him catch up.

'So where we meeting your cousin – what's his name?'

'Lloyd.'

'Right. Your cousin Lloyd. Lloyd. This is your cousin who's a bikie? Not the one who's the manager at Target?'

'You think I'm a dickhead?'

Apologising, I offered the excuse that it was the stress of what we were doing that was making me antsy.

'That's 'kay, mate. And to answer your other question, if you guess where we're meeting him, first round's on me.'

Sitting in the passenger seat as the engine roared to life first go, I had no idea. Dave screamed out of my street and it was clear the first round was going to be on me.

11
LLOYD THROWS A CURVEBALL

'Your lips are moving,' the barmaid with the long bottle-red hair said as she assembled my drinks on the parade ground beer mat.

'Really?' It's a bad habit of mine when I get worked up. Sometimes my internal monologue breaks out on my lips. I think I have it under control until someone springs me. Embarrassing. Not only had the barmaid caught me venting my internal annoyed monologue about the elusive bikie, who was now late, but she had caught me checking out her butt.

'Name's Kirrily. Here's your change.'

As I scooped the coins from the metal tray, Kirrily piped up again.

'No tip? After checking out my arse like that?'

She softly *tut-tutted* until I dropped the three gold coins back onto the plate. That was the end of that twenty bucks.

'Thanks.' She leaned forwards, provocatively flashing cleavage from which I whipped my eyes. Having paid the toll for looking at her bum, I was not going to cop a fine for her boobs. Not when I was about to meet a bikie.

Meeting a bikie, even one on the periphery of the scene like Dave's cousin, is always going to be a tricky thing. There's an element of face that needs to be respected. You can't offend or appear smarter than them, you have to just take things as they're presented. Not too many questions and a good dose of acting chops don't hurt either.

We were meeting Lloyd at an Irish-themed pub down

Hamilton way. It was not the sort of place I'd normally choose but, then again, that was probably a good thing. I prefer old man pubs, the places where the wallpaper is peeling in the corner, not places like this where newly moneyed miners hung out with their pay packets as women tottered by on high heels, drinking piccolos of pink champagne. Money attracted skirts, which attracted men looking for a root, either on the strength of their charms or by picking up the late-night leftovers. Like I said, not my kind of place. It all pointed to Lloyd being either a lot younger than expected or a really creepy older guy.

Carrying the beers back to Dave, I attempted to count how many shamrocks decorated the room. At what point does a shamrock cross from friendly decoration to tacky? One, I decided, as a weedy guy who could have been a jockey if not for his steroid-built muscles strutted in. Lloyd was young, muscle-bound and hair-free. Gone were the days of the hairy biker wearing the same clothes until they rotted and blew off him on a fast stretch of highway. Lloyd was of the new breed, which is why he had chosen this pub.

'Dave.' Lloyd held out his hand to his cousin and then looked at me from behind his wraparound glasses, not that dissimilar to the ones Dave had been wearing. Maybe it was a family thing. 'Yeah, you must be Lach. Sweet. Lach, Lachie, Lach, Lach, Lacho.'

Grimacing like a death's head, I offered to get him a beer. I wasn't about to be intimidated by a twentysomething.

'Cider'll do nicely. With ice.'

I almost stopped right there. Cider – no better demonstration that the blue-collar roots of this once great working city were dead. Next, he'd be asking for a vodka cranberry.

'I'll get it,' said Dave.

'Don't check out her arse,' I said as Lloyd and I eyed one another, each attempting to suss the other out.

'So, Dave tells me you wanted to talk?'

So much for Dave telling me that he hadn't said anything. My fight-or-flight instinct wasn't quite kicking in, but my nerve ends were twitching as Dave returned with the cider, which Lloyd took and sipped without a 'cheers' – poor form that made me wary. But I didn't know anything about this guy except that he was related to Dave. So I played it cool.

'Yeah. Just, y'know. Was thinking of getting a bike.'

And so it began. Lloyd dribbled on about bikes. What sort were the best in terms of reliability, what were good to mod, who had a bike they wanted to sell. This mate had a sweet frame, another had a decent engine. Blah, blah, Harley blah. Lloyd would even help me build up a decent bike if I wanted, or at worst connect me with the men who would sell me the parts.

'So, yeah, man. You wanna bike, me and the boys can get you set up well nice.'

Sitting on the edge of his stool, Dave was clearly puzzling over the conversation. Bikes were as much his thing as mine.

'Awesome. Now I asked Dave and he didn't know. You're not wearing colours. What club are you with?'

Leaning back, Lloyd grinned as he lifted his shirt to reveal a tattoo in the centre of his gut that showed the face of a snarling ape – the Knuckledraggers logo. The ape's mouth was Lloyd's belly button. I told you my instincts had been jangling. 'Knuckledraggers for life, booyah!'

That was why Lloyd was prepared to set me up with a

bike. The Knuckledraggers were rumoured to be up to their nuts in rebirthing Harleys. But that was obviously far from all they were mixed up in. This was the same crew that had run Roxy's boyfriend out of town.

Lloyd cracked his knuckles as he pulled his shirt back down. Seeing that tattooed ape threw me a curve ball that I should have seen coming. Of course Dave's cousin would be in the Knuckledraggers. That should have been the first question. I wasn't ready to talk business, I was just after some intell. The whole thing was moving too fast. Everything I'd learned pointed to this cider-drinking monkey and his mates being linked to running a uni student out of town and either killing Billy Wong's cook-cum-security or Billy Wong's cook-cum-security taking a hit on their behalf. Potential participants in a turf war were not the type of people I wanted to do a deal with. This meeting had been a mistake that needed a careful exit.

'Great. What I was thinking is one of those red postie bikes. You know the ones, I think they're Japanese? Yamaha? Maybe get a milk crate on the back for my work tools. One of those stirrup things the surfers have for their boards, except I'll use it for holding my ladder and extension poles. What you reckon?'

Lloyd smirked and then the smirk kind of slid from his face as he realised I was serious. Turning to Dave, he went a shade of red. 'This joker for real, Dave? I thought I was here to have a family catch up, maybe talk a bit of business. Instead, I get this joker taking the piss talking about Jap crap to me!'

Looking back at me, Lloyd confirmed for himself that I was indeed taking the piss. His finger was still pointed at me and I could see engine grease under his nail. I realised I'd miscalculated in a big way. Holding my hands up as if his finger were a gun, I tried to placate him, tried to say I was just messing with him, but it was too late. The world exploded into white stars and black.

Waking to see Kirrily the bartender looking down on me with concern, I tasted blood on my upper lip. The wall had a bar stool sticking out of it near my head.

I took the paper towel she offered me and gingerly tested to see if anything was broken or chipped. Dabbing at the blood with the help of a little ice, I asked for a shot of something medicinal. A straight-sided glass containing ice and a couple of fingers of spirit was in my hand by the time I'd extracted my stool from the wall and was perched on high. Sipping the cold alcohol stung the point in my cheek where my jaw had been realigned.

Dave hurried back inside to check on me.

'What were you doin'? I thought you wanted to talk to him about … y'know.'

Shaking my head, I told him I'd changed my mind. 'Didn't feel right,' was all I offered, not willing to share any of my other suspicions.

'So you just go from hot to cold?'

'Pretty much. I'm trying to keep us in charge, Dave. Stop some bikies just taking control. So, yeah. I changed my mind simply by talking to him.' I skipped adding that being attacked was another setback to building a healthy working relationship.

Curling his lip, Dave reached for his beer to gather his

thoughts. He couldn't believe my turnaround. He didn't like his cousin either but we had set up a meeting. So for Dave, I should have been more respectful. Maybe.

'Is he still outside?'

Seems that once the bouncers had him outside, Lloyd had got on his bike and hared off before any police arrived. Accepting this information, I drained the last of the icy drink the barmaid had given me. Placing the frosted glass on my cheek, I enjoyed the sting as I watched the staff clear up Lloyd's mess.

'Dave, I was wrong. Lloyd is a dickhead and isn't going to be of any use to us. It was a mistake to think about bringing him in. We need to talk to someone bigger than Lloyd. He's a wannabe, not even a middleman.'

'Why? I thought he'd be perfect. He is a bit punchy ...'

That had to be the understatement of the year but I went for diplomacy. 'Guy's a loose cannon. No idea what he'll do. Not the sort to bring on board something like this.'

'He's fine. Just a few anger management issues.'

Pointing to my blackening eye, I begged to differ.

This seemed to cut through a little for Dave, who started to nod.

'I'm sorry, Lachie.'

I waved the concern away. I'd requested the meeting so I didn't see what Dave had to apologise to me about. Leaning back against the wall, the glass still against my nose and my eyes closed, I relished the darkness.

'I shouldn't've told him anything.'

My eyes opened and I pushed myself off the wall. 'Told him? Told him what?'

'About what you wanted to speak to him about,' said Dave.

'You told him? How much you tell him?'

'All of it. He's my cousin. He said his mates might be interested.'

Seems in Dave's world, family is more important than secrets. Even secrets that can earn you a whole lot of trouble.

It was about then that the police turned up. Refusing to press charges was the least I could do. After all, who wanted the extra paperwork, the hassle? The two young constables agreed. Thank Christ tomorrow I'd be back at work. I needed the peace and quiet.

12
BACK TO WORK

Getting a lift back to mine with Dave didn't do anything to stop me jumping at every shadow and noise. Once home, I checked the front door and every window several times before perching on the edge of the couch with one knee pumping and my head in my hands. Dave and his bloody big mouth.

For all his good mate status, Dave had demonstrated a monumental failing: trust. He trusted that everything would be okay and that everyone was alright. Which was why he was such a good mate. Doesn't change the fact that, cousin or not, he'd told a member of an organised criminal enterprise what we'd found in the sea.

I flicked on the television, then realised I wouldn't be able to hear anything else – like some bikie gangster hitman creeping up to my house to kill me. Stabbing the remote to mute, I listened for any sound that might be out of the ordinary. There were none. It was total suburban quiet. I was quickly developing a sense of why so many gangsters ended up shot – it was a relief from the stress of their daily lives trying to avoid getting shot.

Tomorrow couldn't come quickly enough. Regardless of what I'd pulled from the ocean depths, I still had a day job to do and a life to try to keep normal. Some would say that it was all about balance. What I wanted was to avoid bringing any attention to myself, anything that might make people curious. I just wanted to get back into my natural under-the-radar environment and stay there.

Even not making a statement about Lloyd's assault risked

coming back to bite me. I was certain that my name would get dropped at the police station, triggering some link to the torso. I was turning into a cop magnet at the worst possible time. The more contact I had with the police, the more dodgy things would start to pop up. The more dodgy things that popped up, the more people would know what I was up to. Somehow, I knew, all of this would flow like water on a dusty plain back to Melbourne.

History was at risk of repeating.

In Melbourne, things had got too hot when I pushed my luck too hard. I'd become involved in a shady deal that no one knew I was part of – up to now. It wouldn't take much for some bright spark to work out who I'd been running with in Victoria, track my family history, maybe correlate some dates. It was why I'd ended up in Newcastle, where no one knew me and I was simply a normal guy who painted houses. Nothing says 'under the radar' better than painting a bunch of white walls another shade of white.

So what with the cops, Dave and his big mouth, an angry young bikie and a load of bricks containing illegal powder on my mind, I hit my mattress with a full-body slam and lay awake, knowing I was in danger of breaking my promise to my mother to stay on the path of righteousness.

After a sleepless night I beat the alarm before it chirruped the new day. I stepped into the shower in the vague hope it might help me feel like I was actually awake.

Catching a glimpse of myself in the mirror was a fright. My face looked like a limp balloon, my eye was well and truly black, swollen across my left cheekbone. Breakfast of coffee and Weet-Bix was continually interrupted by the uncontrollable urge to keep touching my face. Even once out the door, I was still touching the bruise. Why are we unable to keep ourselves away from any bits of our body that hurt? Always poking and probing, the jolt of pain coming as a surprise as if this time it'd be different.

The Beast must have felt as tired as I was, because it put up a fight, whining and spluttering smoggy belches from its exhaust. A few loving taps on the accelerator and it coughed to life, a smoker with their first morning fag.

The morning was filled with surfers, joggers, dog walkers and tradies, as always. Tradies are the ones standing in cafés waiting for takeaway coffees, wondering why the squarehead civilians are up. We're getting paid for it, you're … exercising? Madness.

Michael had my coffee ready before I needed to say anything – the beauty of being a regular, walk though the door and they're already making what you want.

'Where to today, Lachie?' he asked, as he worked another order on the sandwich press.

Mumbling was all I could manage but he understood that I was off to Hamilton as I collected a copy of *The Daily Telegraph* – regulation worksite reading material. Paper folded in half under my arm, death grip on my coffee, I clumped back to the Beast, its motor still running for fear of not being able to start it again.

Pouring the coffee into my insulated travel mug, I drove with it nestled between my legs, sipping at traffic lights or give way signs. I was at the address in no time, a townhouse, all made out of ticky-tacky like its neighbours: identical in every way.

Small enough but with a tight main stairwell linking the two levels. Stairs are almost as much of a pain as French windows.

'Big Lachie M, look like I feel, mate.' Maxie was standing at the top of the drive, waiting for someone to arrive. He whistled as he looked at my bruise. 'You cop a belting? You really were sick yesterday.'

'Unload the gear and set up a work pile by the door. Muzz here yet?'

The boss was inside with the owner getting the lowdown on the job. He'd pass it on to me over the morning ciggie and then piss off. All standard operating procedure. Seeing Maxie setting up, I made a decision. Although I was reluctant to involve him in selling my contraband, it was a lesser evil than getting involved with the bikies. All I was looking for was a contact, maybe an introduction. Maxie could have a finder's fee that would keep him at arm's length for safety.

Muzz coming out to smoke a heart starter as he delivered the rundown on the day's job ended my rationalising.

'Okay, boys. I off. Youse call if any problems, but I'll be back by lunchtime.'

Taking me aside, Muzz made sure Maxie was a little way away before telling me the extras that every job has.

'No fuck ups on this one.'

'Muzz, when've I fucked up?'

Before I could answer, Muzz was already lighting a second cigarette. Never a good sign. 'Extra care, that's all I'm saying. This is a big one. Old bastard in there has a lot of property. So, extra drop sheets, keep the place clean. No dust. Perfect.' He looked into my eyes as the smoke jetted from his nose, held my gaze intently for a moment and then grinned as he slapped my shoulder. 'This is why I give you the good jobs, Lachie.'

With a wave, Muzz headed for his family-friendly four-wheel drive, a sign for his prospective clients of how large and prosperous his business was. Watching him drive off, I knew I had no desire to follow in his footsteps. Absolutely zero ambition to run my own business, more than happy to just do as I was told and do it well, Monday to Friday, and take nothing of it home. Despite my resistance, I'd learned from my old man that other than the next pay day and how to spend it, long-term plans were pointless. Kids supposedly changed that but at this stage I was the end of my genetic line. Dwelling on that, I suddenly thought of my mum again, sitting in the kitchen with a cup of tea, sniffing as she said plans were simply ways of telling God a joke.

Shaking free from the memories, I drained the last of my coffee and turned back to Maxie.

'Okay, Max. You heard the man. Set up in the back room, drops down and furniture in the middle. Start with the gapping and patching.'

He ambled off like a white wombat, clutching a gap gun and rag. I called him again.

'Max. Remind me. After work, let's have a chat.'

He wanted to know what about so I told him, 'The future.'

Painting was just what the doctor ordered after the last couple of days. It's the repetition and the way that the job is either done or not. Sure, it's dusty and dirty and different bits of your body ache with every discovery of new muscles, but the meditative nature of the work has its plusses. And at least I wasn't a plumber, hands and arms in shit. Anything that comes from the body is best avoided. That's my motto and

I'm sticking with it.

Max and I made short work of the back room. It wasn't really in need of a paint, probably only three years since the last coat. The owner was one of those anal types, everything in its place and all neat and tidy. The more I saw of the place the more I understood what Muzz had been saying. A far cry from some that are so desperate for a spot of paint that the walls just soak it up, making it impossible to get a good finish. Best of all, the job at hand meant I didn't need to think about the other matter.

Morning tea came about all too quickly.

'Maxie!' I had to yell from up on the ladder in the stairwell. 'Max! Where you at? Break time or want to go a bit longer?'

Nothing. I put my kit down and went in search of my apprentice. He was in the lounge room where we'd started, headphones on, leaning precariously on a ladder, straining to paint a corner of the ceiling.

'What're you doing?'

Maxie very nearly fell off his perch, exactly as I feared. I didn't want him to get hurt but I was also worried about the pot of paint going flying over the expensive leather sofa that was no longer protected by the drop sheets – they'd slipped to a pile on the floor. It was a toss up which would be worse.

'Just finishing up this bit.'

'And giving the couch a nice spray while you're at it, too?'

Chastened, Maxie pulled his headphones free as he got down to the ground, looking so hangdog there was no way I could rub his nose in it.

'If Muzz caught you doing that, he'd have your balls. Now, want anything? I'm going to the bakery.'

Maxie gave me his order.

13
STOLEN

Working with the same crew, you quickly pick up what everyone likes and how they like to have it. Maxie liked a sausage roll and Coke for morning tea. I was more relaxed. Some days were sweet, others were more savoury. Today was feeling savoury so I was in search of a pastie. Maybe a custard tart to follow and another coffee. At a push, I'd accept an iced one.

The Beast still hadn't shaken off its night-time chills and refused to start. After a little coaxing, it agreed and we were off to find the closest bakery. Didn't have to go far, couple of blocks at most. That's another thing about the work I do, you quickly develop an encyclopaedic knowledge of the city's cafés, bakeries and sandwich shops. I left the Beast running outside the shop while I went in.

The queue was long, the service slow and the coffee weak, possibly even burnt. Standing there, making a mental review for next time I was in the area, my mind slipped easily back into the groove of what was waiting for me at home. Could I really ask Maxie? Would he even know anyone? Did I want to deal with the Knuckledraggers? I didn't like to feel out of my depth and, in the world of drug deals, this was a less than perfect place to be.

Carrying coffee, Coke, sausage roll, pastie and custard tart out of the shop, the sight that greeted me made me drop my bundle. I didn't know whether to be furious or dumbstruck. I'd left the Beast running like that pretty much from the first day I bought it. Why would someone want to steal it now?

I know it was dumb, but I stood and looked up and down the street as if the Beast had merely wandered off like a dog to explore the area's interesting smells despite being told to stay. We all do stupid things in times of stress. The Beast was gone – looking up and down the street wasn't going to bring it back.

So I did what any normal person would do: I trotted off in the direction I'd come from with the trot rapidly becoming a jog that soon developed into a run.

Arriving back at the work site out of breath, I found Maxie on the driveway looking even more downtrodden, with Muzz pacing furiously in front of him, waving his arms madly. All signs pointed to something having happened, something that was not good. Seeing me walk up hot, bothered and angry, Muzz turned his rage in my direction.

'Where you been? I leave you here and this idiot ruins everything!'

'What happened?' I looked at Maxie. He was finding the ground more interesting.

Seemed Maxie had decided to continue what he'd been doing. Except he'd lost his balance and spilled half a tin on the leather sofa and carpets while punching a Maxie-sized hole in the plaster wall as he fell.

'He's his own disaster. And you left him here? Alone?'

'I was on the morning tea run.'

Not that Muzz was listening. He was looking past me. 'And where the bloody blue blazes is your car?'

'Stolen. Just now. I need to get to the police station and report it.'

My boss went a shade of red I'd never seen before. 'You sacked! You and you. Sacked. Both of you.' As he yelled, his spit sprayed like a sun shower. 'Fuck off! Get! You with your bloody sickies, coming back to work with a black eye. Never want to see you lazy bloody Aussies again.'

Nodding, every muscle taut, I turned and walked back the way I came. At the corner, I paused as the shock of it all blotted out how to get to the police station.

'Beer then, Lachie?' asked Maxie, running up behind me. 'What you want to talk to me about?'

'Walk away,' was all I could say. Not only had I lost my car and job, Maxie's attempt at renovating had me on the brink of losing it. There was no way I was in any state to talk to him about his shady friends. I couldn't even look at him.

My fury must have been written all over my face as Maxie scuttled away from me, calling over his shoulder that the beer could wait for another time. I watched him walk quickly away, my jaw clenched. He got that right. Way I was feeling, that beer would be a long time coming.

14
COP SHOP SURPRISE

Normally, you report a crime so the police can go do their job and investigate. Only problem was the Beast was uninsured, rego was just about due, and it was over twenty years old and covered in splatters of paint. Adding insult to injury was my habit of leaving it running when quickly ducking into places. None of these things was going to put the investigation at the top of a crime taskforce to-do list. Thankfully, the long trudge along the waterfront gave me time to work out suitable responses, explanations and rationales for all of that so I'd escape a lecture about insurance, road worthiness and security.

The Church Street cop shop looked like it had been designed by an East German refugee after the Berlin Wall came down. Either that or someone with shares in concrete had influence with the government. Entering the lobby, all lino, glass and steel, I went to the counter and told the desk sergeant what I was there for. Without a word or looking up from the latest copy of the police association magazine, he reached under the counter for the forms I needed to fill out. Then he pointed a finger at the seating area before the same finger went to his mouth for a lick to turn the next page. Management speak might refer to us all as 'clients' now but that doesn't mean customer service isn't a dying art.

Sitting on a hard plastic chair, I dutifully filled in the details of where the Beast had last been seen, make, rego and so on. Was I able to claim my favourite CD? The policeman nodded and said to fill it all in. If it wasn't on the form, it was difficult to add later on. He solemnly explained that sometimes the most innocuous item would be the irrefutable piece of evidence needed to secure a conviction. I raised an eyebrow at that. He just went back to his reading material.

Satisfied I'd covered everything, I took the forms to the desk and stood in silence as he glanced over them with little interest.

'All the i's and t's dotted and crossed, officer.'

It was the desk sergeant's turn to raise an eyebrow before he tore off my duplicate copy and poked the other two into an intray. He cleared his throat.

'Mate, we see something, we'll be in touch.'

'That likely?'

He looked at me properly for the first time. 'Gee, I dunno. Twenty-year-old car, full of crap. Reluctant starter. What d'you reckon?'

I glanced down at my copy of the form, which I would have been taking to my insurer if I'd had insurance.

As I got to the door, he called out to me.

'We might have a bit of luck with this CD though. If we find a copy of the Beatles' *White Album*, we'll be right in touch.'

'It was a burnt copy.'

The sergeant shook his head. '*Tsk, tsk, tsk*. Piracy is crime too, y'know.'

It was at that point that Detective Sergeant Jon Baxter and Fisheries Officer Karen Miller entered. She was not happy to see me.

'Hello?' I stuck out my hand, thankfully not too dirty with gapper and undercoat. The white overalls and paint-splattered baseball cap tended to give it away anyway.

'Hi,' she said stiffly. Baxter looked from her to me with the faintest of smiles. Dirty-minded bastard.

'You know him, Karen?'

Karen looked flustered so I stepped in to save the day.

'From Billy Wong's. The inspection. That's all. Just being friendly,' I said, as my head screamed at me to shut up.

'Right. Well. Mr Munro, you've saved me a trip. Was going to come out and check a few things with your statement.'

'My statement? But the Sergeant won't have even started processing it yet. How can you be wanting to go over that now?'

'What are you talking about?'

'My car? Stolen this morning? What're you talking about?'

The detective looked at Karen, who had the best poker face I'd ever seen.

'I'm talking about your statement from Monday. You say your car was stolen?'

Karen was holding her folders close to her chest and looking straight at me as the pennies finally dropped for all of us. The man who reported a body on a beach. His car was stolen. The police were adding two plus two and getting five while I was seeing images of handcuffs.

'I'll leave you to it, detective,' Karen said, making her way to the exit.

'Thanks for keeping us in the loop, Karen. Fascinating to know the goings on in the waters of Newcastle.'

As the detective held the internal door open to take me into the station, I wondered aloud if I needed a lawyer.

'Do you, Mr Munro? You tell me. We're just wanting to

have a little chat, yeah? You're free to leave at any time.'

If you've ever had the misfortune to be interviewed by the police, you know how uncomfortable they make you feel. Everything you say is met with an intense stare and a cloud of silence. Even the purest of saints would crack under that pressure. Especially when the coppers start asking about things in your past.

'I see you've had a little bit of trouble in your youth with drugs, yeah?'

Shifting in my chair, I looked up as Baxter's colleague O'Keefe joined us.

'You have my record there? It'll tell you all about it. I think the court called it a youthful indiscretion.'

'Earned you a good behaviour bond.' The silence again.

See, the trick to surviving an interrogation is to say nothing. Police are naturally suspicious. If you say anything, you'll feed them something to investigate. Keep quiet and they have to think for themselves. Like dealing with a crocodile, if you don't want any attention, don't throw them a chicken.

'Where are you heading with this, detective?'

A shrug and a little tapping of the papers to straighten them was all he was going to give me.

'Just running through a few things, Mr Munro. Have to be thorough, yeah? Where'd you get the shiner?'

I touched my bruised cheek and focused on the discomfort. Like I said, they'd seen something in my record they understood and had leaped on it.

'Well, if you've covered all the bases, I have to be going. My car was stolen this morning and then I was sacked. So ...'

He made notes and I mentally slapped myself. I could

just about see the cogs ticking over – dead body, prior drug conviction, car stolen, sacked, associating with shady characters. As that soured Utopian William S. Burroughs said, once the law starts asking questions, there's no end to it.

Finally, I was shown the door by the detective. Walking back into the foyer, I looked across at the desk sergeant, who was now paying me much more attention than when I'd been just another dolt who'd had his car stolen. As I was about to step into the freedom of the street, Baxter called out to me.

'I wouldn't plan on leaving the city if I were you. Just in case we have any more questions.'

'I'm not going anywhere, Detective Baxter. Nothing's changed since you and Big Bird told me that on Monday.'

'Detective *Sergeant* Baxter,' he corrected. 'I like Big Bird though. Not very original but I'll let Shennae know your nickname for her.'

I stood in the doorway unable to say a thing as Baxter stared at me, daring me to give him a nickname too. My mind clamoured with things I could have called him, but a sniff was all he got as the desk sergeant smirked and shook his head slowly before buzzing Baxter back inside and returning to his magazine.

On the street, my fists clenched, I took my frustrations out on a defenceless Coke can. Booting it into the air, it hit a shiny wagon, setting off the car alarm. How could it have done anything else?

As I walked up the driveway to my front door, I was pleased to see my landlord, old Harry Kinniburgh, sitting in the backyard by the Hills Hoist, smoking his tightly rolled cigarette and sipping a green tea.

'Lach.'

'Harry.'

Simple communication. No frills. Harry never asked about the weather or my day. If I talked of those things he'd listen, but he never asked. The faded tattoos on his once powerful forearms were on display as he sipped his tea: a Hawaiian girl and an anchor. If you studied the blue blurs with a squint you could sort of pick them out.

'All's good?'

'Prick of a day, Harry. Absolute prick. Can I borrow your bike?'

Drawing deep on his rollie, Old Harry peered up at me from under his frayed baseball cap, which advertised a hardware chain that no longer existed. His singlet, faded Stubbie shorts and cheap blue rubber thongs exposed too much skinny old-man flesh. His yes was a given but he left vocalising it until the last minute, continuing to sip his tea and ruminate.

'Lach, my bike is your bike. Y'know that. She's out in the shed.'

The shed was the repository of all things past. Unable to throw anything away in case he needed it again, Harry knew where each and every piece of junk was and how he planned to use it. I watched as he rearranged things to get at his bike.

Maybe that was why he took me in. I'm guessing he could sense I'd left behind a less than perfect life, a life I was happy to forget and make damned sure no one knew anything about. Not that I'd told him and not that he'd asked. But the understanding or recognition of a fellow traveller meant that when I came to look at the place, Harry sized me up and told me if I could pay, the place was mine. Close wasn't the right word for our relationship, but there was respect. I didn't want to lose that.

'Bit dusty. Wheels still hard. She'll treat you well, knows the streets round here better than me.'

Thanking Harry, I wheeled the bike to my front door and leaned it against the brickwork. Bike technology might not have really changed in eighty years but what had improved was the weight. Harry's old bike weighed a tonne.

A quick shower and a spruce up had me heading out the door again, feeling a little more human. Harry was still sitting by his back door, his rollie now minuscule and the mug of tea nearly dry.

'Looks like my bike's the only thing you'll be throwing your leg over tonight, Lach.'

In a couple of hours, I'd think of the perfect witty retort, but now all Harry got was a wave and a noncommittal shrug as I swung my leg over the old racing frame and pushed off. The handle bars were upside-down rams' horns with brake handles for grips. But riding a bike, like swimming, is always relaxing if you know how. The movement makes you smile as the wind flows past. Pedalling, I let myself freewheel on the down slopes, looping back and forth like a teenager. Even as my mind chewed over my problems, riding that bike put back the smile I'd been missing.

Maybe I could take Dave's boat out again and get some more abalone, tide me over until I could get rid of the packages. One of those bricks had to be worth at least five figures. All twenty? Those bricks had the potential to be a big help to all that was ailing me. People were always going to buy drugs. If I didn't sell what I had, the market would still exist, and it made sense to get a piece of it. It wasn't like I was an importer myself. I was just getting rid of a bit of flotsam. Once I found a buyer.

Rationalising anything is easier with the wind blowing through your hair.

15
DAVE DELIVERS A MESSAGE

'You arrive on my doorstep without beer? Why is it you never bring any beer?' was Dave's greeting.

Shrugging, I wheeled the bike down the drive to the backyard as he continued to whine. When I turned around after leaning the bike against the shed, Dave looked at me with an exaggerated sad face.

'Give me the keys and I'll drive to get some,' I offered. 'I need to borrow some cash too.'

Dave shook his head. 'Don't bother. The barbie's just about at temp. There's beers in the shed. Stocked up the other day.'

'Why are you sooking about me not bringing any beer then?'

'Cos you never bring any beers, Lach-stock.'

That was so not true.

'Whose bike's that?' he asked as I headed for the beer fridge.

Wrenching the shed door open, I flicked the lights on and blinked under the harsh fluorescents before idly going to the storage locker to give the wet suits, snorkels and masks a once over. They were all clean and in working order. Dave kept things like that: everything well-maintained — any hint of a problem meant immediate repairs or replacement. It was an admirable quality. Kneeling, I looked over the aqualung, testing the air and gauges and imagining getting into the water. I could almost feel it swallowing me, the ocean's embrace. Illegal as it was, I did love the challenge of diving for abalone.

I lifted the hessian sack and poked at one of the abalone with a finger. The large foot retracted, showing it was still alive. They weren't in any danger yet but they needed to reach their destination. Fresh, as they say, is always best. Dave's setup was fine but they would be better with a stronger filtration system and aerator. Once they were in Billy Wong's own tank setup, these shellfish would live their last few days in abalone heaven.

Taking two beers from the old fridge, I pulled a couple of stubbie holders from the poly-tube dispenser, slid the bottles into their wetsuit jackets and popped the tops. Taking them outside to Dave, I discovered he already had one by the barbecue.

'But cheers. This little lager's nearly done.'

Annoyed, I sat down in one of the camp chairs and drank a long pull.

'So, rough day? Want to tell Uncle Davo?'

I kept drinking until my beer bottle was empty.

'Thirsty?' Dave handed me the second beer I had brought out for him. 'Here. Looks like you need it more than me.'

It helped. Sitting there as the shadows of the afternoon's golden hour grew longer, I told Dave about how much of a shocker my day had been. As the first sausages were cooked and slapped into the obligatory slice of white bread, Dave loaded up the barbie with chops and burgers. It was enough to feed a footy team. The casual stickybeak peering over the fence would assume a party was about to start. What Dave was actually doing was cooking up his week's feed. What wasn't eaten would be covered and shelved in the fridge for later. It was his patented tight-arse bachelor menu system: buy in bulk the marked-down, day-before-its-use-by meat, cook it up and keep it in the fridge. It was how he'd live until he headed back into the mines in a fortnight.

Licking my fingers as the last of my second sausage in bread disappeared, I caught Dave watching me.

'What?'

Without looking up from tending his meat, Dave took another pull of his beer, sprinkled a little on the burgers and shifted his weight.

'Happy to see ya mate. Just happy to see ya.'

Even ignoring the fact we'd seen each other several times in the last seventy-two hours, Dave's shifting body language highlighted something was on his mind and he didn't know how to say it. Sitting there in silence, staring at him, I soon had Dave spilling what was bothering him.

'Me cousin wants to apologise.'

I maintained the silence as any ideas about delivering the abalone to Billy Wong evaporated.

'He's upset about what happened. Wants to say he's sorry.'

'Sorry? For belting me?'

Nodding, Dave drank from his beer like a baby sucking on its bottle. Despite this being a good solution to our little packages problem, I still didn't feel like seeing that prick ever again.

'Lachie, he'll be able to ...' Dave nodded twice to the left. 'Y'know, take care of the ... stuff.'

'But if you hadn't told him about that, would he be wanting to apologise?'

Dave shrugged.

Did it matter? As suspected, the only reason I was being

offered the chance to hear an apology in person was because I had something that the angry Knuckledragger wanted more. It annoyed me that Lloyd was now our best shot at getting rid of the stuff quickly. If I wanted the cash for a new car, a new job and an escape net, I'd have to go through with that face-to-face, accept Lloyd's apology and put aside my reservations about dealing with the Knuckledraggers.

As the meat sizzled, I looked to the heavens, weighing up the decision I'd already made. I needed to keep up appearances.

Like a puppy checking to see if he was forgiven, Dave sidled up to me and held out a third sausage in bread. 'What d'ya say, Lachie? I think Lloyd is being very generous offering to meet again.'

The burn on the sausage mixed with the tomato sauce and soft bread tasted good. Swigging a mouthful of beer to cool the meat, I looked up at Dave and pretended to be swayed. 'Make the call. I'll see him.' My reluctance remained hidden beneath my words.

Dave fist-pumped the air.

'Just make it somewhere safe. No bar stools or weapons, okay?'

Dave got the message but my own reservations bubbled loudly in the back of my mind. I pushed those thoughts deep. I'd meet Lloyd and if it went well, I'd be rid of the drugs. By the end of the week, it might all be over.

If I said it enough, even I could believe it.

16
A NEW DEAL

Insomnia. Not sure if it was caused by Dave's meat selections and dubious supermarket salads or the thought of the new meeting between me and the Knuckledragger. At about two thirty in the morning, I gave up and tried to watch some television. Even the boring early-early morning TV didn't start me snoring.

My problem was that even in a public place, out in the open, Lloyd was still a man of violence, and I, a man of peace. Now, I'd be the first to admit that I've made some dumb decisions in the past – too many to even list – so what difference was another one? Despite this and despite wanting to be rid of the drugs, even for me, this meeting was feeling like a bad idea.

As a commercial came on advertising a set of steak knives and the promise of a second set if I purchased them in the next fifteen minutes, something clicked. Protection. I needed protection for this meeting. And by protection I didn't mean Dave. Heading for the linen closet by the front door, I rummaged until I found an old dive knife. When I first started diving, I bought this knife and then promptly lost it. So I went out and bought another one. When I got home, this knife was sitting on the bench by the fruit bowl. As many a frustrated girlfriend has muttered, I'd clearly been having a man's look.

Sliding the knife free of its sheath, the stainless steel gleamed dully. There were a couple of small spots of surface rust but the blade looked menacing and that was all that counted. I tried to imagine it stabbing into a sea creature, like some diver in a B-grade movie wrestling a huge shark while a giant octopus watched, waiting to attack the victor. Reality was, if a shark decided to chow down on a limb, I very much doubted the knife would be much use. Better to bop it on the nose or poke it in the eye. Or so I'd been told.

Padding back to the couch, my mind shifted gear from stabbing or wrestling a shark to wondering if I could actually stab a 'roid-raging bikie. It takes a long time to train soldiers to the point where they can physically hurt or kill someone. Not everyone can.

Mulling this over must have been enough to send me into the land of nod, as I woke with the sun streaming in and a text from Dave. The meeting was all set for that afternoon by the big carpark at Bar Beach near Memorial Drive. The location didn't fill me with confidence. At least a big open carpark was public. Now all I had to do was wait and hope I didn't lose my nerve.

Lloyd was waiting for me. He didn't realise I could see him waiting up on the ridge as he scurried out of sight to collect his Harley and make a thunderous entrance. Maybe he was nervous too.

As he roared down Memorial Drive, I made my way to the picnic table on the grassy slope overlooking Bar Beach and leaned Harry's bike against the table.

Making a noisy show of parking, Lloyd slow-walked the huge hog back into the parking spot until its rear wheel kissed the kerb. I hoped I was giving off the right amount of confident cool and that Lloyd's hearing loss from his barely muffled exhaust would prevent him from hearing the thudding of my heart.

Swaggering towards me bowleggedly, Lloyd didn't really look like the kind of person who was arriving for an apology.

'Lach.'

I pushed myself off the table and stood, arms crossed, staring at him blankly, ignoring his outstretched hand. My sunglasses weren't dark enough to have any intimidatory effect, so I tried to look tough, waiting for whatever happened next.

Seeing I wasn't going to shake his hand, Lloyd withdrew it and looked about the place as if expecting someone to rescue him too.

'Wanted to say sorry. For gettin' annoyed with you. That was wrong and I apologise.'

'Well, thank you, Lloyd. That means a great deal to me.'

'Cool.' Maybe Lloyd hadn't collected his club sarcasm badge yet.

Surprisingly, he sat down at the table, which forced me to do the same. Leaning forwards, he put his elbows on his knees before bobbing his head as if rocking to his own internal beat.

'So why, Lloyd?'

'Why what?'

'The apology.'

He looked at me for the briefest of moments before looking back to the street as if expecting company. Maybe it was his bikie training, keeping an eye out for cops. Probably learned it from one of his club's *Sons of Anarchy* or *The Sopranos* DVD nights. Those shows have all the lifestyle tips for the criminally aspirational. But I took the hint and made sure I kept an eye on the approaches as well. Couldn't hurt.

'Cos I'm sorry?'

'Okay.'

'You disrespected me the other day. Truth is, I'm a fuckin' marshmallow. I didn't want to clock ya. But someone sees me let you get away with that ... I've got an image, the club has a reputation. We were in public. You get it?' He paused. 'And me sergeant-at-arms told me I had to for deckin' ya. We can't afford the bad press about public brawlin'.'

'Wouldn't that be positive PR for a bikie?' I shifted so I was on more of an angle to him and felt the knife scabbard that was tucked into my sock digging into my leg.

'Y'know, you ask a fuckload of questions!'

I stood up and made to walk off before his temper blew. Nothing had changed my reservations about sharing what I had stashed around my home with this guy. Sometimes, playing hard to get is the best position.

'No. I mean, please? Stay?'

The way he looked at me, I felt like I was being hit on.

'Why? You want to say something else to me, Lloyd?'

'Sit down, would ya? Fuck, you make this hard.'

Funnily enough, seeing Lloyd like this killed off any feelings of fear. He looked kind of pathetic. So I sat down again. I was warming to the guy.

'None of us want any trouble, right? So if we're goin' to be doin' business, we should get all of that into the open. We checked you out. You're clean.'

The way he pronounced 'business', letting each syllable form and adding some of his own so the word became 'biz-zy-neice', was distracting. It pulled focus from the real issue:

that the Knuckledraggers had, unnervingly, carried out an investigation into me that had found me to be an okay dude. These guys were more efficient than any branch of government and equally as terrifying.

'Y'proposition is of interest.'

'What proposition? My desire for a postie bike to get about on?'

Lloyd kept himself in check but both sets of knuckles tensed and his jaw became sharply defined. Then, with a deep breath, he turned and smiled.

'No. Not. That. You can look after all that on your own. The other thing.'

How much had Dave told him?

'Don't look shocked. Dave is family. He told me all about … the stuff. And I think I can be of assistance. I've got connections, got the ways and means, man. You, you're just a house painter. And you discovered some nasty shit on the beach the other day.'

Was there nothing that Lloyd didn't know?

He grinned as if reading my mind before adding his next stipulation. 'Need a sample. To see if what you got is the real deal. That the sea water hasn't affected it in some way.'

'It was well sealed. There wasn't any water contamination.'

'Best be safe. Also, it'll tell me you're not a pig or somethin'.'

Now the burble of fear percolating in the bottom of my guts started to rush up. 'Really? But you said you'd checked me out.'

'Lach, mate, you came up clean. But cops, they can be well crafty. And so if you are a cop, you could have been planted here months back, just waitin' for the green light.'

The idea was terrifying in its illogicality. That the police would have the resources to plant an undercover so deep for so long on the off chance they could be activated when required made my mind boggle. And with the boggling, the tide of fear came flooding back in.

Breathing deeply to quell my terrors, I decided not to tell Lloyd that supplying a sample would also be exactly what an undercover police operative would do. Instead, I stuck out my hand to shake on it. He instructed me on how to get him his sample in the next few days – a small amount, less than commercial, for testing.

He grinned. 'Mate, I'll be in touch for the drop-off.'

Sitting there on the bench, I took stock of what had just been agreed to as Lloyd stood up and walked back to his bike. Swinging his leg over, he set about the intricate order of switches and checks in preparation for ignition.

As the echoing Harley exhaust disappeared over the rise, I looked at the waves crashing on the shore as they had done for thousands of much simpler years. Despite my reservations, I'd just agreed to deal with the Knuckledraggers.

Next time I saw a large suitcase shape in the water, I'd leave it there. Some salvage just wasn't worth the effort. Unlike the abalone. The bloody abalone! Still sitting in Dave's tanks. I wondered how long we had before they went off.

17
SURPRISE VISIT

Any feelings of urgency regarding the abalone disappeared as I approached my granny flat and saw what was outside the front door.

'Lachlan Munro? Detective Sergeant Jon Baxter. You remember my colleague Detective Shennae O'Keefe. Just wanted to have a word about Monday? Mind if we come in?'

Everything was getting too close.

'You okay, Mr Munro? You look pale.'

'Big night,' was all I could offer.

'Not like I haven't had my fair share.' He winked at his colleague.

Showing them inside reinforced to me how small the place was. Three people and it looked like a party.

'Just wanted to run through a few things in your statement, yeah?'

'Didn't we cover all that yesterday?'

I offered them a seat on the couch, dirty as it was, and tried to look cool, calm and collected – like having two cops in my lounge was normal – and to forget about the drugs taped in various bolt holes around my place and the stash of poached abalone sitting at my mate's.

'Look nervous, Mr Munro. Relax. This is pure routine. Not every day someone finds a body, no.'

'It was only a torso.'

'True.' Baxter nodded, fixing me with that laser-drilling gaze people in authority have.

Detective O'Keefe opened a lever arch folder she'd had under her arm. 'We wanted to see if you recognised any of these people.' She slid the folder across the coffee table. Idly, I flicked through the pages of mug shots and missing persons. None of them looked familiar.

'Take your time,' O'Keefe said.

'These the victim or the killers? What am I looking for?'

'Do you recognise anyone?' Detective O'Keefe was staring at me closely now, watching me for a tell. I hated to disappoint, but none of the faces triggered any sort of memory.

'Oh, well. Always worth a shot, isn't it, detective?' Baxter leaned back in his chair and looked at his colleague, indicating it was time to leave.

O'Keefe was still looking at me, to the point where it was seriously unnerving. Without shifting her gaze, she agreed with her colleague that it always was worth a shot. Was there a hint of a smile when she said it? Being unable to read her was even more unnerving.

'Isn't this a little unorthodox?' I asked. I don't know where the question came from but maybe the kilos of drugs hidden in my flat heightened my criminal senses. It did seem odd to have a couple of cops doing house calls with a photo album of crooks.

'A little. Normally do this down at the station, yeah?' said Baxter. 'But we were in the area on other matters. And a man has not only been killed but horribly dismembered. Kind of allows for a little unorthodoxy, yeah?'

Detective O'Keefe was still watching me as she flipped her folder shut and made ready to leave. 'Call if anything comes to mind?' She touched my forearm and smiled, leaning close to be out of earshot of Baxter. 'Big Bird? Come on, been getting that since high school, Lachie. After everything I've heard about you, I thought you'd come up with something a little more original than that.'

I watched, puzzled, as Detective O'Keefe caught up with her colleague. What had she heard? Who was talking about me? Once they were gone, I bolted the door and collapsed in a nervous heap on the couch, hyperventilating, my mind spinning with theories and scenarios. Dave and his paranoia. It was contagious.

Every now and again, the paranoids are the only ones who can see the truth. I needed to see Dave. We were ditching the drugs. Deal or no deal with the Knuckledraggers, I was calling it off.

18
BACKING OUT

'Was not expecting you, buddy.' The suds from the large sponge dripped onto Dave's thongs. The waxy sheen on the HSV Maloo ute was immaculate but that didn't stop it getting another wash from its besotted master. 'Perfect timing, but. Had a word with my cousin.'

'What'd he want?' I asked, still rattled by my visitors.

'Nothing. Just said that you had a good catch up and we'd do beers again soon. All very nonchalant and casual. Threw in a few yeah, maybe, okay thens. But he told me to keep my mobile close and on.' Leaning towards me, Dave translated, unnecessarily, 'It was a code. Means your meeting went well.'

I sat down on the edge of the deck, leaving Dave standing with one hand raised for a high five. It was happening. Lloyd was setting up the exchange. Dropping backwards, I lay with my hands over my eyes, trying to blot out the world and the badness that was quickly swirling around me.

'I want to pull out.'

Dave didn't understand. 'You shook on it. You'd be going back on a deal.'

'Nah. I want to get rid of it. Find a hole and bury it, flush it, pour it all back into the sea.'

Even with my hands over my eyes, I sensed the large shadow hovering over me. Peeking, I saw a beer held out to me with soap suds sliding down the sides. Taking it, I pulled the ring and took a sip. Dave dropped the sponge into his bucket and set about caressing his ute with a chamois.

'I don't even have a fucking car,' I sighed.

'What's that got to do with the price of fish?'

'Don't have a job. Everything's gone to shit since we pulled that thing out of the water. It's a curse. We got to make it right.'

'Bullshit. You're just getting cold feet. We're about to score. You need to relax. Finish your beer.'

Moan shared, I sat and sipped as Dave wiped his car down then joined me on the deck. Washing an already clean car was thirsty work as Dave necked his own beer in one long pull before tossing the empty over to the ground near his recycling bins. Satisfied, he pulled over one of the collapsible camp chairs and sat himself down. I could see he was mulling things over in his mind, tasting them, sucking in air, swilling to see what he thought. Looking to the sky, he slapped at one of the hairy mosquito lures protruding from his shorts.

'Nothery?' he asked, standing and heading for the shed without waiting.

'I'm good,' I said, because I'd had a new idea. 'Guess if anyone can find the Beast, Lloyd can. Maybe you can ask him to find it? Tell him I need my car found. I need it for work. I need it to get around and I can't afford another one.'

'Why can't you tell him?'

'He's your cousin. And I don't have his number. Tell him to find my car or the deal's off.'

As he came back to the deck with the fresh beers, he popped the lids. 'Is the gear still safe? Hidden well?'

That came from left field – very left field. But Dave persisted, wanting reassurance that the drugs were safe. Now Lloyd was involved, Dave's view was that the risk should be shared.

'You saying you don't trust your cousin? If you are, you've picked a fine time to share it.'

'I'm just saying, two minutes ago, you were talking about throwing away our one shot at making some serious fuck-you money. If it's split, you can only throw away half.'

I could see where Dave's concern was coming from as he voiced another: making the return of my missing car a condition of the deal had the potential to delay or even derail the sale of our contraband. Worse, the buyers could decide to just cut us out of the equation all together.

'Get Lloyd to find your car, no wuckers. But don't make it part of the deal. And yeah, we should split it. Bring some here for safe keeping? Just in case.'

'You worried about me or your share?'

'Mate! I'm just being, y'know, proactive.'

'You shat yourself after having the package for a couple of days. Now you want to help hide it again?'

'Maybe some. Split the difference, share the load. It's a lot of money, Lachie.'

Sure it was a lot of money, but I wasn't having a bar of any schemes to divide the stash. If it all went to plan, the drugs would be gone by the end of the week. We'd have our money, our lives would be easier and we'd never mention this again. Dave liked the sound of that.

'Never mention it again. Apart from our money. Can't wait to get my hands on that money.'

That was what was worrying me.

19
HORACE HAS A SOLUTION

When I got home my next-door neighbours, Mario and Jess, were unloading their shopping under a deepening blue sky sprayed with deep orange cloud. Their black labrador, Horace, came bounding over to me, arching her body into a banana as her back legs decided they wanted to be front legs for a change. As she thudded into my knees, her heavy tail slapped about my legs.

Loaded down with shopping, Mario waved as Jess stood smiling. I pushed against Horace and crossed to the back of their car to do the neighbourly thing.

'You're looking great, as always, Jess,' I said.

And she was. Having just beaten off a bout of breast cancer that had left her with a sizeable collection of head scarves and a weakened immune system, she was slowly coming back to her old self as remission became a reality.

'Hey there, Lachie. How you been? What's news?'

Most people aren't really interested in hearing an answer to that question, especially when the answer involves fishing a fortune of narcotics from the ocean, discovering a dead body and chats with the local police while setting up a deal with the local bikies. So I went for the safer option. 'Nothing much. You?'

'Still getting used to going out into the world without worrying about catching a head cold.'

Horace finished rolling on her back and took herself inside as Jess invited me around for dinner.

'C'mon, buddy. Come in. Have dinner. We'll whip something up in no time,' Mario pressed.

'Nah, nah. Busy, mate. Places to be. Another time.' I made my excuses.

Mario accepted them and headed in with another load of shopping under the loving gaze of his wife. Jess was determined to set me up with a friend or a sister, convinced I was the perfect catch. As much as I'd been the good neighbour during their cancer experience, I really had little in common with them other than a postcode.

'We worry about you,' said Jess.

'Me? Nah, I'm fine. All good.'

'I don't think Mario would have coped without you keeping an eye on him.'

'I really only did it after I saw the high quality drinks he enjoys. Pure selfishness, Jess.'

'Rogue. But a good heart and you'll always have a place in ours. Anything, any time, just ask,' Jess said.

I hate it when things get sentimental, when the emotions come too close to the surface and hay fever pricks the corners of my eyes. I had really done nothing except look out for how Mario was tracking, offer him someone to talk to, and make sure Horace was walked on the weeks Jess had chemo and Mario was sleeping in the hospital by her side.

At that point, Horace decided to follow Mario out of the house with a massive thigh bone, all blue, white and red, between her jaws. I was transfixed as my head filled with images of the torso on the beach. One hand on my chest, legs weak, I emitted a gargled scream that scared all four of us.

'Sheesh,' I said, catching my breath and feeling like a prize idiot. 'Watched a sick horror film last night. Caught me by surprise.'

Bemused, Mario told me to pick better movies.

Nice neighbourly chats and a dog's bone being what they were, I made my farewells and headed for my place and the siren call of bed, slapping Horace's solid flank a little too sharply.

As I hit the sheets, my mind insisted on an all-night replay of everything that had happened along with all the what ifs, what might have beens, and the downright paranoid.

Organised crime is a business. In business, nothing is personal, everything is about ensuring maximum profit. Nothing can stand in the way of those profits. There are no friendships, only associates. To maximise profits and protect my share, I had to get smarter.

Flat on my back, staring at the ceiling, I realised it wasn't so much about trusting Dave as eliminating temptation. Why did Dave want to know if the packages were safe? He didn't want them at his place. I'd taken care of them for him, but now he was interested? Money, money, money.

Unable to sleep and unable to forget, I got up to make a cup of camomile tea. Sipping the hot liquid that tasted of hay and summer, I heard Horace barking, and the solution came to me. Wasting no time, I collected all the bricks from their hidey holes around the flat and stacked them on the coffee table. Seeing them all piled up, I decided to leave a couple hidden under the kitchen sink in case of emergency. It made sense at 2am.

Bundling the brick paver-sized packages into the green shopping bags once more, I drained the last of my tea.

Next door, Horace barked again, no doubt scaring off the local possum. Man's best friend, an ever-hungry labrador had given me the answer, Now all I had to do was implement it.

Picking up the bags, I slipped into the yard and checked that none of Harry's house lights were on. Darkness. Tiptoeing along the perimeter to avoid setting off his sensor lights, I made it to the fence. Whispering Horace's name, I was rewarded with a full-throated *woof*. I peered over the top of the fence and looked down onto Horace's head, her thick kangaroo tail was wagging furiously.

'G'day, mate. Gonna let me in?'

I hoisted myself up and over the fence, dropping ninja-silent to the ground, careful not to let go of the bags. Horace with her insatiable appetite would assume it was sausages or something, and she'd eat it before it hit the ground. Thankfully, Horace trotted off and returned with something in her mouth. The chewed teddy bear would hopefully help muffle any barks. Horace slept in the old cubby house. Despite the chewed collection of kids' tables and chairs, no one went in there anymore. Jess and Mario were hoping for grandchildren to one day appear like garden gnomes and repopulate their backyard.

Creeping through the Hobbit-sized doorway, I squatted and looked for a good place for the stash. Judging by the cobwebs, the wooden play oven was just the thing. I opened the door and packed the space with bricks, making sure they were well hidden. With the door closed, the oven looked completely innocent. I hoped no kids would suddenly decide to make mud pies while I was trying to offload the junk. How to explain that to my neighbours?

Crawling out of the cubby house, I took a moment to stretch the kinks out of my back. Horace stood in front of me, wagging patiently, her muffled barks telling me she was ready to play.

'Not now, mate. Another time.'

As I leaped back over the fence, I caught a glimpse of Horace's morose face looking up at me as if I'd just broken her heart. Maybe labradors were good guard dogs, after all – not as a deterrent or attack dog, but for melting the heart of any intruder.

I followed the same route back to my granny flat to make sure the sensor lights stayed off. Now when Dave asked me if the packages were safe, I'd know they were as safe as cubby houses. And all the safer for him asking.

Thank you very much, mate, for the reminder that when it comes to drug deals, no one is your friend.

20
A DATE

Having spent a good part of the night awake, thinking – or stashing drugs in the neighbours' backyard – I slept until midday. It was very out of character. Years of getting up at sparrow's fart to be out and on a worksite by seven made the habit so ingrained that even on days off I couldn't stop waking at dawn. Sleep-ins were an alien concept.

As I blinked at the bright daylight, the plan of getting up early to scour the newspapers or hustle my contacts for a job flew out the window. Instead, the day had become mine – an enforced holiday. With the sun shining, it was the perfect time to hit the beach.

I'm not a surfer. Never have been. Body surf, yes, but balancing on a board? I'm no Hawaiian. After sizing up the sea at Bar Beach, I stripped off to my bathers and did the manly thing of running at the water until a wave slapped my testicles. It was bracing, as only a slap to the nuts can be.

Diving under, all I felt was peace and calm. Breaking the surface behind the wave, I stroked out to where more waves were and waited. Whenever I have problems, feeling the pull and push of the ocean helps wash my woes into perspective. In the ocean you're nothing but a speck, fertiliser for the microbes in the darkness far below.

Catching the next wave in, I began porpoising, windmilling my arms furiously before being dumped in the fizzing foam. When I say I body surf, if anyone on the shore was watching me, they'd run for the lifesavers.

Swimming out again to the deeper water to wait for more waves, I relished the rise and fall, how I could touch the sand with one toe at the low roll and soar skywards on the high roll. As I rose up, my eyes and nose appearing above the surface like a saltwater crocodile's, I missed the next wave. It dumped me tumbling and spluttering into the foaming churn. Staggering up the beach, water pouring from every orifice, I slunk in the direction of my towel, relieved the beach was empty but much happier for the experience.

I sat on the sand, towel over my head, and toyed with my phone. No one had called but my finger was already thumbing the contacts to display Karen Miller's number. Should I ring? Too late, my fingers had decided for me.

'Hello?'

'Karen? It's Lachlan. Lachlan Munro. I must have dialled you by mistake, how about that?'

'My number's in your phone?'

Without a reasonable excuse to explain why I'd entered her number in my phone, I ploughed on. I'd either crash and burn or fly like an eagle. Just so long as I avoided looking like a dickhead. 'Feel like a coffee?'

'Not really. Are you at the beach?'

'That a problem?'

'Not with me. Surf, swim or something else?'

Confidence creeping in again, I made up a story about being a champion bodysurfer. She laughed and I knew I wasn't crashing and burning.

'Come on, meet me for a drink.'

She said yes. 'You caught me at a weak moment. A drink. That's all.'

She agreed to swing by mine in an hour or so but had hung up before I could ask her how she knew where I lived. Had the good Detective Sergeant Baxter said something about me? Then I started to worry if this was a date or social. What do you wear to these sorts of things? And what does an hour or so mean? An hour? Shorter? Longer?

Jeans, a moderately clean T-shirt and a newish hoodie were my decisions. Then at the last moment, I splashed on some aftershave. Casual but with the hint of extra bergamot. The fragrance had me changing my hoodie for an informal jacket. Checking myself out in the mirror, I realised it was all for nothing. If Karen saw inside my place, it wouldn't matter how much aftershave I threw around, she wouldn't be hanging about. Couldn't even remember when I last changed my sheets.

The doorbell rang before I had a chance to do anything about it. Small blessing.

'So. Worked out where we're going?' Karen stood on my doorstep, hand shielding her face from the glare outside. She looked like she'd got some sun since I'd seen her last. She was wearing a T-shirt with sparkles on it, jeans and leather sandals. She looked good and she smelled good. Her perfume reminded me of frangipani – she was wearing perfume!

'The Beach Hotel is around the corner? Or there's a café, if you just wanted coffee.'

She wobbled her head from side to side, pulling a face, but I picked up that the pub would be fine.

'Is it safe to leave the car here?' she asked.

Okay, maybe I should have changed those sheets.

The pub was a locals' place so it was comfortably daggy with good views of the ocean. Surfers colonised the verandah and front seats so they could stare at the swell or lack of it. But we managed to find one tall table and a pair of stools.

'What do you feel like?'

'A beer? Fourex?'

'Jesus, what are you? An old man? From Queensland?'

She punched me in the arm good-naturedly and it felt like she'd been doing it all my life. 'Make it a Fosters then.'

'That's not much better,' I said. 'I'll see if they have a Fourex. I'll even get one to make you feel better.'

I had no intention of ordering a Fourex for myself. At the bar, it turned out they did have the Queensland brew, so I ordered one for Karen and a pint of Coopers for me. Some beers are old man beers. I am not an old man. And if this was a date, I also didn't want to look like the guy who agrees with everything in a cringeworthy performance of the 'me toos'.

'Here you go.'

'Ooh, big ones. Cheers.' Her eyes twinkled with good humour over the top of the pints. 'You did get Fourex. I got a taste for it when I had to work up north a few years back. Nothing else seemed to taste right in the heat.'

'Never been further north than Port Macquarie.'

'Don't bother.'

'Newcastle's got it all?'

'Wouldn't go that far.'

'So what brought you here?'

'Work. The great mobiliser. You?'

'Same. Work. It was the great Newie house painter shortage. Probably remember it, all over the news. Economy at risk of grinding to a halt. Practically a gold rush for those of us who can hold a brush.'

'You mean, a paint rush?' Karen bit her lip and winced at her atrocious pun. 'Come on, that was worth a chuckle.'

'Maybe a little one. But more a sympathy chuckle.'

'How does that go?'

'You'll know it when you see it.'

'Kind of like this?' She gave a tight smile, tilted her head and nodded, perfect condescension that went right for the jugular. She was funny.

We sat watching the ocean for a bit, basking in the warmth of the gag, a silence that seemed odd for a date. Unless it wasn't a date. I was pretty sure it was a date. All the signals seemed to say so. Silence getting too much, we both started talking at the same time.

'Sorry,' I said as she smiled. 'I interrupted.'

'I was just going to ask if you missed Melbourne.'

'Melbourne? I'm from Melbourne?'

'You swap your A's and E's like a Melbournian. What's that suburb? The one that trips up everyone but a local?'

'You mean Prahran?' I pronounced it correctly, like a local.

'That's the one. How you get Prahran to rhyme with tram, that's pure local knowledge.' She laughed.

'What about you? Where are you from?'

'I'm boring. Let's keep talking about you,' she said, and I realised she had her hand on my arm. I could feel the warmth through my jacket and the absence when she realised and pulled it away. Now, the silence was awkward.

'Did you want another drink?' she asked, already standing as she fetched her purse from her oversized handbag. As she went to the bar, I looked to the ocean. Why was this uncomfortable? We'd already had a lot of the getting-to-know-you conversation the other night. I knew enough about her, we'd shared some laughs, she looked great and she was funny.

'Here you go. What's on your mind?'

'Well, I was wondering why this all felt a bit ...'

'Awkward?'

So it wasn't just me.

'I think,' she said, pausing to sip her Fourex, 'it's a little odd because we're doing it all backwards. We've met and had dinner, you ended up at my place. Now, we're trying to fill in the gaps to catch up.'

Maybe that was it. This was a catch up before we decided what was next.

'So what did you want to know?' I asked.

'What did you want to tell me?' She looked innocent but her question was all flirtation.

That was how the afternoon played out. Friendly, chatty and flirty, as if we'd known each other for years.

21
OCTOPUS

'More than two shakes and it's a wank, brother.'

Generally a shove in the back while standing at the urinal is seen as very poor form but Gary Newman had never learned that lesson.

'Get fucked or I'll piss on your leg.' Shaking off to reholster, I turned to grin at Gary, who loomed all deeply tanned and sun creased. His faded Hawaiian shirt and cheap jeans gave him the air of exactly what he was: an ageing beach bum and possible former rock god. 'Jesus, Gary. What the hell are those?'

He looked at his feet, which sported a pair of fluorescent orange Croc sandals. Hideous.

'Play your cards right, Lachlan, you might see a spot of Croc wrestling before the night's out.' He grinned.

I'd been bumping into Gary for years. He claimed to divide his time between two states: the ocean off the Newie coast and the dry South Australian desert. Almost like he had to bake himself dry then rehydrate for a spell. He was only about ten years older than me but his lifestyle made him look about fifty. He always made me nervous. Never been able to put my finger on it but you couldn't get a straight line on what he did, where he'd been or what he was up to. I'm all for privacy, but with Gary, it was a whole different super-spy level of secrecy.

'So you back then?'

Toilet conversation is never easy. I washed my hands and stood with them under the ineffectual dryer as Gary made his usual show of pulling free his member and leaning forwards, both hands on the tiles above his head to piss hands free. The whole thing was unpleasant and I just wanted to get back to Karen.

'Got back yesterday. A friend called. Told me the waves were coming good and he might have a spot of work for me. Perfect timing.'

His story was that he did a bit of prospecting: gold, tin, opals – made some money looking for likely places for claims that he then sold. I found it hard to believe this story but it never wavered from visit to visit.

Shaking from the knees up, Gary turned as he zipped to tell me he had just made a small fortune in geothermal so he was back in town to party.

'Geothermal? Hot rocks? How do you prospect for them?'

'I just walk around barefoot till I feel something hot.' His face crinkled at his joke. 'Just got a knack for reading the lay of the land, brother. There's a fortune to be made. I could retire next year if I play my cards right.'

Gary was also always on the verge of retiring. I listened as he went on to tell me what he was planning to do while he was in town. How long he would be in town was as yet undecided.

'Which begs the most important question, you flirting or closing the deal out there? Have t'ask. Been a while and that is a fine filly you're talking to, if y'catch my drift.' Just in case I didn't, he waggled his bushy eyebrows as he thrust his hips back and forth.

'What's it to you?'

Leaning back, hands out to the side like a dodgy salesman, Gary assured me he was only trying to get a handle on where I sat. 'I'd never cut a brother's lunch without good reason.'

Slapping me on the shoulder, he grinned as he held open the door. 'Gonna at least introduce us?'

'No. But good seeing you.'

Unfortunately, when I returned to Karen with our drinks, I had picked up a shadow.

'Karen, this is Gary Newman. Gary, Karen.'

Karen did the polite thing of saying hello but Gary was going to have to work hard to get anything more than that. Maybe she was put off by the spectacles hanging about his neck on their plastic nanna chain. That or the way he sat next to her in my spot with his arm instantly draped up over the back of her chair. My lunch was being cut.

'Gary, you're in my chair,' I said.

Gary made a show of looking confused before apologising and moving to the other stool.

'And how do you two know each other?' Karen asked.

'Mates from way back, Kaz –'

'Karen.'

Gary smiled. Karen looked blank. I felt really uncomfortable.

'Karen. I've ordered some calamari. I'm sitting on the other side of the bar. Why don't you two come and join me? I can tell you all about Lachlan,' he said.

'I don't eat calamari. Or octopus.'

'Them suckers, freaky stuff, hey?'

'No, I just don't think I should eat the most intelligent thing in the ocean.'

'Vegan?' asked Gary, still ignoring me.

'No. Discerning.'

'Right. Well. Dry argument? You two up for another round?'

'No. We're good, Gary. Another time.' I said. Apart from picking him up and carrying him off, I didn't know how to play this. Was Karen the type to enjoy a bit of macho action?

'And I'm driving,' said Karen.

'Can't shoot a guy for trying. Another time, then.'

'Maybe,' Karen said, appearing friendly as the subtext said, *No way, not a chance, just keep walking.*

Finally accepting the temperature drop, Gary made a show of waving at someone across the pub before beating a retreat with an excuse about needing to go say hello to an old friend. As he left, he blatantly raised his eyebrows at me to indicate what he thought of her.

Watching him leave, Karen turned back to me stony faced 'What a wanker. Sorry, I know he's your mate, but please!' she said as she stood up.

'He's not my mate. I know him but that's as far as it goes. Mate is so far from what we are …' I was blabbering, trying to save whatever the afternoon had promised. 'Want to get out of here? Go somewhere without calamari?'

Karen was polite but the spell was broken. She claimed she was meeting a girlfriend. When I made to walk out with her, she told me to stay and finish my beer.

'I'll call you.'

'Yeah,' was all she said.

Hardly a rip-roaring endorsement. She did at least give me a little wave from the door when she caught me watching. Embarrassed, possibly blushing, I drank some more beer only to catch Gary watching me from the other side of the bar. Karen was right. He was creepy. Like a next-door neighbour who insists on being called uncle, creepy.

As a waitress passed me with a large serve of calamari, I directed her to where Gary was now sitting. Watching the passing calamari, I thought Karen was right. It was a complete waste that an intelligent creature had died simply to be crumbed, deep fried and eaten by a mug like Gary.

I gave Gary the finger and made my exit.

Outside, the air was cooler and the sun had disappeared behind the blocks of apartments. The landscape had taken on the peace of the end of day. The tradies were done, the kids were home from school, the early edition of the television news was playing in the countless lounge rooms I walked past, alone. Without Karen.

Finding Dave perched on my letterbox when I got home was not the antidote.

22
MISTAKES ALL ROUND

Lloyd had found the Beast. Which felt very quick to me. Even if Dave had called his cousin as soon as I left his place the night before, it had barely been twenty-four hours. Yet Lloyd had not only found the Beast but reacquired it.

'He has a good handle on the local car scene,' said Dave, as he drove me to where we were to meet Lloyd and get back my Beast. If nothing else, it would be great to have freedom again. Walking was fine but wheels and an engine were better. The hills of Newcastle were killers on a pushbike like Harry's.

'So did Lloyd say anything about my tools and stuff?' I asked.

The question had Dave shifting in the driver's seat as he offered to text Lloyd and ask. Watching him flick his eyes back and forth from the dark road outside to the bright screen of his mobile, a wave of weirdness washed over me.

'Dave, you all good?'

'What d'ya mean?'

'For a start, why are we meeting Lloyd out here, wherever the hell we are, and not just at my place? Or yours?'

'I know. I mean, at least somewhere we could have a drink. I'm drier than Jesus' sandals.'

A beep from Dave's mobile announced the latest incoming message. 'Lloyd's sent some directions.'

'You mean you didn't even know where you were going?'

'I knew the suburb,' he said. 'The general area. I was just waiting for him to send an actual address.'

'No time like the present then,' I said, grateful I'd moved the packages from my place and guilty for feeling that way. Better to feel bad about thinking the worst of a mate than to have those fears realised and kick yourself for not acting when you had the chance. I was happy to be wrong.

'Maybe we can swing past Gino's after. Grab a pizza?' said Dave, ever hopeful and ever hungry.

'Sure, Dave.'

Looking out into the inky night, the city illumination highlighting the sky, I settled into silence, wondering how the evening was going to pan out, trying not to think of Karen.

Standing by the fence around the docks on Cormorant Road, the night cool rising off the sea, it felt like a bloody gangland cliché. Although I had to admit it was beautiful. The bright white lights on coal-loading equipment, the contrasting yellow tungsten lamps and, overhead, pinpricks of blinking red that warned low-flying pelicans to steer away. Industry and purpose, as unseen night crews readied the ships for the next high tide.

Behind me, Dave stamped his feet intermittently. It was cool but not that cool. As the occasional heavy truck roared past I didn't turn around, just continued to cling to the cyclone fence, each hand clawed by the sides of my head.

'You've gone quiet,' he said.

I let the statement sit there for a bit before turning to him. In the light flooding from the port, his face was hidden in the shadows. Mine must have been better lit, which reminded me I was hopeless at wearing a good poker face.

'Why here? Why so far away? If he's found my car, why not bring it to my house?' Even I could hear the whine in my voice.

Struggling for an answer, Dave was rescued by the sound of a car approaching, its exhaust death rattle loud.

Pulling up in front of us, Lloyd got out and slammed the door to stand like a showman before the dark green utility with canopy. 'Tah-dah! Cop that, pussies.'

His outstretched showman's arm stance wilted as I slowly crossed my arms and stood stock still, feet planted in the dirt.

'At least you should be thankin' me, you ungrateful cunt.'

I let the silence build and thicken around us like a fog.

'What?'

My wingman took a subtle step to the side. So much for backup.

'What is it about the colour silver you don't understand, Lloyd?'

'They painted it. Were gonna sell it to some backpackers in Victoria.'

'Really. Victoria. Lot of trouble for – what? Car's only worth a grand at best.'

'Kids. No concept of profit.'

'And my tools? Where're my tools?' I started walking away, leaving my trusty wingman to deal with the colour-blind bikie.

'What's his fuckin' problem? I got him a car. He said he needed a car, one shit box any different to another?'

'The problem, Lloyd, is that inside my car is the thing that you want. No car, no package.'

I have no idea where that came from, but the look on

Lloyd's face was priceless. He now took on my predicament with laughable seriousness.

'You stashed it in the car, Lachie?' Dave was deadpan as he soaked it up as well.

'Yes, Dave. Hidden in the car. That plain enough for you both?'

'Crystal, chief,' said Lloyd as he pushed past Dave to get closer to me. I resisted taking a step back.

'Lach, I'm sorry I didn't take your request with the seriousness it required. If you tell me all the details of your vehicle, I'll tear a new arsehole for the scum who took it.'

If I hadn't just dug a huge hole for myself, I would have laughed. Instead, I yet again dutifully gave Lloyd the details of my Beast, every tidbit I could remember. He scribbled notes on a scrap of paper he pulled from his pocket. It was easier than the police station.

'Now, can I give you a lift home?' Lloyd asked.

'You know what, just fuck off.' I was serious. After a shit afternoon, here I was standing on a road by mountains of coal, having my time wasted on a fool's errand.

'Lachie …' Dave began, a note of diplomacy in his voice.

'No, you too, Dave. Just fuck off, the both of you.'

Lloyd nodded, his lips tight.

'I let you down. I hear ya. I apologise again. But trust me, this will be sorted.'

But I was already walking. As the two utes sprayed gravel behind me, zooming off in opposite directions, I scowled at the tail lights until they faded into the night. Then it was just me and the seagulls in the streetlights as I walked home along one of the scariest deserted streetscapes in the world.

It was only by some minor miracle that a passing taxi slowed to see if I was suitable to be picked up. Seated in the cab as the driver agreed with the late-night talkback, it was the perfect end to an ordinary day.

Fate, though, had other plans.

Harry came out to greet me as I arrived home, all agitated and irritable.

'Flaming heck, Lachlan. Hope you bloody got that out of your system. What the blue blazes you been doing in there?'

'Harry, it's been a shit of a day and most of it I spent a long way from here.'

'Then who's been in there?' he said, pointing down the drive to my flat.

From the look of my front door, it was clear my keys weren't going to be needed – it had been kicked in but pulled shut so a casual observer wouldn't notice. Not that this was an area where Neighbourhood Watch was popular, other than to learn who was shagging who.

Carefully, I pushed the door and stopped. Everything was upturned, slashed, tipped over, pulled out and trashed. Every tap in the place was running full bore. The plugs were in every sink, turning each one into a mini waterfall. Carefully stepping through the ankle-deep water over the squishy carpets, I turned off the taps and made my way through the place. From what I could see, nothing was missing. The TV was still there as were the DVDs and CDs. The swim probably wasn't going to do them much good other than to make a strong argument for video on demand. Surveying the place, hands on hips, I heard a noise by the front door.

'Christ, Lach. Hell's bells, if I'd known ...' Harry was

genuinely shocked as he shuffled into view. He didn't come in, peering around the doorframe like a kitten.

'Thanks, but probably better you didn't come and tell me off. Whoever was here meant business. Never know what might've happened,' I said, tossing a slashed and dripping cushion onto the upturned couch.

'Too right. But I coulda done something. At least stopped the taps. You want me to call the cops?'

Did I want the cops involved? Nothing seemed to have been taken. I didn't have insurance. What would I tell them anyway? 'Officers, I think I have been done over by criminals looking for drugs I'm trying to sell that I fortuitously decided to secretly stash in my neighbour's cubby house'? Yeah, probably wouldn't go down so well.

'I'll be fine, Harry. I'll fix the place up. Make it look good as new.'

'Bloody dump needed a freshen-up anyways. I'm real sorry, son. Real bugger 'bout your things.'

Then I swore.

'What they take, Lachie?'

'I'm sorry too, Harry. They've taken your bike.'

Harry looked about the small room, hoping to see a wheel poking out from some of the upturned mess, before looking at me again with a slump to his shoulders. 'All that for me bike? Bugger.'

Funny enough, he seemed almost relieved to hear his bike was gone. I suppose it was an old clunker that weighed a tonne. I was positive I'd spot it soon enough being ridden by some bearded hipster, ecstatic to have picked up a vintage model bike from a guy at a pub.

'I'll replace it.'

'Lad, I think you got bigger problems than replacing an old bike I didn't even use.'

He left me to it without even a stick of advice as to where I should start. Not that I needed any. As soon as he was gone, I headed straight to the kitchen sink. Taking a deep breath, I swung the half-open cupboard door wide and reached in past the cleaning products to feel behind the sink. I was desperate to find the bricks. But no, they were gone. All that was left was a dangling strip of tape.

I sank to the ground, my head in my hands. I felt like I was going to be sick.

23

ENLIGHTENING

It took me a long time to get started on the cleaning. It took me a long time to get up off the kitchen floor. But somewhere near dawn, I moved. Like Harry had said, it was, in a weird way, an opportunity for a spring clean. As the first rays shone over the horizon, I'd already marched in and out of my place a dozen times, carrying armfuls of all sorts of bits and pieces I'd collected that were now wet, trodden on or worse. They were heading for the bin. Buddhists say getting rid of possessions is an essential step to enlightenment. By sunrise proper, I had stripped the place and dumped the worst of it. What to do about the carpets was trickier. Good thing I was between jobs or I'd never get anything done. It was taking a lot of effort not to think about the missing drugs. As for enlightenment, I was clearly heading for reincarnation as a cockroach.

Somewhere in the bare unit, a packet of cereal had escaped the attack. Eating it by the handful, I hoped Harry would be up soon to stick his nose in with an offer of a cuppa. I'd have to make a trip to the supermarket or the op shop to replace my broken mugs.

Harry gently knocked on the splintered doorframe. In his hand was a blessed mug. 'Took the liberty. Worker's brew.'

'You are a scholar and a gentleman, Harry,' I said, mouth clogged with dry cereal paste. 'How'd you know?'

'Think I'm blind?' he said, sniffing as he held up the handle of a broken mug from the sink.

Sitting on the kitchen floor sipping the hot milky

sweetness, I could feel myself rejuvenating. Amazing how a cup of boiled leaves can do that. You can be slaving away on a worksite, eyes filled with dust and drips, and then smoko comes along. You have a brew and all's suddenly well with the world again. Even the worst boss in the world knows the benefit of giving his staff a tea break.

'Worked out what you'll do, son?'

'Not yet.'

'Don't worry, cobber. Can always kip on the couch if you need it. Rattle about in my place as it is.'

Sometimes the kindness of your neighbours catches you.

'Thanks, Harry. Very generous. Means a lot. Probably won't need it but I'll keep you posted.'

Looking about the place, Harry sniffed again before asking me if I had a better idea what was missing. Far as I could tell, nothing was gone except his bike. Everything was just trashed.

'Looks like they went through your kitchen, too?'

'Nothing left untouched. Except this box of cereal.'

'Bastards,' he muttered. 'Keep the mug. Drop it back when you replace your broken ones.' With a nod, he turned and headed back to his own place. 'And don't you worry about the rent. I'm about to come into a bit of moolah, so get yourself back on ya feet. Then we can worry about all that,' he said over his shoulder as he left.

Humanity at its finest.

Things started to look a bit more normal as I cleaned up the last of my stuff. Now that it was about mid-morning, I did a bit of a ring around to see who I could convince to help get my place shipshape again. Thankfully, the favour bank was open. My chippie mate, Chas, said he had a spare solid core door he could fit later. He was working on a large housing estate – one door was about to find a new home at mine. Unfortunately, I didn't know any carpet layers. I could get the unemployed Maxie on board. After all, he owed me. Not sure if this was something I wanted to cash in just yet, or if I had the headspace to make sure he stayed on task and did the right thing. I held off and got stuck in myself to give the place a bit of love where the worst of the water damage showed. I promised Harry I'd have the place good as new and I was going to be true to my word. If it took longer, I'd call in Maxie.

Yet a nagging thought had sprung up and refused to go away. It was very convenient that Dave and Lloyd had me away from my place on a fool's errand at the time of the break-in. When doubt takes root, it becomes a cancer, and I was going to have to work hard not to let the symptoms show. I had to keep on acting as if everything was normal. It could, after all, just be my suspicious mind. Except, when it was all added up, Dave looked very guilty. Problem was, the more I thought about it, the more I knew Dave didn't have the imagination to plot such a thorough job of destruction. It looked like the work of a meth-head hunting for the next day's bender money. Dave didn't have the brains to cover his tracks like that. Did that mean someone else – a professional – was responsible? The culprit or culprits had made off with two bricks of smack under the sink. They must have known there was more.

So was it Lloyd? Was he the brains? He'd arrived late with what wasn't my car. He could have done it. But my gut was saying no.

Nothing made sense. Nothing offered the perfect answer to fit all of the facts.

Which brought me back to Dave. That did have my gut twitching – he was involved in some way. I could smell it. Now I had to play along and pretend all was peachy-keen until there was some proof that it was my mate trying to do me over and I figured out what I was going to do about it.

Maybe it would have been better to hand in the keys to Harry and walk away. Except curiosity made me determined to find the truth and my suspicions made me more determined to make sure Dave got nothing. It was only fair. So after organising some real mates to sort out my place, I trooped across the water to look Dave in the eye and voice my doubts. Only then could I tell if he was in on it.

But he wasn't home. So I had to ring him, which annoyed me even more as I could have saved myself the journey. And the ferry ticket.

'Mate, I'm just out for a bit? Why?'

'Where? I'm standing at your front door and you're not here.' My belligerence was annoying, even to me. Dave had every right to not welcome me with open arms.

'Um, the shops?' He paused. 'Lach, you're sounding a bit wired. Spare key's under the mint pot by the shed. Let yourself in and I should be back in an hour. Maybe talk about last night too.'

Standing there at his front door, staring angrily down the street, the calmness of his words made sense. I was knackered. The wave of exhaustion dumped on me like a bad wave break. As promised, the spare key was under the mint pot.

Sliding the door closed behind me, I trudged to his couch

and flopped down. The remote dug into my kidneys, so I pulled it free and thumbed the television on. A midday movie started but that was all I got. What do they say about letting sleep sort out your problems? I passed out before I could remember.

24
SUSPICIONS

The sound of Dave arriving home woke me. I looked at my watch and rubbed my head.

'Beer?' Dave was pulling a can free. 'Went shopping. Me kids are coming.'

I didn't feel like it, but the can was already flying through the air towards my head. Popping it open and taking a sip, I watched Dave unpack groceries and shuffle through his junk mail, his running commentary competing with the afternoon TV newsbreak.

'So you better? Sounded pretty rough earlier.' He held up a tin of hotdogs in gravy. 'Love these. Get 'em for the kids for after-sports snacks. But really, all mine.'

I let Dave use up his conversation quota. Every word he said was another nail in his coffin of guilt. He was rabbiting on, blathering, digging a hole, condemning himself with his words. He was so guilty. Guilt was practically oozing from his pores. I could see the guilt, the guilty, guilty, guilt, guilt, guilt.

'You good? Your lips are moving but there's no sound, like one of those ventriloquists: "Hello, my name is Lachlan and this is Mr Spanky."' Disappointed at my lack of reaction, he went on: 'Come on, that was funny.' He held up a pizza home delivery menu. In my dark, sleep-ruffled mood, pizza sounded perfect.

'Aussie?' I suggested.

It was music to Dave's ears as he trotted to the phone and flipped the handset up high in the air then caught it as it fell. The well-rehearsed manoeuvre was impressive. More so because he had somehow dialled the number as he lifted the headset to his ear.

'What about Mr Spanky? What he feel like?'

I gave him the finger then listened as he placed the order, wondering what I was going to do next. Did I confront him or let it sit, see how it played out? Maybe I was just being paranoid. As Dave came over to join me on the couch, he took the remote and started surfing the stations.

'Got burgled last night.'

Dave thumbed the TV to mute, looking at me with what looked like genuine shock.

'You right? They get much?' Then after thinking for a moment, 'Shit! The gear! Oh, no, that's right. You stashed all that in your car.'

I shook my head.

'The drugs were never in the Beast, Dave.'

'I knew it! I knew you were foxing. The Lachie Munro I know would never stash the bricks in his car. So, they're all still safe?'

Felt nice to get a compliment as I nodded my little white lie that, yes, all the drugs were safe.

'You got anything else worth nicking?'

I was looking for a tell, a sign that he knew something. I wasn't seeing it. 'Don't think so. You're right. Not much worth anything in the place. Weird thing was they turned on all the taps so the place flooded.'

'What's with that? Sounds like kids. Good thing they didn't shit in your bed.' He thumbed the mute off. His attention was now split between my predicament and the screen. 'They didn't shit in your bed, did they?'

'Might as well have.'

'You need to crash for a spell? You look whacked.'

Maybe Dave was innocent. Maybe all of this was just lack of sleep and pressure and all the rest. Then he spoke again.

'Anyone would reckon you thought I had something to do with it, way you're carrying on.'

'Why would you think that?' If Dave was looking for a tell from me, he would have had it in spades. I could feel the corners of my mouth pulling into a frown.

'You seemed a bit agitated, punchy, when you called. That's all. Then last night ...'

He had me there. But I used the legitimate excuse of the lack of sleep, which he seemed to buy. Annoyingly, in my mind, having just put him in the clear, his suspicion of me threw him back on the suspect list. Even as I told him I agreed with his idea that it must have been kids who broke into my place – who else? – every time I added it all up I was getting a different answer.

Sitting there in silence, we looked straight at the TV like guilty teenagers. It was Dave who broke the silence.

'So, the abs?'

'Fuck. I keep on forgetting them.'

'Maybe tonight? Get our beer money off the guy who wanted them. Take my car if it helps.'

The thought of the abalone still alone out in the shed under the hessian was an annoying embarrassment. The way the deal worked was that Dave handled the logistics, I did the deals. He didn't ask who I was selling them to and I didn't tell him. Not that it mattered, but it seemed safer to keep things separate. Collective deniability was what we called it. The courts would probably call it something else entirely but when we started playing the abalone-poaching game, it seemed like a good idea. If only we'd done the same with the package instead of working as partners.

The doorbell rang, and Dave loped off to get the pizzas, leaving me to feel like a prick and righteously scorned in equal measure. I tried to think about other things but failed. If Dave was dodgy, it would have a way of working itself out into the open. If not, I had to hide my thoughts better or I'd lose a good mate, one who had always been there for me. I needed to practise my poker face and keep cool.

By the time Dave wandered back in with the two large pizzas, garlic bread and large bottle of soft drink, my poker face was working again.

'Should I get plates?' I asked.

'Mate, we're not animals,' he replied, already scooping up two from the dish rack and reaching for the roll of paper towel. Back in front of the TV, a master at balance, he laid the food out and we started to eat like everything was the same, that we were best mates and the world was a bright, happy and sparkling place once more.

Eating was a help, the pizzas not so much. Greasy, doughy and covered with dubious meat, there wasn't really much to like in the cold light of day. Much like me on a bad day.

Collecting the remnants, I took them with me outside to dump in the bins before heading into the sheds. Inside, the filters working the water-filled drums softly burbled beneath the hessian sack cover. Reaching into the cool brine, I pulled up a second hessian sack and opened it to see the collection of abalone sitting higgledy-piggledy, happily unaware of their fates. Dumping them sack and all into a polystyrene box, I carried them outside to the tray of Dave's ute before going back in to collect the keys.

'Just watch the temp. Engine seems to be running a bit hot. Nothing to worry about.'

I climbed into the cabin. It felt good to be behind the wheel again, overheating engine or not.

As I reversed down the drive, left arm pulling me into a twist to see where I was going, I had to smile. With my luck, the stupid car would conk out halfway to Billy's and that load of shellfish would be the end of me. Way my life was going, it could've been a good thing. Planting my foot, I sped away far too fast down the suburban street.

25
FRIED ICE CREAM AND LYCHEES

It's a roundabout drive from Dave's to Billy Wong's. You start driving north through the fibro country-town landscape of Stockton before a stretch of derelict buildings that will no doubt one day feature in a low-budget horror movie. Hitting the Stockton Bridge takes you high over the water before looping back through the industrial part of town with the mountains of coal waiting to be loaded for China, then the appearance of the lawns and trees of the suburbs that lead you into the city.

At night, with the headlights leading the way, it's peaceful. Driving has always been a pleasure for me. Not the stuck-in-traffic-looking-out-your-window kind but actually moving driving. Music always sounds better from a car radio with road noise. The passing view and the sound of the car travelling make a space perfect for meditating. Didn't give me any ideas about what to do about Dave though. Too soon I was pulling into the laneway behind Billy's.

'Ah, Lachie, you found somewhere else to eat? You break my heart.' Billy welcomed me like an old friend as I entered the kitchen. Taking the two sacks of abalone from me, he grinned and nodded with delight. 'Lovely, lovely. What's my discount? Two, three days you're late.'

I didn't really care. It'd been a crap few days that hopefully would all be erased when I got rid of a large load of illegal narcotics.

'Go through and I'll bring you something special. Upstairs.'

'Upstairs? Really?'

'Of course, Lachie.'

Sitting to the side of the gamblers in the shadows, I watched as the players studied their Mahjong tiles, agonising over quick decisions. The place hadn't changed, echoing with the *clack clack* of the tiles and the loud proclamations of runs or cooing at winning combinations. It all had me wanting to join in, forgetting for an instant what happened the last time I felt that way. But once bitten, and all the rest.

Arriving with a dessert plate of deep-fried ice cream and tinned lychees, Billy didn't have to ask if I wanted some. There's always space for fried ice cream and lychees.

'So what's up, mate? Why the hold up?'

My mouth full of orbs of sweet lychee and ice cream, I held up a hand to signal I needed him to give me a moment to swallow and for my teeth to defrost.

'You normally so happy and cheery. Now when you come in, the world weighing on your shoulders.'

'Having a rough trot, Billy.'

'I know. You never forget my special delivery, yet now, what has it taken you? Three trips to bring me my stuff?'

Scooping up another spoon of dessert meant I avoided his eyes. 'Like I said, been a bit of a rough time of late. But don't worry. You'll get your discount. Have to admit though, was kind of good how it worked out.'

'How you think?'

'Well, with the raid by Fisheries. You might have got done if I'd brought those things in earlier.'

Billy squinted, appraising the information before waving it away. 'Is it girls? Lachie having trouble with the ladies?'

Laughing, I assured him that problems with my love life were not the cause of my grief. For some reason, seeing Billy sitting there in attentive silence, I felt able to tell him some of my woes. Without mentioning names or specifics, or that the biggest problem was the stash of heroin hidden in my neighbours' backyard, I shared my tale of the Newcastle blues that had befallen me since finding the dead body on the beach. I changed a few elements to make a good story. I also made it sound like Lloyd was some random bikie I'd had a run-in with, nothing more. In fact, by the end, even I was surprised how clean I sounded.

Listening as he sipped his cup of jasmine tea, Billy nodded and pursed his lips to suck in air at the appropriate moments. 'Ah, mate, you got some problems there. I thought having my cook disappear and turn out to be a member of a Triad gang was bad. Nah, that's nothing compared to what you dealing with. Bikies. You got it bad.'

Scraping the bowl clean, I leaned back in my seat. 'Worst part I haven't even told you yet, Billy.'

Billy was all ears. 'Yes! I knew there was a woman in all of this. Does she have a sister?'

'No ladies involved. I think a friend is trying to do me over.'

Raised eyebrows and a long exhale of air showed how much of a deal this was for Billy. No matter what culture you come from, mates don't do over mates.

'How hard?'

'All the way.' I hesitated. 'I'm not sure, but I think the break-in is his doing.'

'But why?'

Why would someone – worse, a friend – rob me? 'He's always been jealous of my PlayStation?'

Clearly Billy didn't believe a word of my story, but he accepted what I said. Sipping his tea, he let the flavour expand in his mouth, noisily sucking in a bit of air to assist, then leaned back in his chair. Looking down his nose at me, eyes starting to squint, he weighed up my options.

'You like this friend?'

'Most of the time.'

'He worth it?'

'Most of the time.'

'You want to forgive him?'

'Not sure.'

'All for your PlayStation?'

'Nuts, isn't it?'

Billy didn't need to say that he agreed with me. His look told me exactly what he thought. 'I have a mate in town. Helping with my problem. You remember how I have problem too?'

I had a flashback to the torso on the beach and realised that Billy was much calmer than when I last saw him. I hoped I'd never get to meet that mate of his.

'I can have a word,' Billy continued. 'But you need to choose if you want to end your friendship or teach him a lesson.'

A lesson. Hadn't thought of that one. 'Lesson'd be good. Don't think I'm ready to call in your mate.'

'Then you better get thinking, Lachie.'

In the background, a player at the Mahjong table won and the short yell of victory along with the clattering of tiles being pushed back for shuffling changed the subject.

Billy was right. Thinking was in order. Work out if Dave was doing it, why he was doing it, and then what to do about it. That was what I needed to do. Sitting there in the room was as good a place as any to think. Not like I had a home to go to. And so my problem went, around and around in my head like the players at the Mahjong table. Billy even brought me a glass of complimentary rice wine. Sipping it, I found that the ideas just became even crazier as the burn went all the way into my belly before the return trip up into my nostrils.

What did become clear was that I needed to get out of the gambling den, because if I kept drinking the rice wine, I'd feel a winning streak coming on. Good thing I had Dave's ute to return.

Reluctant but happy for the solitude of the road, I drove back the way I came, foot heavier this time, pushing the speed limit to get the trip over and done with. Turning into Dave's street and then into his driveway, the sight of his house lights seemed welcoming. Dave, standing on the back deck, gave his car a once-over to make sure it was all in order.

'She run alright?'

'No problems.' I tossed the keys back to him and he caught them mid-flight.

'Drink? Hot or cold?'

It was late and the ferry was going to stop running in a short spell. Besides, I wanted to get away from Dave for a bit. So I declined. Pulling my wallet out, I counted his share of the abalone money from Billy and held it out to him.

'Mate, don't worry about it. You need the money more than me at the mo', sorting your place out.'

'No, fair's fair.'

'Mate, keep it.'

'Dave, stop being a dick and take your share.'

Making a show of the refusal, Dave shook his head. 'But you do owe me for petrol.'

That took me completely by surprise. Counting the petrol money, I held it out to the tightarse. It felt like a humiliation, that I was some sort of loser in need of charity. Seeing Dave pocket it with a smile confirmed all of my suspicions.

'Who knows, mate. In a month, tables might be turned.'

'Which is why you should take your share now, mate.'

Dave shook his head. 'This is how mates work. Looking out for each other.'

He made it sound menacing and sinister as he coolly looked at his watch and offered me a lift to the ferry. I wasn't interested, I just wanted to get out of there, and in the time it would take for him to get ready and drive me to the wharf, I'd have walked the distance.

With a friendly wave, I ambled off towards the dock with no idea where I was heading once I got across the water. As the ferry pulled in and a young couple got off, hands all over each other with much giggling, I had an idea.

26
WE GOT A PROBLEM

I didn't feel great about the idea either. Which is why I was still standing at a forty-five-degree angle on the street, looking at Karen's place, unsure if I could do it. I liked her. I really liked her. I wasn't sure if I'd be welcome, rocking up at her front door. So just like in my dilemma with Dave, I chickened out, opting to put off a difficult decision and instead pray it went away. My place might smell and feel hideously empty but it was a roof. I had bigger things on my plate than booty calls.

Digging my hands into my pockets and hunching like a burglar on the prowl, I thought I'd better not risk it by knocking on her door, and started home. Which was when she ran into me. Literally.

'Eee-yow, watch – Lachlan?'

We were both on the ground, sitting on our bums, looking at each other. She was wearing tight compression skins, a tank top and an iPod – jogging gear. Her face was red and sweaty; I couldn't tell if she was blushing or flushed from running. Ever the gentleman, I helped her to her feet.

'What are you doing here? You looking for me? Your place is miles away,' she said, plucking her earbuds from her ears. Her eyes narrowed. 'Were you looking for me?'

I lied and said no, then thought better of it and came clean. Sort of.

'Actually, I wanted to apologise. For Gary. At the pub. But I'll get out of your hair.'

'You're here now.'

The universe was smiling.

Sitting in her place again, this time actually knowing who she was, felt good. Karen had opened a bottle of wine and let me start on my glass while she had a post-run shower. She was singing, hushed and low, thinking she wouldn't be heard. Sinking into the lounge, I smiled, relaxing. When she came out in a fleecy tracksuit, her hair still wet, it made the world seem right. She was positively glowing from the shower and her run. Outside, there were bikies and bad men, but here, here there was just me and her.

'Sorry. After seeing me in my running gear, you only get comfortable and homey.'

'Homey's good. I like homey.'

Flopping onto the couch next to me, Karen lifted her glass for a silent clink of cheers.

'Bad day?' I asked.

'God. Where to start?'

I was more than happy to hear all about it. Seeing that I was watching her, she looked away and took another sip of wine to gather her thoughts.

'Still no progress in my investigation. Getting grief from my boss about the lack of said progress. Then to top it off, I go for a run and bump into the guy I seem to be having this ... I don't know what, a thing ... with, only to end up sprawled on my arse.'

Thing. The word rattled around between my ears. 'A thing,' I said.

'Yeah.'

The way she drew the word 'yeah' out was wonderful. My phone vibrated with a message alert. Ignoring it, I poured more wine into her glass as she finally looked at me, both knowing and expecting. My phone vibrated again. I took it from my pocket and put it on the coffee table without looking at the screen. I settled in, placing an arm across the back of the couch, and Karen responded by leaning back, eyes looking into mine.

'So this … thing …' I said looking straight back at her.

'I guess the word would be … flirting?' she said, looking gently puzzled.

On the coffee table, my mobile started vibrating skittishly like a six-year-old needing to go to the toilet.

'Seems important,' she said.

I shook my head as I reached for it, intending to turn it off. But it was too late. Karen leaned forwards for her wine glass and left me to take the call.

'*Yes?*'

'We got a problem.' Lloyd.

Damn straight we had a problem. I was sitting on a couch on my own after getting the sexy bedroom eyes, so yeah, we had a problem.

'Lachie, I'm serious.'

I looked up and saw Karen reflected in her kitchen window, her hands covering her face, thinking I couldn't see her.

'Can I call you later?'

'Need to do this now, Lacharoonie.'

Watching Karen's reflection, I knew tonight was not going to be the night. I listened to where Lloyd wanted me to meet him and ended with a promise he'd see me there in twenty.

'Something come up?' Karen asked, too brightly.

Something had come up but, unfortunately, Lloyd's call

had killed it off like a cold shower.

'I'm sorry. A friend. In trouble. Reckons I'm the only one who can help. I have to go.'

'That's okay.' But that tone said it wasn't really. 'Should go to bed – I mean, I have an early start.'

Nodding, I thanked her for the wine. She showed me the door and we stood in silence for a moment.

'You're a weird guy, Lachlan Munro.'

That was as good an opening as any. I reached for her and kissed her, slowly and deliberately. It was everything you want in a kiss and then some.

'Didn't you have to go?' she whispered, but neither of us stopped. Hands pulled at clothes as we pressed against each other and the wall and, damn it, I should never have answered that call but her hand was, yes, and my, it was, and it was high school all over again but this time experienced as she nibbled my ear ...

Breathless, I looked into her face and brushed her messed-up hair back with my hand. I breathed a sobering lungful of oxygen and rested my forehead on hers.

'I ... Bit out of practice but ...' As her hand slowly went to my crotch.

Adam was tempted by a bloody apple? Deep breath again as I kissed her and nodded in that odd way that really means no. 'I want to. Really, really want to. If I stay, I won't go, and I have to go do this. I'll call you.'

She pulled back and smiled, nodding in that silly way we do when disappointed. Her hand ran down my arm and paused before opening the front door. Standing there, neither of us knowing what to do next, she straightened as she exhaled, as if making a decision.

'Maybe there is a point where we actually grow up. Start acting like adults.'

'Maybe,' was all I could manage.

'You'll really call?'

I nodded and then stepped out into the night. As the door shut behind me, I was ready to kill Lloyd and his stupid problem. Until it dawned on me I really did have a problem.

How the hell did Lloyd get my mobile number?

27
A CURLY ONE

Lloyd had suggested meeting at the Great Northern in what had once been the ladies' bar. I wasn't going to comment on that, or the bizarre tiki decor that ignored the decidedly un-PC 1950s Aboriginal motifs pressed into the ceiling. In the corner, Lloyd was nursing the standard bikie Jack and Coke, chatting with the barman about who knows what: muscles, tattoos, the Middle East peace process?

'Lachie-loader, glad you could make it.'

'No cider, Lloyd?'

'Felt like something stronger. That okay with you?'

I signalled for the bartender to get me a beer as I sat on the vacant stool next to Lloyd.

'How'd you get my number, Lloyd? Generally pretty careful with that. Even told Dave not to give it to you.'

'Dave had nothin' to do with it. Simple six degrees of separation, mate. All it took was me phone. We have our ways.'

'Enlighten me.'

Lloyd slumped theatrically as if he was about to share nuclear launch codes. 'Fine. I know you're a painter. I know you lost your job in a particular suburb. Painters and tradies tend to stick to the same areas. So I simply asked the painters known to work in that area if anyone knows my cousin Lachie Munro. People share all sorts of things if you ask nice enough.'

The answer seemed almost too easy. I was kind of disappointed. 'So none of that stuff about bikies infiltrating government departments?'

'We're everywhere. Doesn't mean we have a hotline. It's no different to you. You want something, what do you do? You ask some mates. Someone always knows someone. Difference is my gang of mates is much bigger than your bunch of buds. Not all bikies are long-haired and unwashed.' He pointed a finger at his club ring to show how big his group of mates was.

Thinking about the all-knowing bikies had me reaching for my beer.

'Besides, this was more a freelance operation.'

I was confused.

'I needed the cash so this ... bit of biz, the club don't know I'm doing it. To be honest, it's really way above our pay scale. We talk a lot but really, we just like bikes and chicks. Bit of fightin', a lot of rootin'. But I was happy to step up, had some good leads on where to go with ... the gear.'

'You gotta be fucking kidding me.'

'Don't rag me out. This was all just a bit of bluff for me cousin. And that's the problem. Me cuz.'

I paused, beer almost to my mouth. 'Dave? You think after that little speech, Dave's the problem?'

'Yeah, I do. I think he's dirty.'

'*Dirty?*'

'You going to repeat everythin' I say? I think Dave is dirty.'

'Why?'

'His missus has been tellin' me he's gone all cagey. Hasn't been himself.'

'He hasn't been himself since the marriage ended. No argument with you there.'

'Yeah, true. But she's sayin' much more recent. Cagey. He was the same with me. Asking about money, anything I had going on the side. Everyone is doing it tough at the moment unless they're digging something outta the ground, but this was different. This was kinda persistent … not right.'

It was almost too much to absorb. I'd been wrong about Lloyd. He was actually pretty sharp – sharper than I'd been. A whopping great liar, but I was impressed as much as I was kicking myself for being so rusty about who to trust and neglecting due diligence.

'In fact, I very nearly didn't come and meet you the first time simply 'cos it was Dave doing the arrangin'.'

'So why did you?' I asked, sipping at the unwanted beer. I could feel it just sitting in my gut, leaden.

'He's family. But he's fuckin' up somewhere. And I don't want to be nowhere near it when he does.'

'Why are you telling me this, Lloyd?'

Lloyd cricked his neck and looked to the bar door as though he was expecting trouble.

'Lloyd, stop looking at the fucking door and tell me what you expect me to do about it?'

'I don't expect you to do nothin'. I'm just tellin' ya. I was happy to do business with you, even if you did tell me to fuck off. But not him. That's the issue. You're a good bloke. Felt after everything youse was owed a warnin' before Dave went off the rails.'

Now I was understanding the size of the problem. The universe was telling me that, like it or not, I had to deal with Dave. Question was how. Did dealing with Dave mean I would have to cut him out? This was a bloke who knew everything I was up to. Cutting Dave free meant a loose end. Loose ends could become trip hazards.

'I can see you understand the pickle,' said Lloyd. 'It's a tough one. But when a brother strays, you can't do nothin' about it. Just have to accept it and do what's necessary.'

'What's necessary? What would you do, Lloyd?'

'Cut him off. If he keeps goin', he'll end up with somethin' else cut off and who knows who else will be there next to him.'

Massaging my temples, I just wanted all this to be over. My life would have been so much simpler if I'd just tipped the shipment back over the side to float free once more in the ocean. Better yet if the drugs really had been stolen from my car. I confessed the truth about that to Lloyd. Seemed only fair.

'Wait. So the stuff's not in your car?'

'No. I just said that to get you to work harder to find it. I'm kind of stuck without wheels.'

'You stashed it at your home? What are ya? Fuckin' mental?'

'Not all of it. I took precautions. The two I had in my place were taken. The rest of it is safe.' I was feeling like a teenager being told off for coming home late.

'You deserved to lose it. The rest of this stuff had better be safe. All of this will be a bit of a non-event if it ain't. The people I reached out to have a funny idea about time wasters.'

'What if I gave you the ...' Now it was my turn to look about the place. Not sure what I was looking for but I was following Lloyd's lead.

'The package? Nope. I'm a middleman, that's all.'

'What if I give it to you gratis, no strings? I just want to be rid of it.'

'How's that gonna look? I turn up with a load of somethin'. People are gonna ask questions.'

'And how is it different from me turning up with a load of stuff? Aren't people gonna ask questions?'

'They are, mate. Don't you worry about that. But the questions are about you. Not me and my imaginary friend who gave me a huge whack of smack.' Point made, Lloyd drank the last of his Jack and Coke, crunched some ice between his teeth and rammed home his last gem of advice.

'But don't worry. If you can keep that stuff safe for a bit longer until me connections come through, I'll have someone interested in dancin' with ya. You just got to work out how to ditch Dave. Cos until you do, I'm not introin' you to no one. I can't. Thanks for the drink.'

Alone, my guts flicked onto a heavy-duty spin cycle. Draining my beer, I signalled for something stronger to settle them. How to get rid of Dave? That was a curly one.

28
HORACE HAS A BELLY ACHE

It was late when I approached home but the neighbours' place was lit up like Christmas. Seeing Mario pacing on his front verandah with a cigarette, I detoured to find out what was going on. As I got closer I could smell the greasy sweetness of marijuana. When Jess had been on the chemo, I'd helped Mario out in sourcing some from Maxie for her nausea. They must have had some left over. Or got a taste.

'Everything alright, Mario?'

Looking like death, Mario gave me a tight grimace as he gently pinched off the lit end of the barely smoked tobacco ciggie.

'Lachlan, terrible day. Terrible. The dog. Jessie let me have one of these – that's how the day has been.' He held up the cigarette before going on. 'Then I had to have a joint for my nerves, which meant I needed to have this one to mask the smell. We had to get the vet ambulance to come and get her.'

Even I could tell my face had blanched as I wobbily enquired what the emergency was.

'Horace ate something, got crook. Thank God for the ambulance.'

'A pet ambulance?'

'Godsend. The emergency vet told us she was this close.' He held up two fingers pinched together.

'They have an ambulance for pets?'

'Yes. Included in the pet insurance. Why wouldn't they?'

'Just had an image of a labrador in the back of a normal ambulance.'

Mario looked at me with what I took to be horror. We both let it slide.

'They know what she ate? I mean, she's a labrador.'

'She's a labrador ...'

'And they eat anything. Was it something she picked up on a walk or ...?'

'They'll pump her stomach and do some tests tomorrow so we'll know what caused it. But they don't know if she'll pull through – we could still lose her.' Mario started to cry, snickering whimpers rather than full-blown howls as he tried to hold it together in a macho display of bravado.

Awkwardly, I placed a hand on his shoulder and squeezed. 'She'll be right, buddy.'

He mistook this for permission to suddenly embrace me and cry on my shoulder. I patted him on the back as images of Karen hugging me tight flitted into my brain along with the nightmare scenario of the vets retrieving the remains of a package of heroin from the labrador's stomach.

'Thanks, Lach. You're a good man. Got some funny ideas. But a good man.' Mario wiped his eyes as he pulled himself together. 'A good man.'

Thankfully the man-hug was over, but one hand still pressed on my shoulder.

'That guts of a dog will eat anything not moving. I blame snail bait. That crazy bitch on the corner. Garden's covered with the little blue bastards.'

Excusing himself, Mario went inside, leaving me standing on the lawn wondering how he would react if the vet told him his labrador was a junkie. I was gutted. If Horace died because of me ... I needed to be sure.

If I got really close to the kitchen window inside my spartan flat, I could see into Mario and Jess's place. From there, I watched and waited until their lights went out, chewing at my nails. It took an age. Maybe Mario needed to unwind after what he'd been through. Finally, the front lights flicked to black. As each inside light turned off, I traced Mario's path through the house until the only light still burning was in the front bedroom.

I snuck outside again and crept around the garden to prevent the sensor lights coming on. Throwing myself over the fence was easier knowing that poor Horace wasn't there to woof at me on my way to the spider-filled cubby house. It was a huge relief to open the play stove and see all the packages just as I'd left them, none of them missing or chewed. To make sure they stayed that way, I shoved a warped and faded old colouring book in front of them as additional protection before shutting the door.

My commando escape back to my yard was much easier without the burden of thinking I'd poisoned Horace. But dropping over the fence, I got the fright of my life.

'Lachlan, evening stroll?' His cigarette burned bright on his inhale, the glowing red end the only thing visible as he sat on a crate by the shed.

'Harry! You scared the crap outta me.'

'What comes from leaping over neighbours' fences.'

I started to stutter an excuse but Harry cut me off with a wave of his hand. Standing, he turned on his head torch to grind out his cigarette.

'I don't care what you're up to. Seen nothing, know nothing. Not my problem. Until you bring it here.' With that his long legs loped him back to his place, leaving me to my own thoughts.

Inside, I pulled out a sleeping bag and found a space to lie down that wasn't too smelly as distracting thoughts of Karen drifted through my head. Dave kept on intruding. Like in real life, his goofy head would materialise in my thoughts to deliver a message too soft to hear but impossible to ignore.

Lloyd might have wanted me to cut Dave loose but I knew doing so could jeopardise everything. Dave knew it all. What we had been doing with the abalone, the drugs that he himself was up to his neck in. Like the old saying goes, keep your enemies close … and whatever the rest of that is. Dave needed to be kept in the game, close enough that I could keep an eye on him. Which raised the next problem. How did I make it appear like he was still a player while I kept him out of the loop?

Somewhere in there I fell asleep to dreams of labradors of all colours fetching syringes from the sea and dropping them at my feet while Harry sat on the beach silently watching and smoking, and the limbless torso of Dave rolled up and down the sand at the water's edge, laughing.

I didn't need a dream dictionary to work out what it all meant.

29
DECISION TIME

A buzzing by my ear woke me when the sun itself was barely up. The labrador army with their syringes still played behind my eyelids. I fumbled for my phone.

'Hello?'

'I woke you.'

The sound of Karen's voice had me instantly awake.

'Was going to suggest getting together for breakfast but then thought dinner would be better.'

'We could do both.'

'How about we just pick one.'

'Dinner it is then.'

'Great.' She paused. 'How was your meeting?'

It took me a moment to remember she meant Lloyd. Flattering to call him a meeting. 'Not as positive as hoped.'

'Your friend, she alright?'

She? Then it twigged. Karen thought I'd had to deal with an ex.

'It wasn't an ex. It was a mate of a mate. He ...' What could I say about Lloyd?

'You don't have to say anything. I'll see you tonight. You can sort your story out and tell me then.'

Stretching, I felt very pleased with myself. And determined today would be the day I solved all my problems. I'd be lying if I didn't admit that my solution was simply to pack up everything not waterlogged and damaged and get out of town. Start again anywhere. Somewhere warmer, somewhere with four seasons:

desert, coast, tropics or ski field. This was nothing more than a fantasy. While I might have nothing left in this town, no job, no prospects, I wasn't a quitter. Deep down, I knew I needed to take the reins on this thing and stop other people telling me what I needed to do. Taking out my mobile, I dialled Lloyd.

'Yo,' his voice came down the line.

'Lloyd. It's me, Lach.'

'Lll-aaaaaaaarrrrr-ccccccckkk?' he drawled my name out stupidly. Was he stoned?

'Don't do that.'

'W-hhhhh-aaaaaa-ttt?'

My finger hovered over the end call button, so very tempting. But I needed this to be done and Lloyd was the only one in my corner.

'Lloyd. I need you to reconsider.'

'What you talkin' about, Lachie-licious?'

Speaking in simple short syllables, I spelled it out. 'It's about Dave. If you're right and he's bent, the longer the package stays near either of us, the more chances Dave has to do us over. So I need that meeting.'

'Oh, Goldie-lach, so forceful and manly, all –'

'You're wasting my time. Yes or no?' I said.

'Lachie, come on. You got to see it from my end. I'm the one stickin' my neck out here.'

'We're both knee-deep in this, Lloyd. This goes pear-shaped, no one's coming out clean.'

'You a lawyer now, Lacho? He's me cousin.'

'So what was all that shit you were spinning about cutting a brother off?'

'Blood's thicker than water.'

'My experience, Lloyd, water dilutes blood. Every time.'

It was true. People said blood was thicker than water but I knew: family means diddly. If someone wants something you got, they'll sell you out in a flash. The more mates you got, the stronger you are.

'We are on the same page, Goldie-lach.'

'Don't call me that. Just do as I ask and get me a meeting.'

'Okay. Give me a couple of hours and I'll meet you at the pub.'

'Which one?'

But he was gone. I guess that's what text messages are for.

Now fully awake and energised by my decisiveness, I felt the day stretch before me. It was time to make my place more liveable. Shower first though. Start clean so you know where you been, as one of my first paint bosses liked to say.

30
VISITORS

When your home has been reduced to a gutted shell, cleaning doesn't take long. Which gives you a lot of thinking time as you walk thirteen steps in one direction and thirteen back waiting for a call, text or some other form of contact from a bikie named Lloyd. Surprises me that more philosophers don't emerge from our prisons. You also notice a lot of flaws in the surfaces. So, along with the pacing, I started doing a bit of gapping, filling and surface prep.

In between pacing, gapping and filling, I found a couple of milk crates that had been sunning themselves in the backyard. I thought they might enjoy the chance to come into my place to live as chairs. A couple of the not-so-damp cushions softened the hard plastic grid. Used to perching on all sorts of odd lumps for morning tea or worksite lunch breaks, a hard seat didn't trouble my backside but any visitors might not feel the same way.

'How's the redecorating, Lachlan?' Harry was at the front door, silhouetted by the bright afternoon sun. 'Looking good. Love the crates. Amazing what we have these days. I remember growing up, me da made chairs out of old packing crates, few planks of wood. No cushions, maybe an old pillow if you were lucky.'

'Wood floor or dirt, Harry?'

'It wasn't the Depression, ya cheeky bastard.' The old man stretched his arms and scratched his belly. 'Fancy a beer? Tell you some more about the old times?'

The ringing of my phone gave him his answer.

'No worries. It'll keep.' Harry turned and waved me off as I answered the phone.

'Lach, I got your answer. Where are you? Been waitin' for ya.'

'You never told me where to meet you, Lloyd.'

'Oh. Well, where are you now?'

'Home.'

'Be there in ten, then.'

It was more like twenty before I heard the rumble of his motorbike echoing up the street.

Watching the small man in his leathers walk up the driveway trying to work out whether my place was the house or the granny flat was mildly amusing. But I put him out of his misery by standing in my doorway.

'Lloyd! Down here.'

Seeing me, he trotted over and gave me some sort of weird bikie handshake with a shoulder bump.

'So I came around to your thinkin' and did the askin', and me contacts came through. But this is serious stuff, Lachie Munro.' Lloyd crinkled up his nose, sniffing. 'Jesus. What's that stink? Leave a tap on?'

'Not me and not just one. Guess someone was trying to send me a "fuck you".'

Lloyd gave a slow whistle as he took in the waterlogged possessions now in the garden by the front door. 'Pissed someone off.'

'So I guess you see why I'm so keen to get this over?'

Lloyd looked me in the eye and handed me a scrap of paper. 'That's your man.'

On the scrap was a phone number and an address in

Sydney. 'Marrickville?'

'The Fishy Man.'

It was a nickname that didn't give me great cause for joy.

'He's the big man. Does most of the big deals. Controls, like, sixty per cent of the market. If he can't help you, no one will.'

'Is he expecting me?'

Lloyd nodded. The meeting was set for tomorrow.

'What if that wasn't convenient?'

'You want this all over? You'll find it is convenient. Can I use your dunny?'

Pointing him in the right direction, I looked again at the piece of paper, hoping it truly held the answers to my prayers. By the time my toilet was flushing and Lloyd was coming back, I'd pretty much convinced myself it was.

'Sorry, brother. Might be best if you stay out of there for a while. That turd did not want to leave the nest.' Slapping me on the shoulder as his farewell, Lloyd headed back down the driveway. Then the stink hit me.

Thankfully, it didn't follow me outside where Harry was sitting with his beer, staring at the greenery.

'So you did come out,' he said.

'Felt like hearing about the old days.'

'Bullshit.' Swigging his beer, Harry kept one eye on me, watching. 'So what's with the bikie?'

Shrugging, I told him it was a nuisance that wouldn't go away. The old man accepted this.

'There was another bloke who was sniffing about too. Hawaiian shirt. Older. Know him?'

Now Harry had my attention. 'When?'

'Day or so ago. About dinner time?'

This was news. Why was Gary looking at my place? This was not a welcome development. Was Gary in on this too now?

'You seen him before, Harry?'

Harry shook his head while pulling on his beer like a baby on a milk bottle. I sat in silence, pondering this development, until Harry smacked his lips, signalling the end of his beer.

'Right. Best I go think about making some dinner.'

Recapping his empty beer bottle, Harry left me with my thoughts. The idea of having nothing better to do than think about what the evening meal was going to be sounded very appealing. But Harry's bombshell had elbowed out any consideration of the merits of chops versus sausages.

How did Gary fit into all of this? Did he fit in at all? He'd never been to my place before. I didn't even think he knew where I lived. Which made me put him in the box marked 'involved'. Was that with Dave though? Having turned back up in town like a turd on the tide, was Gary involved by way of Dave? Maybe he was in cahoots with the original owners? Or was he freelance, having heard a rumour and decided to do a bit of prospecting of a different kind, hoping to make a score? It was all bad news though, if he was sniffing around my place. None of these thoughts made me feel any better. I had to stop being so suspicious. There had to be a simple, rational explanation. Had to be.

Over the top of all that were the police trying to get to the bottom of a torso on the beach, which they'd decided I must know more about than I was letting on. My stolen car just added to their view that I was dodgy. And all of this was having a negative effect on my pursuit of Karen. With everything going on, I was not going to be in any state to see her tonight.

The old brain box was spinning with possibilities. My anxiety was telling me that when it stopped, I'd be the one thrown off. Maybe, if I was lucky, my trip to see the Fishy Man would provide a soft landing.

Deep down, my lizard brain, the one supposed to control all the fight-or-flight responses, was screaming at me that the Fishy Man could be a setup. Would Karen visit me if I went to prison? What would the sentence be for trying to sell some flotsam and jetsam? Does finders keepers still hold for narcotics?

The sun was making me drowsy and my thinking crazy, a combination that did not point to a positive outcome. I needed to work out where in Marrickville I had to be and how I was going to get there by public transport.

Having a purpose changed my mood as I locked up and headed for the train station. Walking the streets allowed the world to show me its indifference. Which was reassuring. In the great scheme of things, my problems were of no consequence: the sun still shone, the grass grew and the birds sang. The ocean would keep on waving at the shore long after I was not only a distant memory but reduced to base elements once again. This realisation, melancholy as it was, made me feel happy even when I discovered I would be forced to walk the extra distance to Hamilton train station thanks to the government's closure of the local train line. It was a wonderful coincidence that the line earmarked for closure also happened to be the only Newcastle land not riddled with old coal mines. Convenient for any developer who might want to put up some more expensive apartment towers.

The State Rail employee at the station didn't really care for my lament on the changing face of the city.

'What you don't get is once it's gone, it's gone,' I said.

'Yeah, yeah. They paved paradise and put in some parking spots. Called progress. Anything else I can help you with, sir?'

'When's the Sydney train leave tomorrow?'

'Timetable's on the wall. Or download the app. App's easier and you get alerts. Next?'

I headed back home. The sun was burning, the grass now seemed to house dog turds and the waves pounded the shore, dumping dirty, foam-filled monsters, proving once again that everything is relative. Life always comes down to perspective.

Realising I was close to the Department of Primary Industries office by the waterfront reminded me about Karen. Reluctantly, I dialled her number.

'You can't make it.' It was a statement.

'I'm really sorry, Karen.'

She didn't ask for my excuse. She wasn't asking anything at all. All I could hear down the phone was her breathing.

'I have a few things on tomorrow. Have to go to Sydney. Short notice. Got to see a mate.'

'Another mate,' she said.

'Not really a mate. An errand.'

'That's fine. Probably for the best. Where you going?'

'I'll call when I get back?'

'If you want. I am very busy, so, y'know, probably for the best.' She didn't need to say it. I'd blown it.

I thought maybe if I was lucky, when all the trouble was sorted, I'd get another shot. But at that point, I also felt like my luck had run out – over without even starting.

Regrets? I've had a few. This one was heading straight to the top of the chart with a bullet.

31

MARRICKVILLE

As the train to Sydney weaved its way along the waterways, I was still sulking over Karen. Even the early morning sun glinting off the oyster beds and mudflat inlets of the Hawkesbury failed to lift my mood.

But as the scenery changed I had to admit that it was easy to see why this part of the world was loved by so many. Every turn of the track presented views that would do a landscape artist proud, showing the bush all the way to the water's edge, human presence at a minimum. Maybe one day I'd have a place somewhere along there, hidden from the rest of the world and only accessible by boat. Or sea plane. Only contact with the world the postman and deliveries of supplies. Not sure what I'd eat as I don't like oysters much, but the idea seemed pretty seductive as I stared out the train window at the blue sky and the boats, about to go and meet a major drug supplier.

By Mooney Mooney, the view really started working and I was feeling more optimistic about Karen. I'd make it up to her. I'd get a second chance. When all the business was settled and life got back to normal, I'd sort things out with her for sure. By the time the train was approaching the urban sprawl, I was convinced I'd win her over.

A quick change at Strathfield for the leg into Newtown and a bus down Enmore Road before a longish walk over the hills and I was in Marrickville. It's an odd place, Marrickville. On the surface it's an inner-city suburb populated by the young and familied, its industrial roots still evident – a bit like

Newcastle but unpolished. There were working men's pubs, some renovated and trendy, others turned into apartments, strips of artisan coffee bean polishers or local gin speakeasies. Low-flying planes, their wheels dangling so close they threatened the chimneys and television aerials, drowned out everything in their final airborne moments. I wanted to hate the place but there was something about it.

The address I was looking for ended up being a warehouse. Nondescript, in a street of other warehouses, the front door made of checker plate steel. After knocking then thumping with my fist, I waited, a lone figure in a streetscape of pigeons and asbestos roofing.

Turning at a sliding sound, I saw a pair of eyes peering at me through what could have been a half-sized letterbox slit set at eye level. The eyes looked up then back to me again. Puzzled, I squinted as if that would give me the answer. When the eyes looked up again, I followed them and saw the security camera.

'Now you get it. Smile!' said a disembodied voice.

I did as I was told and heard bolts being withdrawn and locks being undone before the door swung out towards me. Stepping into the gloom, I noted the thick reinforced door and the seriousness that it communicated. The darkness swallowed me as the door closed. I couldn't see much at all.

'Lift your shirt. You understand, we's got to check.'

I'd seen enough bad TV shows to know what I was being checked for.

'Turn around. Like a ballerina. What's that word?'

'Pirouette,' I said as I did a clumsy turn, not quite en pointe, with my shirt hoisted up to my armpits. As my eyes adjusted, more of the space became visible. I was in a square cage, a kind of security airlock. I'm guessing they really didn't like Jehovah's Witnesses. I should never have agreed to come to this place.

'He's clean.'

The call triggered the cage door in front of me to click open. Standing to the side was a very large Maori guy with a sawn-off and further back in the room was a smaller man in a leather jacket with a bum-fluff beard and a short ponytail. He couldn't have looked any greasier if he swam in a deep fryer for a week.

'You Lachlan Munro? He's been waitin' for you,' said the greasy one. 'Need ya phone first.'

I stepped through the cage door and into an office-sized empty space. At the back was another door, where Greasy stood. Behind him, a set of stairs. The whole room was covered in the same checker plate steel as the front door. Really made you feel safe.

'Homey,' I said as I handed across my mobile.

He grinned. 'You ain't seen nothin' yet.'

It was then that I noticed a familiar face sitting in the corner reading the day's newspaper.

'Damo?'

It was Roxy's ex-boyfriend. As the blond dreadlocks shifted and he looked up from the paper, I remembered why I hated him. Private school wanker.

'Lacho?'

I shook his hand. We'd met a couple of times at a party and I'd never really warmed to him. Didn't help that he was doing the horizontal rhumba with the lovely Roxy.

'You spoken to Rox?' I asked. 'She's worried about you.'

Damo shuffled and wiped hanging dreads off his face. 'It's complicated. Y'know. I mean, Newie was getting a bit intense. And Rox is a great chick. I love her, man, but love doesn't have to be forever.'

I let him hang. He filled in the silence, too quickly.

'I'll send her a Snapchat. Or something.'

Greasy was watching us both, puzzled. 'I thought this was a business meetin'. Instead, you're organisin' family reunions?'

Damo started to say something but Greasy shut him down.

'Get the fuck out of here, Damo. You're only here as a favour. Do y'see Tiny chattin' away to visitors? No. So sit your arse down and don't move or say nothin' until we need you to do somethin'. Get it?'

Tiny must have been the large guy at the front door with the sawn-off shottie. Greasy led me upstairs to yet another corridor. The place was a rabbit warren. 'What the fuck's a Snapchat?' he asked.

'You're asking me?'

Arriving at a door, he tapped out what I assumed was a secret signal.

'Yeah?' was the gruff response from behind the door.

'It's me. I got the guy.'

'Who?'

'The guy. Lachlan. I got Lachlan Munro here,' said Greasy.

'Give me a minute.'

Standing there next to Greasy, I looked up at the ceiling, hands clasped before me like I was trapped in a lift, patiently avoiding eye contact. It was an awkward moment for both of us and the sound of a toilet flushing made it even more so.

Heavy deadbolts thunked before the door swung open to reveal what can only be described as a palace. Directly opposite the doorway was a massive fish tank that looked like a chunk of the Great Barrier Reef had been sliced off and captured in a bottle. It was the first fish tank I'd ever seen that came close to capturing some of the amazing richness of life you see under the waves. I was mesmerised. It reminded me that I needed to get in the ocean again without any poaching or fishing baggage, to just be. I was overdue for a saltwater recharge.

It was then that I noticed him standing in front of me, getting as much of a thrill from my gob-smacked reaction as I was from his tank.

'Mr Munro. Welcome.'

32
THE FISHY MAN

'Fuckin' peach, ain't it? See that?' His workman-like finger pointed to where a moray eel was hiding in some rocks. 'That's Nessie. See the anemone next to her? Poisonous. Most things in the tank? Deadly.'

He was gauging my reaction. I tried to deny him one and failed. Behind me, Greasy pulled the door shut, leaving me alone in the room with the Fishy Man. It didn't help the mood.

With a small chuckle, the Fishy Man slapped me on the shoulder. 'Stop lookin' so worried. You think I'd bring you all the way in here to kill ya?'

The weight of his hand on my shoulder had my attention and I felt relieved when it was gone. He walked over to a bar that was bigger than most nightclubs' and leaned backwards like a kid who owned a lolly shop, showing off all of the spirits on display.

'Drink?' he asked. 'Dark spirit? Feels like a dark spirit kinda day, yeah?' He looked at me, squinting one eye and cocking one finger as he decided what sort of dark spirit drinker I would be. 'Rum. Am I right?'

Before I could say no, he was pulling a tall, thin bottle from the shelf and telling me a story about how special it was, smuggled over from a small distillery started after East Timor became independent.

'Not only does that country grow my most beautiful marijuana, but they have this distillery no one knows about. In ten years, it's gonna be the choice of celebrities everywhere.

Mind you, by then it won't be any of them Hollywood starlets with their bobble-headed anorexia, no. It'll be Bishaka from Bollywood or Chi Lei from Guangzhou. People do not realise the cultural tidal wave about to hit the West.'

No one it seemed, except the Fishy Man, who handed me a tumbler of rum and gestured for me to sit on his enormous leather couch.

I did as he'd indicated and joined in his toast. He was right. The rum was good.

'So, Mr Munro. I hear you got somethin' you want to sell.'

Confessing the truth about my predicament, I told him how I'd found the package and about my desire to get rid of it. The Fishy Man sat and listened, nodding and sipping his rum. When I was done, he got up and stood in front of his fish tank, his back to me.

'Don't believe a word of that,' he said, scooping a goldfish from a small bowl and dropping into the giant tank. 'So, Lachlan, do you have a taste for me?'

'Taste?'

'For testing.'

'No.'

That stopped him. Pursing his lips, the Fishy Man looked from me to the dazed goldfish in the saltwater tank with an expression that even I understood: Can you believe this guy?

'Hard to sell somethin' without the buyer taking a test drive.'

'I thought this meeting was more the meet-and-greet type,' I lied.

'You want a wooing? Bunch of flowers, box of chocs? That make you more comfy?'

'Just trying to keep everyone safe,' I said, clearing my throat to stop the wavering in my voice. 'You can't be too careful these days.'

The Fishy Man liked that, raising his rum in silent toast to the sentiment. 'So what's your plan, Mr Munro?'

Now we'd met, my plan was to arrange a new time and place to deliver a sample. Preferably somewhere closer to me that was most definitely neutral ground.

'I do like that. One that *you* don't have to travel too far to.' The Fishy Man leaned back and looked at his rum. The caramel liquid rolled in the tumbler, an oily swirl.

Softly, the Fishy Man started to speak again. 'I think you've forgotten your place, Mr Munro. Forgotten that I'm the buyer here. And as we all know, the customer is always correct, and the seller must aim to please.'

Stalling, I raised my glass to drink, forgetting it was empty. The Fishy Man noticed and the corner of his mouth hinted ever so slightly at a smile.

'You want me to come back here. Again? That's a risk for both of us. The Central Coast has many places we can meet,' I said.

The Fishy Man wasn't having a bar of it. 'No, it'll be Newcastle. I've a spot of business there needs checkin' on. You still livin' at your place by the beach? Merewether, right?'

I felt sweat on my forehead. In the tank, the now panicking goldfish darted away as several mean-looking fish came hunting for it. It ducked into some coral and straight into the mouth of Nessie the moray eel.

'You really think I didn't check you out? I know everythin' there is to know about you. You been scanned and prodded and probed and didn't even know it. That's how big I am, that's how I work. That's why you got to come through my front door and sit there admirin' my fuck-off fish tank.'

Why is it the crooks who have all the answers? I go to the police with a problem and they look into it, but every crook and dodgy dealer I've met in the past week already knew the answer.

Dazed, I sat through the rest of the meeting, listening to what the Fishy Man wanted me to do. Before I knew it, Greasy was at my elbow, escorting me out. As we reached the door, the Fishy Man called out to me.

'And Mr Munro?'

Turning, I waited as he finished his rum and placed the glass on the coffee table.

'Last guy who tried to fuck me over ended up burley for a fishin' trip. I think you met him?'

He must have mistook my look of terror for confusion.

'Asian guy, chinky-chink? Dragon tattoo on his chest? Or was it his back? Can you remember?'

Picturing the torso on Nobbys Beach, I had no desire to end up the same way.

'That guy let me down. Don't do the same, dig?'

'I just want this over,' was my soft reply.

For some reason, the Fishy Man thought this was hilarious.

As Greasy shuffled me through the security grille, he made sure it was shut tight before turning to signal with a nod that it was okay for the outer door to be opened. As the sunlight flooded in to erase all the details, Greasy grabbed my sleeve.

'Mate, you realise this is never over, don't ya? Like that song, "Hotel California",' he said, holding out my forgotten mobile.

'Been getting that impression.'

'Good. See youse in Newie, then,' he said as he started to softly sing the lyrics to the song while shutting the door.

I've always hated that song.

33
HOSPITAL

I was now trapped in a world that I had no desire to be a part of. Exhausted from my meeting and the trip back to Newcastle, all I could think of was how close I was to breaking the promise I'd made to my mum. I was sliding towards becoming exactly what she'd feared – my old man.

I couldn't let it happen. I'd do the deal and get my life back, return once more to the straight and narrow and live under the radar. Maybe I'd get lucky and have the money to replace my car and get myself out of trouble, even if that meant getting out of Newcastle too. Somewhere I could make a new start. Maybe even with Karen. The flip side to all this I didn't want to think about. I did not want this story to end with a Lachie-sized lump of 'ambergris'.

As the train finally stopped and the heavy door released, it felt good to be back in Newcastle. For all its faults, this place was home and even the teenagers at the end of the platform, grunting rhymes to an imaginary gangsta beat, felt familiar and bizarrely comforting.

I toyed with the idea of calling Karen. Remembering our last conversation, I realised it wasn't a good idea. Having her yell at me I could live with. What I feared most was silence. And her right hook.

'Got a light, brother?'

I shook my head at the skinny tracksuit-wearing man as his tongue ran across his toothless gums.

'No worries, brother. God bless.'

As I watched the man weave up the platform searching for a kind soul to light his ciggie, my world didn't seem so bad. Even at our darkest, sometimes all we need is someone to give us a light to make things right again.

An onshore wind had come up, bringing whitecaps with it. My mother always said an ill wind blows no good and, sure enough, Dave rang.

'Mate, where the flamin' fuck you been?'

I wasn't about to tell him my plans so I told him I'd been looking for work and running a few errands.

'It's Lloyd. He's been beaten up. And run over. He's in the hospital.'

As Dave filled me in on the details, I raced for the taxi rank. By the time I was closing the door, I had the lowdown and was heading for the hospital.

Lloyd was in a bad way. Seemed he'd been jumped about midday after a spot of bother at a roundabout. Road rage and 'roids, never a good mix. Lloyd telling an SUV driver how to drive prompted the bloke to demonstrate his black-belt jujitsu skills to his twin boys, who were watching from the back of the family car. It wasn't so much the beating that had damaged Lloyd as the chest punch that sent him falling backwards off his bike and into the passing traffic.

At the hospital, I saw the evidence for myself. A heavily sedated Lloyd had one leg in plaster and a beatific grin on his dial thanks to whatever they were drip-feeding directly into his veins.

'Hey, Lach-o. How you goin' man?'

'How you feeling, Lloyd?'

'Never better, man. Hey! How was Sydney?'

I stayed silent. Who was on my side? Who could I trust? Was someone chilling out on an IV line the best person to tell about my meeting? Watching Lloyd as he blissed in and out of the moment, I debated what to tell him. Then he surprised me.

'It was Dave. No ...'

He had my full attention.

'Not Dave. Some mate of his. Positive. Recognised him from a school fete.'

A bikie at a school fete. I hoped he wasn't offering the kids rides.

'The guy who beat you up was a mate of Dave's?'

'No! Keep up. I was being followed! I stopped to eyeball the prick and this arsehole in an SUV started honkin' at me. Is the door wobblin'?'

'The door's solid, Lloyd. Did you get a good look at the guy following you? Know what he looks like?'

'Nah, that SUV got in the way. But they're onto you. They're tryin' to put the wind up us. Scare you. Take me out of the picture. That door is wobblin'. Must be that dragon out the window. He looks a right mean bastard.'

As Lloyd drifted off into his own thoughts again, I let him be. I had enough to deal with without adding dragons to the list.

In the hospital carpark, I ran through what Lloyd had said, trying to nut out what the hell was going on. If Dave had a friend following Lloyd then the stakes were definitely being raised. Either Dave was a meaner bastard than any of us thought or he was under pressure. What was his end game? Mates being mates, it seemed like there was nothing left to do but call him on it. When a buddy's being a dick, you tell him.

Don't you?

34
CONFRONTING THE PROBLEM

What do you say to someone who is up to the wazoo in crime, a co-conspirator in some, if not bad, then certainly dodgy activities with you? Is it a question of 'Hi, how you doing, you trying to rip me off?' Rehearsing it in my head didn't make it any easier. Nothing I thought of sounded right.

Walking up Dave's driveway, I still didn't know how to play it when the man himself appeared with two beers in his hand.

'Your Lordship, Sir Lach of House Painter. Brewski?' The tinnie was already sailing through the air towards me – head height, I noted.

'Went and saw Lloyd.'

Dave looked concerned, taking a sip of his drink before asking how Lloyd had seemed.

'Pretty much away with the fairies.'

'Lucky him,' was all Dave managed. He must have felt my eyes burning into him because he turned and looked at me, his face a look of pure puzzled innocence. 'What?'

'Bit harsh. He's your cousin.'

'Who runs on the bad side of the law.'

I didn't know what to say to that. But a mouthful of beer and my Dutch courage was up. 'And what? We're a couple of cleanskins?'

'It's a one-off!'

'And the poaching?'

Dave shrugged and stuck out his lower lip.

'Where were you the other night? When my place was getting done over?'

'With you!'

'What about when Lloyd got beaten up?'

'What the fuck's up your arse? You accusing me of something, come out and fuckin' say it.'

'Just asking the question, mate.'

Dave stood up. I'd never really noticed it before but his lanky AFL footballer frame was intimidating when he switched it on. Not that I was going to let him. As he placed his beer carefully on the ground, I did the same and stood to meet his glare, hands on hips, jaw jutting forwards.

'Then you better say what's eating at you before I get the wrong idea,' he said.

So I did. 'Are you trying to do the dirty on me?'

With one push, Dave had me back in my chair.

He stood before me, shaking his head. 'Mate, you're going all paranoid. You're jumping at shadows. This stuff you got hidden, it's messing with your mind. The sooner you get rid of it the better.'

He had a point. All I had was Lloyd's word to go on, a man of dubious character and limited vocabulary. That and my own instincts. Pinching the bridge of my nose, I shook the weariness from my shoulders and replaced it with more.

'Yeah, you're right, Davo. Sooner all this is over, the better. Get back to doing what we do best, hey?'

His meaty paw gripping my shoulder in a friendly squeeze felt good. Maybe a little too strong but that was Dave.

'Nong. What are ya? You really think I'd do over your place? What else is spinning around in your brainbox? Christ, mate. Drugs are bad, mmmkay? I should be asking you the same questions anyways.'

'Like what?'

'Like where were you today? Your phone was off.'

Thinking fast, I remembered my story that I'd been looking for work. I explained that my phone had been off when I met a project manager interested in working together. It seemed to be accepted without question because Dave had bigger things on his mind.

'After getting robbed, still think your place is the safest for the stuff? I said it before but I'll say it again. Might help take the edge off if we stowed them here. What d'you say?'

'Drink your beer, Dave. Leave the thinking to me.' Pretending I was joking, I worked hard to create a believable smile as Dave tried again.

'Just offering. Share the risk, maybe help ya sleep a bit better?'

'No one's found where I stashed them yet,' I said, meeting his gaze.

With a grin, Dave accepted that and left the topic alone. 'Good thinking. You want a feed or heading home?'

Finishing my beer, I made my excuses. Going home seemed like the best option.

35
THE ROT

Sitting in my lounge as the morbid fascination that passed for television news played, I kept chewing everything over in my mind, hoping I was wrong, hoping for a solution, hoping for the best. Despite Dave's reassurances, the rot had set in. I didn't trust him.

It didn't matter what the truth was. In my head I had a mate trying to do me over, and a dead and dismembered kitchen hand on a beach who was connected to a major drug dealer with a love of tropical fish. It all had to be related. For good measure, I also threw in the disappearance and then reappearance of Roxy's ex-boyfriend Damo in Marrickville. In the middle of it all was me, a sticky beak with a nose for trouble. The schmuck who reeled in what he thought was the biggest prize of his poaching career. Don't forget my brilliant decision to explore what looked like a dead seal on a beach. Nice way to involve myself in two things that I had no business being interested in at all.

'You in, Lach?' Harry was at my door, poking his head around the frame. 'Brought a cleanser. If you feel like a bit of company.'

Hard to refuse an offer like that. Harry shuffled over to settle on one of my milk crates and popped the top of a longneck.

'S'pose you don't got glasses. You want help scrounging some up, let me know. That or anything else, you just say the word.'

He was a dying breed. His gesture touched me and I felt

the prickling of tears. If I let them escape, that would be the end of any help being offered. Sad truth.

'Harry, I appreciate it. I really do. If I think I'm in over my head, I'll let you know.'

Harry looked at me, leaning back slightly, eyes wide. 'When you *think* you're in trouble? Your car's stolen, your place is broken into and turned into a pool, and a bikie keeps wandering up and down the drive? Nah, that's right. You let me know when you think you're in over your noggin'.'

Shaking his head, Harry took another deep pull on the beer, finishing it off. He popped the top of the next one without taking his eyes off the television weatherman explaining how the next few days were going to be wonderful.

'Bloody dickhead,' Harry muttered. In truth, I wasn't sure if he meant the upperclass twat of a weatherman or me.

36
ROXY'S FEARS

My head was filled with fumes and the tank was empty. They say a hangover is the dehydrated membranes around the brain shrinking as the body digests alcohol, turning one substance into another even scarier one. No wonder I felt rough. The only antidote was going to be a decent black coffee, baked beans, eggs and sausages. None of those were in my pantry or fridge. So when the cupboard is bare, it's best to make like Old Mother Hubbard and do something about it, and I'm not talking shopping.

Roxy beamed from ear to ear as she saw me amble towards the counter. 'Hey, Lachie, been too long.'

Seems a week is a long time in Newcastle. The café was relatively empty so I got the plum window seat and gorgeous Roxy's undivided attention.

'The boss spent last weekend away. So positive he's having an affair. With the coffee rep!' She proceeded to list all the indicators that her manager was on the pull.

'Heard from your fella, Rox?'

She made a sad face, a genuine one, not one of those pouty duck-faced ones. Not a peep from old Damo. 'Not even on Facebook. He was always updating where he was, what he was doing.'

Little prick not following through on his word. How hard is it to send someone a quick message? Karen popped into my mind, causing me to shift uncomfortably. I could hardly judge on that score.

'Nothing at all? How long's he been gone now?' I asked.

'Too long.'

Should I let her know I'd run into Damo? Or was it better to just let him disappear?

By the time she'd taken my order and brought out my coffee, I'd decided it was best to spill the beans.

'Damo's in Marrickville? In Sydney? That Marrickville?' She seemed to struggle with the geography.

Nodding, I improvised a little. I told her I'd seen him on a trip down to the city, a chance encounter in a café where he was with another girl. 'They looked pretty happy. He was under the thumb, that was clear.'

'She a redhead?'

I shook my head. I'd said too much already. A good lie should be light on detail and easy to deny.

'I caught him once looking at photos some chick had sent him. She had red hair. Figured he was probably heading there next.' She sighed and pulled out the other chair at my table. 'Guess I always knew he was a toad.'

And just like that, she was over him.

'I'm just glad he's okay. I was starting to get worried he was in trouble.'

That got my undivided attention. My guts were twitching and it wasn't just from the coffee.

'Charlie, you remember her? The blonde with the big norks?'

I nodded, not wanting to interrupt her thoughts on what trouble Damo might have been involved in.

'Charlie said just before Damo left, he was telling her he had some big meetings lined up. Then that guy washed up on the beach. I was worried that was something to do with Damo.'

Seems Roxy had good instincts as well.

'I just hope he's staying safe, wherever he is,' she said.

Safety. She had a very good point. The more the word rattled about my head, the more scared I got.

37
STEPPING UP

'You want *what*?' Billy Wong's face screwed up like I'd just handed him a bag of dog poo. Had I overstepped the friendship and overestimated Billy's abilities and criminal involvement? Made me glad I hadn't brought up the package.

'If it's too hard …' I tried to play it like it was no big deal.

'Why do you want a gun? What sort of trouble you in, Lachie?'

I shook my head. Where did I start?

'This about that friend who was doing the dirty on you over your, what was it again … your PlayStation? Or his sister?'

'PlayStation,' I said, regretting my poor excuse.

It didn't seem to get me over the line with Billy. 'You want a gun for a PlayStation?'

'Look, I know how it sounds but I think there's some bikies involved.'

'*What?* You outta your mind. Bikies? And you come here? To my business? Because of a PlayStation?'

Feeling like a prize country bumpkin, I took what Billy had to give. His advice was normally pretty sound.

'You in that much trouble, I can get you out of town. Back to the city, interstate. I have friends in Melbourne.'

As attractive as that offer sounded, I was not ready to cut my losses and flee just yet. It may have been suicidal but I wanted to see where this was going to end. Plus, bailing on a deal with the Fishy Man made me feel I might never need my superannuation.

'I really just want a gun, Billy. I don't want to use it but I'll sleep better knowing it's there.'

'You even know how to fire one?'

Truth was, I did know how to fire a gun, but I was rusty. I'd used rifles, done a bit of rabbiting in the past. I'd been in fields firing a gun in the darkness or held a spotlight while others fired. As far as I knew, I'd never hit a thing but I'd probably sent a few rabbits and kangaroos deaf. I told Billy about the rabbits and rifles. Not the handguns. Especially not the last trigger I'd been near, which went bang on a Melbourne street one cold winter night.

Billy sat there, watching me. Sipping his tea thoughtfully, he reached for one of the spring rolls on the plate he'd plunked on the table when he first sat down. 'You really want a gun.' His exhalation threatened to send a spray of spring roll into my lap.

Leaning forwards, he suddenly turned serious. The conversation became all business: what calibre; long or short; how much I was willing to spend.

'No idea. That's why I came to you. Had a feeling you might be able to point me in the right direction. Really would prefer if the gun was a lender rather than −'

Leaning back, his hands fanning wildly, Billy interjected before I could even finish. 'No way! You want a shooter, you own the shooter. Any trouble goes down, it's not coming back here. You understand that? I don't do no boomerang, baby.'

'Course. Understood, Billy.'

'No, I serious, Lachie. From me to you, it's then yours and yours alone. Nothing will trace it back to me. I know nothing. I give you that advice for free and suggest you use it. Save a lot of hassles, long run.'

His terms seemed acceptable. Not like I really had a choice. And scary as it was to be in a situation where the idea of a handgun was not only acceptable but required, the thought of having someone like Billy to go to was a comfort.

'I know nothing,' I repeated.

'Damn right, you don't. Every time I see you, you make sure of that.' Plucking the last of the spring rolls from the plate, Billy grinned. 'I know a guy. He might know someone.'

Of course Billy only knew 'a guy' who 'might'. It was a story like mine about my PlayStation, one we pretended to believe but both knew was a long way from the truth. Which made me decide to stop pretending. The game I was playing was serious.

'I want something common. A twenty-two. Happy to go up to a thirty-eight. But standard, no mods. Ten rounds max. Smith and Wesson, Glock, don't care. Just has to be in good condition and reliable. Your friend able to do that?'

Billy slowly took the spring roll from his mouth and placed it back on his plate. He looked at me, reassessing me. I sat still and let him. I could see I had gone from some idiot who got into trouble gambling to someone with a past at odds with everything he'd assumed. He was struggling with the mismatch.

'You never fired a pistol.'

'You're asking the wrong question.'

Again, Billy did a reassessment, straightening himself in the chair and leaning forwards. 'Won't be cheap. You want it quick. Cost extra.'

'What's the ballpark?'

'Five. That's thousand. Not dollars.'

It was a dig I didn't bite. I simply nodded because I didn't have that money, and he knew it – I was up to my neck in debt to him after all. 'So you'll ask around? See what you can find?'

Billy made a show of how unusual this was. My request needed a down payment.

'Or do you want it on your tab?'

Without the money for the down payment, I didn't have a choice as I played nonchalant and agreed to an IOU being added to Billy's ledger next to my name once again.

Deal done, Billy leaned back, grinning ear to ear, and held out his hand for us to shake. 'Because I know you. And you got me interested.' Dropping his hand, Billy pointed one finger at my chest like the pistol I'd just ordered. 'Lachie Munro, man of mystery. Full of surprises.'

I guess I could live with that.

38
ROSCO

How long Billy would take sourcing a gun was anyone's guess. I was sure it wouldn't be more than twenty-four hours. Preoccupied with what was to come next, I was home in no time and nearly walked slap-bang into the distinctive late-model dark grey Holden parked out the front of my place. Despite having failed to register the car until too late, I knew exactly who owned it. Cops.

Approaching with great caution, I could hear Harry's voice before I spotted him sitting on his front steps, squinting up at Detective Sergeant Jon Baxter, who had his back to the street.

'Nope, no idea. I stay to meself, don't mix with no one. Can't help you, detective.'

Noticing that the neighbours' car was missing from their driveway, I scooted up that way towards their backyard. Edging carefully through their gate to find a better spot to eavesdrop on Harry and Baxter, I was greeted by the sight of poor Horace lying listlessly on the back deck. She must've still been feeling crook, as she made no attempt to get up from her blanket. But that didn't stop her thumping a slow greeting with her kangaroo tail. I gave her a pat, hoping she'd stay quiet.

Peering through a hole in the fence, I could see Harry calmly sitting on his step with Detective Sergeant Baxter before him, hands on hips.

'Harry, we go way back. I'm just trying to get in touch with your tenant. He could be in a bit of trouble and –'

'Jon, I told ya. I keep to meself. I don't have any interest in what my tenant says or does. So long as he pays the rent on time, all good with me.'

'Fine, Harry. Just like the docks, yeah? See nothing, know nothing.'

'You're learnin', son.'

I could see the exasperation on Baxter's face as he turned to walk back to his car. Waiting until the sound of the V8 engine faded down the street, I scrambled over the fence into my backyard.

'Thought you must be about.' Harry was ambling down the drive, smoothing the edges of his rollie. 'But don't worry, mate. Like I said, I got ya back. When you think you need a hand, I'll be here, like always.'

'Thanks, Harry. Really appreciate it,' I said.

'No worries. You just remember to tell me when you think you're over your head, alright?' he said sharply, clearly annoyed.

'Harry, I just need a bit more time. Then it'll be sorted.'

'Yep, you're handlin' things just fine.' Harry looked at me as if trying to decide something before lighting his rollie and inhaling deeply. 'All I'll say, son, is that whatever you're up to your pie hole in better be bloody worth it. You hear much of what that dee was saying?'

'A little.'

'I learned quick, you see nothing, you say nothing. But I like you. And I seen too many blokes not call it a day until it was too late, thinking they were gonna get rich quick. You following?'

Harry watched me nod as he chewed his cheeks as if that was how he formed words. 'Cash in your chips, lad. Live to play another day. The dead just get memorial stones.'

'I'm being careful, Harry.'

'So careful the cops are knocking on me door?'

'Might get a bit rougher than that before this is through,' I said, instantly wishing I hadn't as Harry angrily swatted a hand at me as if trying to flick away a blowfly. He ambled back to his place and barked at me to stay put.

Dutifully, I waited where I was until he returned with an old shoebox under his arm.

'Inside,' he ordered, waving me towards my place where he dropped what he was carrying on the kitchen counter with a *thunk*. Inside was an old rag.

'Too bloody pig-headed, that's your problem.'

The shape of the rag made it clear what was in it. The box of ammunition helped too. I lifted the cloth and a well-maintained Smith and Wesson slid into my hand. The pistol sat naturally in my fingers as I checked it was empty, sighted the barrel and tried the trigger action. All seemed clean as a whistle.

'No serial. Unlike you, I *am* careful.'

'Harry, I don't want to involve you in anything.'

'Bit late for that, isn't it? Take it. Be our little secret.'

Feeling the gun's weight, hearing those words, I was eight years old again, sitting at the kitchen table as my dad leaned close. On the lino tabletop were his pistols and sawn-off. I was allowed to hold each one as he taught me how to clean and care for them while my mother was out. Every session at the table ended with my dad saying, 'Don't tell ya mother. Be our little secret.'

I hesitated a moment as the memory tempered any feelings of cockiness holding the weapon generated. It's easy to feel cocky with a gun in your hand. But on the inside the old belly was doing burpees, cartwheels and backflips.

I tucked the pistol into the back of my jeans and the weight felt unnatural, wrong. The metal caught at my skin as I took a couple of steps, then settled. In my hand, the box of bullets faintly jangled like little bells on a hippy skirt. Walking quicker made it worse.

I could see Harry watching over me.

'Don't go playing the gangster. You pull that out, you gotta be prepared to shoot it.'

'Harry, I've no intention of ever pulling this rosco out unless I have to. But if I do …' I let my words hang.

Nodding, Harry agreed with the sentiment as we both absorbed my use of such an old-school term for a gun. It seemed to spark something in me as the memories flooded back in. I saw my father handcuffed in the court dock. My mother crying. The journalists. Seeing myself on the TV news that night being pulled through the media throng on the court steps, a terrified and confused twelve-year-old. And my mother's tears then and again years later as she held my face in her hands, making me promise not to turn out like my father.

Pulling the gun from my pants, I handed it back to Harry with the box of bullets.

'I've changed my mind. Keep them. I don't want them. I made a promise to someone I'm gonna keep instead. But, if I need it, I'll let you know.'

Harry took the Smith and Wesson and carefully wrapped it once more in the oily cloth. As Harry laid the gun with the ammunition back in the shoebox, I made a mental note to tell Billy to cancel my order.

'Good lad.'

Hearing that felt good.

39
OLD MATES

Alone again, I felt the glow from Harry's approval fade. I was in too deep.

I needed a good long swim to clear my head and forget about all this for a spell. Sitting on a hard milk crate, the TV softly playing nothing of interest, I daydreamed of the waves and the sand, the suck and pull of the ocean. Then my mind wandered to the little fish swimming beneath the waves, skirting the sand floor, pale and camouflaged for protection until they grew too big and made a mistake that caused them to end up as a bigger fish's dinner. Then my phone rang.

'Lach. We're gonna be in town. Wanted to catch up.'

The voice sounded familiar then the penny dropped. Greasy from the Fishy Man's.

'Oh, hey, man. You're in town? Great. Let's do it.' I was ready. I wanted this over, I was sick of trying to appear cool when the weight of every word and action could mean at least twenty-five years in prison. I think I pulled it off.

'Nah, I said we'll *be* in town. Heard you had some good abalone and fishin' spots.'

'Well, great. Let's meet and I'll tell you all about it.'

'Yeah, course. That's the plan. All I was doing was being courteous, givin' ya a heads-up, make sure your diary isn't full in the next couple of days. Jeez!'

Greasy hung up. Now I really needed that swim. I changed into my togs, pulled a towel from the bathroom and was all set to jog down to the beach when my phone went off again. I was tempted to ignore it then thought better of it. I could wash away whatever further stress it might cause with my swim.

It wasn't Greasy this time. It was Dave. Never rained, but poured.

'Lach, Lach, Lach-a-ling. What you doing?'

'Going for a swim. Why?'

'We need to clear the air. Have some fun,' he said.

Dave's usual method of clearing the air and having a bit of fun was to go fishing. I hoped to heaven fishing was all he wanted to do. But he was right – we did need to talk, and the sooner the better. After that chat, I really would need a swim. Looking forlornly at my towel, I apologised for getting its hopes up.

Approaching Dave's, I had one of those moments where you're thankful for the lessons your mother taught you. As I kneeled on the footpath to tie my shoelace, a dirty old Toyota LandCruiser roared past, its throaty diesel exhaling a dirty cloud in its wake. I knew that car. It belonged to Gary.

Puzzled, I walked a little more slowly. Sure enough, when I got to Dave's, Gary's Toyota was parked in the driveway. My hackles went up, prickling the back of my neck like sunburn after sunset. Despite Gary being a local Newie identity, the sort of old surf dude everyone has a chat to if they pass him on the beach or at a bar, I'd never known anyone to have Gary around for a beer. His car in Dave's driveway was as normal as hearing from Old Harry how Gary had been wandering about mine.

Swinging the front door open as I walked up the drive, Dave came out and waited on the porch. Gary followed him.

'Didn't expect to see you here, Gary. Didn't realise you and Dave were mates,' was my first salvo.

Gary grinned as he slapped Dave on the back. 'Dave and me go way back. Plus, now I'm in town, I've decided I need to be better with my mates. Need to stay in touch, share the love a bit more. Y'know, friends are not just for Christmas.'

Dave chortled. 'Fuckin' classic.'

'That love extend to bringing beer?' I asked.

Gary pistoled his fingers in my direction and scuttled inside to fetch me one as I stepped up to the front door.

'Gaz was interested in doing a bit of deep-water fishing. You keen?'

'Really? Does he know how to fish?'

'Know how to eat them and been known to have my hands around the right end of a rod on occasion.' Gary was at the door with a can of VB at his groin, hands wrapped around it to illustrate what he meant by rod. Which left me hoping he didn't open that can he had pointed at me.

We made our way to the back deck, chewing the fat about fishing. Dave and Gary competed in sharing the tallest fishing tales. Sitting in silence, I grinned and nodded at all the right places, hoping I didn't appear as unnatural as Dave and Gary were acting. They were being chummy in the way only two people up to something can be. They were like those two friends having an affair who think they're covering it really well with lots of unconvincing joking and laughter.

But it seems I was expected to believe they were good mates from way back, despite the fact Dave was my mate and I'd never seen them together. Apparently they went fishing every now and again, liked to catch up over beers and, weirdest of all, played each other online nearly every week in some Xbox shoot-'em-up. Annoyingly, the only part of their story I believed was when their conversation shifted to who shot who, where and when. I knew Dave was an Xbox fiend but he had never shared these epic gun fights with me before. In that moment, I realised I barely knew the guy.

Gary popped his next can, spraying up another wasteful fountain of foam. 'Wha-hey! So how about it? Gonna come fishin' with us?'

I needed an excuse but didn't have one. 'No. Tomorrow's not good for me. I'll catch you next time.'

Gary pulled a face. 'Mate, you'll be missed. Gonna be you-beaut tomorrow.'

His insistence that I go along was unsettling. I drained the beer and stretched. 'Love to, guys, but I've gotta go and see a man about a car.'

Dave seemed unhappy now. 'Want a second opinion?' he asked.

'You know me. Decision's always easier when I've only got myself to disagree with.'

'What sort of car?' said Gary, staring at me without a smile.

'Just a work ute.'

'What price they asking?'

Dave came to my rescue before I had to answer. 'Fuck, Gaz. What's with the questions? So what about after? Will we see you then, Lachie?'

'I told you I can't.'

'Not even 6.30 for barbecue and beers? Another week and I'm back in the mines.'

I stood up and shook my head. As I made to leave, Gary

was by my side, wrapping his heavy arm about my shoulders. An inch or two more and that hairy piece of leather could have me in a headlock. Instead, he murmured in my ear.

'Mate, shame you're going. Would have loved a natter. Bit of a chinwag. Hear more about this car of yours.'

I offered nothing, just returned his stare. He broke first.

'Yeah, would've very much loved to hear your thoughts on skin diving. Hear you're the man with all the scuba answers.'

I looked at Dave, who was by the barbie, beer raised high with one hand, the other scraping burnt meat remains from the grill. 'Dave tell you that?'

'Nah, he tells me nothing. Does not say a word. Nah, I just heard it on the grapevine, a little birdie, the whispers. They say you're the man who knows all the secret fishing spots. Especially for a bit of abalone.'

My blood ran cold. I always thought that was just a saying, like your life flashing before your eyes when you die. But I can assure you it is very real. And very unpleasant.

'Well, you shouldn't listen to what people say on the grapevine. Most people are full of shit. Like abalone.'

Gary smiled, eyes narrowing as he evaluated me. 'Nah, I don't think most people are, Lachlan. Some, yeah. But not most. And abalone are clean creatures. No shit there. You're thinking of mussels and prawns. Prawns, particularly – filthy critters. Eat anything they see. Particularly the dead.'

He let that sink in before whipping his arm away from my shoulders and smiling. 'Still, you gotta go, you gotta go.'

I took my chance and headed for freedom. Dave called me. I only just managed to turn in time to catch the cold tinnie flying in my direction.

'Traveller for the road.'

Behind Dave, Gary watched me closely, grinning almost as widely, as I turned back down the driveway.

The threat had me rattled. I should have taken Harry's gun.

I didn't want to go home. I didn't want to go to any of the usual haunts. All I wanted to do was run. Except running was out of the question. With the deal on the verge of being done, it was too late. I needed somewhere no one was going to be watching, or waiting, for me.

40
DIRT DIGGING

'Thought you were going to call?'

Karen barred my way in, eyeing the large bunch of flowers I held out to her.

'Was in the area.'

'And the flowers? They for me or someone else?'

I didn't say a thing, just pushed them towards her, smiling.

Accepting the flowers, Karen looked at me over the top of them as she sniffed their perfume. Then she waved me inside. 'Funny you should turn up. I've been running through the Lachlan Munro pros and cons. Wondering just what I'd say or do when I saw you next.'

I listened as she spelled them out to me. Upshot was we could still be friends but she had her job and she didn't have time for anything more.

As she finished her list, I swallowed and took a half-step closer. 'That all?' I asked.

'Pretty much,' she said.

I broke into full mea culpa, giving her the works. Unlike other times, I meant every word.

'I'm sorry. I know I've been a dick. My life is complicated. I've got all these things going on which have made the timing for us really bad. If you just want to be friends, I can live with that. But give me another chance, when I've sorted my shit out. Please?'

She looked at me. It was clear she was weighing up whether she believed me or just wanted to.

'When you sort your shit out.'

I nodded and she smiled.

'I can live with that,' she said. 'At least you're honest. Want a cuppa? Kettle's just boiled.'

She headed into the kitchen, leaving me in the lounge where I felt awkward, unsure what was next. I dropped onto the couch, making myself at home as the sounds of tea-making came from the kitchen. Looking at the folders of Department of Primary Industry material and the open laptop on her coffee table, I had an idea.

'Can I ask a favour?'

Returning with the mugs of tea, Karen seemed surprised by my question. 'You serious?'

'Just saw your work there and was wondering … I need some info on someone. Is that possible?'

She stared at me, then glanced at her open laptop and folders. She closed the laptop and packed away the folders, asking if I looked at any of it.

'No. Just saw the logos on the folders.'

'So what's the favour?' she asked cautiously.

'That guy, Gary? That mate of a mate from the pub? Thought you might be able to look into him, see what's on file. If he has a record. That kind of thing. I think he's up to something dodgy with a friend of mine. Wanted to find out a bit more about him before I do anything else.' I wanted some serious dirt to be dug on Gary. I didn't like the way he'd suddenly reappeared in town and I wanted to try to work out if his stories about fortunes in far-off dusty country towns rang true. Fuck it, I just wanted to know more about who this elusive surfer dude was.

'Why do you think I'll be able to investigate your friend?' she asked.

'Don't you have access to all those government databases?'

'I'm a Fisheries and Wildlife Officer.'

'Do you have a friend you can call?'

She crossed her arms and glared at me.

'Look, if I've crossed a line, forget I asked. But this guy has always seemed dodgy to me and I want to be sure.' I sounded like a teenager.

'What you're asking is illegal.'

'Really? I just thought, y'know, in your downtime you could maybe ...' I mimed tapping at a keyboard. 'Take a peek for me.'

'No. Highly illegal. Charges-laid illegal. Instant dismissal illegal.' She suddenly sounded distant and cold, her body language reflecting how pissed off she was.

Then she surprised me.

'What do you have on this guy? Not promising anything. But there are ways to look around the edges.'

I could feel a grin splitting my face as I asked what she needed.

'Everything you got. Government databases are not like Google. I need reference points.'

So that was what I gave her. I told her everything I knew about Gary Newman plus a bit extra. Karen took notes and asked a lot of questions and became interested in what I was stringing together.

'Yeah. He was asking me about abalone. And I know how you DPI officers get all excited over those suckers. He has also offered me crayfish in the past,' I added for good measure.

She paused and looked at me just the same way Gary had, seeming to weigh me and my story up one more time. She sucked on the end of her pen in a completely non-sexual way. 'Why now? Why are you suddenly so concerned about this guy that you're asking me for help?'

'He's hanging around with a mate of mine and acting like they're up to something together. I want to know if he's real or not. I've known him as an acquaintance for years but never asked the question – haven't needed to. For some reason, I just think he's a bit dodgy dodge-wah. Can't say why, just a feeling I got. And that would usually be none of my business. Let sleeping dogs lie. But I don't want my buddy – or me – to be in the wrong place at the wrong time and get sucked up into anything he's up to.'

'Well, for what it's worth, never discount a feeling. Instincts are sometimes all we have. Might be wrong but most of the time they're telling you something.'

I realised that while talking about Gary, we had moved closer to each other on the couch. She realised it as well as we fell into an embarrassed silence. Smiling hesitantly, she leaned a fraction towards me. That was enough.

It was as though we were magnets, positive and negative, attracting each other at the lips, as we crashed backwards on the couch. Somewhere in our fumblings, she found my phone.

'Need to get rid of this.' As she went to toss it over her shoulder, it started to ring. 'Again? Really?' She rolled her eyes and handed it to me.

Stupidly, I answered it. I don't know why. 'Yes?'

As Karen pushed me away and stormed off. All I could do

was watch her and listen to the last thing in the world I wanted to be hearing.

'That you, Lachie? Caught you at a bad moment?' It was Greasy.

'Yes.'

'Good. We're all set to catch up tomorrow. Slight change of plans though.'

This was not good but I stayed silent, listening to what had changed, hoping it was still do-able. In the kitchen, I heard cutlery tinkling as a drawer slammed and a cupboard door crashed.

'We want a sample paver. Not a colour swatch like we talked about.'

'A paver?' I said as I realised what he meant.

'Yeah, a whole one. Give it to us on-tick, take it out of the order. Bit curious to know more about these pavers, see where they come from, that sort of thing. You understand.'

Sample or whole brick didn't bother me so much as the on-tick bit. This was not a good development in anyone's book. This had the hallmarks of a set-up for a rip-off.

'My boss isn't gonna let me do that.'

'Your boss?' asked Greasy. 'We thought you worked for yourself.'

'I do.'

'Then stop dickin' around and make it happen. We'll text you in the mornin' with an addy for the meet up. Somewhere near yours. Laters.' The line went dead.

Leaning against the doorframe of the kitchen, wine glass in hand, Karen stood staring at me.

'You actually answered the phone. I cannot believe you

answered that call.'

'I don't know what I was thinking.'

'Why would you take that call? What was so important for you to take that call? Right then?'

'Work. Was about a job.'

She didn't believe me. Talk about phonecall interruptus. She came back to the couch, drinking her wine. Going to her, I tried to rekindle the moment but she pulled free.

'Lach. I get a Pavlovian response with you. Good thing we're just friends because when I hear a mobile phone ring, all desire? Pffft.'

Slumping back onto the couch, I wished I felt the same. 'Promise I'll leave my phone at home next time.'

'Next time? Bit presumptuous.'

41
C.I.

I'd only just got home when someone started thumping on my door. Opening it, I discovered my favourite detective standing there. On reflection, he must have been parked in the street waiting for me.

'Lachlan Munro – bad time?'

'For you, Detective Sergeant Baxter, is there ever a bad time?'

I could see his mental gears spinning as he took in my redecorating. His eyes went from the floor and the water stains to the lack of furniture.

'Had a flood,' I said.

'But you're on a hill.'

'After a break-in.'

The detective looked at me and shook his head. 'Lachlan, the more time I spend talking with you, the more confused I get. Was this break-in when your car got stolen or another time?'

All I gave him was a shrug and an open arm indicating for him to pull up a milk crate.

'I might stand.'

He proceeded to pace the room like some cowboy sheriff, hands on hips, suit jacket hitched back to reveal his holster and handcuffs. All he lacked was a tin star and forty-gallon hat – black, because this is my story.

'You think we're on opposite sides.'

This was furthest from what I was thinking. With all that

was going on in my life, Baxter wasn't even on my radar other than as an occasional annoyance.

'I pulled your complete file. Took a look at what you've been up to in the past.'

'My past is not a secret.'

'No. But what else in your life is, Lachlan?'

That earned him a short-lived smile but nothing else.

'Did your employer know about your old man? That why you lost your job?'

'What my old man did has nothing to do with me. I've had nothing to do with him since you lot dragged him off to prison when I was twelve.'

'Where he belonged. Bad man, your dad. Killing those security guards when that armed robbery went wrong. You know what they say about apples falling from trees, Lachlan?'

'We don't even share the same surname. I'm doing nothing wrong, detective. I'm just going about my days, trying to find another job since my boss decided to punish me for having my car pinched. While, I might add, I was getting my crew morning tea.'

'You finished?'

I shrugged. I could have gone on but, clearly, the detective wasn't one for stories.

'I know you're up to something. Everywhere I go in this town, you appear, yeah? So what have you been meeting with Lloyd about?'

'Who?'

Glaring, the detective explained that Lloyd Dobbin was the bikie I'd been dealing with. Playing dumb meant I now knew Lloyd's surname.

'I know you're up to something simply because I know who you are. I know who your friends are. And I know none of us can change our DNA. We are what we are.'

Again, I didn't feel like pointing out that the detective didn't know boo about me.

'Look at it from my point of view. A guy with a criminal record finds the partial remains of an Asian gang member. He then loses his job, his car is stolen and his home gets redecorated.'

'I was burgled.' I had to correct him on something.

'Fine. Burgled. This same person is seen on several occasions associating with a member of an outlaw motorcycle gang. These gangs are known for their tribal wars over who controls areas up and down the coast in the supply and manufacture of illegal substances, namely amphetamines. One of this guy's best mates works in the mines, a world riddled with amphetamine use. You see the picture I'm painting, yeah?'

I did and it was not pretty. But the guy had suggested we might be on the same side so I was waiting for his wonderful illustration to be framed.

'I don't care about you or what you've done, Lachlan. What I care about is getting a big fat arrest so I can stop dealing with small shitty crimes and leave this shithole of a town for the big smoke. Get a promotion into a real squad. A significant crime bust that'd see me pick and choose where I headed next.'

'So how do I fit into this plan?'

'You're gonna become my CI.' He took great glee in stepping closer, conspiratorially. He obviously thought the idea of forcing me to become a criminal informant, a dog, was a stroke of genius.

'Well, as attractive as that offer is, detective, two things: one, I don't have life insurance and, two, I have nothing to share. You're seeing isolated pieces and forcing them to fit your jigsaw puzzle. You're getting a picture but it's not the right one.'

A great silence descended as he stood before me, glaring at me, trying to intimidate in his cheap grey suit and blue-spotted tie. I knew the drill: whoever spoke first lost. So I simply sat and waited it out. It didn't take long. He broke eye contact and sucked in his lips, cleaning his gums with his tongue while he seethed.

'You change your mind, yeah?' he stated, placing a business card on the nearest milk crate.

'I promise, you'll be the first to know.'

Again, he stood looking at me. Softening his expression, he appealed once more. 'Lachlan, I can protect you. Trust me. You're not heading for a happy ending. But I can do things to ensure your safety. You think those –' his thumb jerked over his shoulder in a gesture that I assumed meant Lloyd and the Knuckledraggers, 'knuckleheads are interested in you? You think if one of them is offered what I've just offered you, they wouldn't be rolling onto their back like a puppy rescued from the pound? They'll sell you out for nothing. You're not one of them. You're nothing to them. Just a means to an end, yeah?'

His words made sense. Except for the part where he saw me as some criminal linchpin. He stepped towards the door, telling me he would let himself out.

I waited until he was just about to leave before responding. 'Detective? Sergeant?'

He turned to look at me, eagerness written all over his face.

'If something was going on and I decided to take up your offer, those knuckleheads who, as you said, are willing to rat anyone out? How would I be any different to them?'

With a sigh, he turned and stepped outside. Then his head reappeared around the edge of the door. 'You enjoy Marrickville?'

This hit home hard. To remain blank took a lot of effort.

'Most people visiting Sydney take a look at the Opera House, the bridge, maybe a museum. Not you, not Lachlan Munro. Listen to what I've been saying. There is no mystery. I know you. I know your story and I know how this is going to end, yeah? You'll carry the burden of all this when we pull you in. Judges like people who cooperate. Even little fish like you.'

The detective's revelations sank in as I listened to the sound of his car driving off. The police knew I'd been to Marrickville. If the police knew I'd been to see the Fishy Man, or, at best, visited Marrickville, then the bet was that others would know about the trip too. The cops wanted me to go undercover and rat out everyone I talked to. It made me feel like my life was becoming an open book for cops and crooks alike. People on both sides wanted to know more about what I was up to and didn't like not knowing the answers. I was becoming a series of known knowns, known unknowns and unknown unknowns. Every one of those made people nervous. If you wanted a pickle, this was it.

The street lights flicked on to shine away the night. A car backfired, sending me sprawling to the floor in fear. Lying there panting, I prayed like I'd never prayed before to just make all this stop. No one answered.

Left with no choice, I still had to do what needed to be done. I had to go and retrieve a brick for tomorrow.

Sneaking out, I made for the fence line and hoisted myself over yet again. Horace was nowhere to be seen, which was both good and bad. Hopefully she was inside eating and wasn't about to come bounding from the shadows to raise the alarm with a love attack. I reached the cubby house without incident and was inside with the spider webs in no time.

I took out one of the bricks and weighed it in my hand. It seemed less the source of all my problems and almost a bad joke. How could something with the weight and density of a parcel of vacuum-packed coffee cause so much trouble? In a lot of ways, it was easier to just hand over a brick. I mean, how much was a sample? A teaspoon seemed stingy. How much was a commercial quantity? Sitting there, cross-legged, weighing the brick from hand to hand, I finally gave up. As much as it felt like a setup, I was sick of these stupid things. One less brick. The less I had to worry about, the better off I would be. All of a sudden, it felt like the end was near on this whole adventure.

This line of thinking was not only unhelpful but the path to failure. Lose my fear and I'd make a mistake that would kill me or ensure the good Detective Sergeant Baxter got the ending he'd painted, the one where I headed off into the sunset in the back of a paddy wagon. I had no intention of letting either take place. Shoving the brick down my shirt, I made my silent way home again.

Having nearly dropped the package several times, I realised I needed to practise carrying it for the drop off. There are a number of places on the body you can hide a hard-surfaced object and all of them are awkward. Slipping it under my armpit didn't work. Trying to hide it against my gut under a shirt looked odd, and adding a bigger shirt to wear over the top just made it worse.

I had a brainwave of using the dust jacket for a hardcover book I'd been meaning to read. The brick slid inside the dust jacket fine. It might work. Then I decided against it; the idea of Greasy carrying a 'book' was probably more suspicious than anything else.

So I settled on the one thing that was left. Sliding the brick into the front waistband of my underpants, I jiggled and bounced to let gravity find the perfect position. Then I loped about the room, twisting and popping my hips to let the brick find a home. Bending over or sitting down wasn't going to be easy. I was also going to have to walk a bit wider than normal. But it was the best I could do. A pair of trackie dacks over the top and I'd just be another paunchy dude out for a bit of cardio.

Happy with the result, I pulled the brick from my jocks and looked for a place to keep it overnight. The dirty laundry pile on the floor seemed as good a place as any. At worst, any intruder would have second thoughts before shoving a hand in to dig about. I was kidding myself, but I was comforted by the thought that at least it wasn't out on display. I tried to settle in and get some kip.

Tomorrow was going to be a doozy.

42
THE DROP OFF

The text with the details came mid-morning. I shoved the brick down my pants, and it bounced around until I did a bit of readjusting. It was sort of like a cricket box, a little uncomfortable, but after a few on-the-spot test jumps, it settled and I was all set.

The meeting place Greasy had chosen was very big and very open. Foreshore Park at the foot of Fort Scratchley was a popular place for families, bike riders, soccer games and the occasional kite enthusiast. At 2pm, the designated time, I wandered along the waterfront, seeking the park bench where I was to meet Greasy. In the channel, a container vessel headed for open water outpaced me as it pumped a cascade of bilge water into the sea.

Sitting on a bench by the pilot station soaking up the rays, hands clasped across his chest and his head slightly back, Greasy was also watching the vessel through his sunglasses. He looked like a stunted rock-and-roll vampire. As I approached, he turned and grinned.

'Lachlan. Beautiful day for catching some vitamin D.'

We shook hands before I stiffly sat down next to him.

'How we do this is simple. You leave what we want on the bench when you get up and walk away.'

Nodding, I saw another man down the walkway talking on his mobile and looking in our direction. My panic rose quickly. How was I going to pull the brick from my pants and then walk away without anyone noticing?

'There's a slight problem with your plan.'

Greasy smiled as he looked at me, lowering his sunglasses so I could see his eyes. Then he realised I was serious. The weight of the brick suddenly felt like a tonne. I adjusted my crotch, and Greasy's eyes opened wide in horror as he caught my wave of panic. Like a couple of surfers, we were going to ride it together.

'It's down your fuckin' pants? Wear a jacket with pockets, a backpack, somethin' you drop and leave behind. That's how you do this. How green are you?'

'Just come with me to the toilets and I'll hand it over,' I said, pointing to the large brick amenities block on the other side of the small duck pond.

'You kiddin'?' Greasy had started to look nervously around the park. 'You … you wearin' a wire? This a setup?' he hissed as he slid away from me on the bench, searching for any undercover cops as I tried to reassure him it was all square. He wasn't listening. He started to look like his nickname should have been Shifty, not Greasy, as he stood up and straightened his clothes. Pointing a finger at me, he attempted to clear himself in the event this was a sting and I the bait.

'I don't know you. I thought you were someone else when you sat down. What are the coincidences you havin' the same name as my friend,' he blurted in a lame attempt at an alibi if any police were listening to us. Then he tried to laugh but it just sounded like a B-movie villain. And it pissed me right off.

'Sit down. Stop being a dickhead. If this was a shakedown, you'd already be done. So we'll continue as planned, just with a small modification. I'll go to the toilet block and leave what you want in the last cubicle behind the bowl.'

He went to protest but I wasn't interested. For once, my tone left no room for argument.

'Cut me some slack, you know I've never done this before. The sooner this is over, the better. Keep talking and this all just takes longer.' I had no idea where that came from. Probably read it in some Elmore Leonard novel.

The thing is, though, it worked on Greasy. Maybe he'd read the same book, was probably imagining the movie adaptation with George Clooney playing his role. Casting a quick glance about the park, Greasy slowly sat down again with a half-nod, accepting what I'd said.

I headed in the direction of the toilets. Glancing back, I caught Greasy still doing his surveillance sweeps of the park and me, clearly still convinced I was some sort of undercover cop. I really didn't care. All I was interested in was getting to that hideous burnt-orange 1990s toilet block on the other side of the pond and making the drop.

There were no urinals in this one, just four toilet cubicles, making me think I'd walked into the ladies'. But no, the design was simply an attempt at a better toilet. The natural light and stainless steel had all the welcome of a prison cell. The block also had a back door, perfect for a quick escape.

Head down, it was into the far cubicle as decided. The lock was broken. Retrieving the package from my pants, I looked at the wet concrete and tried to work out the best way to get the package behind the bowl without having to touch anything. Squatting, I reached around to shove the brick out of sight, but I lost my balance and my hand hit the ground. I swore as I imagined the many diseases and bacteria now crawling on my skin.

'Hello, mate. What're you doing?'

Looking up, I saw Gary grinning as he peered over the cubicle wall, arm hanging down like a strand of cooked spaghetti.

'What're *you* doing here?'

'I asked first, mate. I seen you walking and disappear in here. So I waited. Only you seemed to take a bit of time. Thought to myself, the mad bugger must have fallen in. Or he's just a bugger.'

'Neither. Just a dodgy curry. Then I dropped some coins hoisting my pants.'

'Better left for the next in a place like this. I mean, a bit of shrapnel in a puddle of piss? You really that hard up?'

Fear created a genuine nagging in my gut as I stepped from the cubicle.

'Aren't ya gonna wash your hands?'

It seemed an innocent question but Gary turning up like this wasn't right. I kept heading for daylight. Gary followed.

'Why are you here, Gary?'

He looked to the sky and shrugged. The gesture would play for innocent. 'Like you. Needed the facilities. Heard a familiar voice. Thought I'd say g'day. But don't worry.' He tapped his left nostril for emphasis. 'Your secret's safe with me.'

Any past soft spots I might have had for Gary evaporated entirely. I wished he would just leave me alone and disappear in a blur of Hawaiian shirt and baggy shorts.

'How'd the car go? Buy it?'

He saw my hesitation and smiled.

'Oh, well. Maybe the next one. Better to take your time with these things. Don't want to get ripped off.'

Standing in the sun, Gary stretched, looked at me again and then started a casual amble back into the park. Waiting a moment, I skedaddled in the opposite direction, back through the toilets for freedom via the rear exit.

43
DEATH

How long does it take to test a sample? What did a test involve? Getting some hapless sap to have a go? Did they supply the spoon and syringe? Be only fair. Or was it more along the lines of a high school chemistry test, a few drops on a piece of litmus paper to see a chemical reaction change its colour as someone fires a spitball at the back of your neck? Was the test something I could Google without the police kicking in my door? The internet might be the repository of all knowledge but there are some things that it never pays to look up.

I realised there was no point in going home – I needed distraction as I waited for my phone call. Maybe a pub would be a good place to wait.

Lost in my thoughts, I arrived at the ocean baths of Newcastle Beach with no idea which way I'd gone. The day was a great one, clear sky and even clearer water. Standing there, admiring the view, it was hard to imagine the heavy industry that went with the deep-water port of Newcastle twenty or so years ago. Earthquakes change that. Although the writing was already on the wall for the steel industry before the quake. Nature just sped things up.

Even with the Gary run-in, the weight of the deal was lifting like a morning mist. All I wanted was to receive a phone call from Greasy and the Fishy Man to say it was all going to be okay, that the deal was done and the cheque was in the mail. Well, not a cheque. A pile of cash was what I wanted.

Coming to a viewing platform, I leaned on the green treated-pine railings and stared out to sea, then back down south. Staring at horizons always evoked the future for me, but my reverie was rudely interrupted as a police chopper in a hurry roared low over the sea, heading north.

A couple walked past talking quietly, holding hands then draping their arms about each other. I shifted slightly so they would have space to stare at their future as well. But they were focused on thoughts of a more mortal nature, talking about a shooting that had happened down at the point. How the area was sealed off and crawling with police. How things like this didn't happen in Newcastle, how their city was changing.

Nothing I was hearing was good. Turning to the couple for answers, my pulse pounding, I was positive my guilt would be written all over my face – the face of a man whose future had just collapsed.

'You okay, mate?' he said.

'You don't look so good. Want some of our water?' she said.

'I heard you talking – about a shooting?' I asked.

'They're saying it's a drug deal gone wrong. Guy got shot in the toilet block? Saying he got six in the chest.'

'Why drugs?'

The girlfriend shifted and looked up at her fella. 'That's what I was saying. Why drugs? Everyone knows it's a gay beat. I reckon it's a gay hate crime. The guy's dacks were around his ankles.'

I'd heard enough. Leaving the beaches and the sea, I returned to reality. I just knew the victim was going to turn out to be Greasy. Having heard the couple say no one had heard the shots or seen the shooter rammed home that I was probably the only one with an idea who the victim was. And if I was right about the victim, I also had an idea who might be the shooter.

Shootings like this might not happen often in the once safe city of Newcastle, but my world had just jumped up the scale of dangerous. Somewhere way ahead of bomb defusing or shark wrangling. Bad guys not only knew I had a stash of drugs and was looking for a buyer but that one of their own was now dead after meeting me. They knew where I lived. To say I was scared didn't even come close. I was shitting bricks.

44

LOVE IN THE AFTERNOON

She answered the door with her phone to her ear, waving me in with the other hand without missing a beat in the conversation. I followed her into the kitchen where she pulled two beers from the fridge and popped the tops without even asking. Silently clinking the bottles, it struck me how comfortable all this was. I barely knew her and yet just being here felt right. Being here made me feel calm, and calm was what I needed right now.

'Hi. Sorry. Girlfriend on the phone. You heard about the shooting?' Karen said.

Clearly the hottest topic in town.

'Brazen,' she continued. 'Has to be a drug deal gone wrong. Odd place for it to happen. Broad daylight too.'

Nodding, I sipped my beer. As she ran through her theories, I felt myself relax. Had no reason to relax, but I did. I could have listened to her read the tide tables.

'Wonder if the police have any leads?' It was the most innocent question I could muster.

'I'll be buying the paper tomorrow. Even if they don't have any ideas, bit of excitement in Newie for a change.'

Karen opened the door onto her small courtyard and we sat in the patch of sun.

Maybe it was the alcohol, maybe it was the events of the past few days catching up with me, but either way, my world crashed in. I felt like I was caught in a dumping wave, not knowing which way was up, not being able to tell where I was heading, not sure how much longer I was going to be able to hold my breath before my mouth opened and the saltwater flooded my lungs as I bottomed out on a sand bar.

'Lachie? You okay? You've gone all white.'

My dark thoughts must have left me looking as blank as a zombie.

Concerned, Karen pushed my head down between my legs. 'Breathe. Breathe in slow, slow.'

There was nothing to do but what she said. With each breath, I began to feel better. I straightened up and looked into her eyes, seeing her concern and feeling like a right prick. What was I doing here? What was I doing involving her in all my mess?

'What are you thinking? You're a million miles away. This'll make you feel better. Ask me what I found out about your man Gary.'

Shaking my head, I started hyperventilating again.

'Nothing. He doesn't exist. Nothing on record.' She was clearly impressed with her own detective work. 'You know how hard that is to do these days?'

'I've got to get out of here,' I said suddenly, standing up to leave.

'What? Home? No "Thanks, Karen, I know how risky that info was to get"? You're just going to walk away?'

Struggling to form a thought as I caught my breath, Karen wasn't interested in hearing it anyway.

'No. You know what? Fuck you, arsehole.'

She was standing facing me now, toe to toe. Her eyes were so mad, so intense. She wanted to hit me. I was ready to grab her wrist if she came at me.

Then it happened.

Passion exploded as we kissed and tore at each other's clothes, as all the past interruptions and missed opportunities gave way just like our buttons and zippers. Right there in the courtyard on the mossy pavers and straggly maidenhair ferns, quick and hard and unscripted. It was as fantastic as it was unexpected.

Lying back panting afterwards, I reached up to pull a dead leaf from her hair.

'I'm still mad,' she said with a smile.

Man, that smile.

The next morning, that smile was the first thing I saw.

'Probably shouldn't have stayed,' I said, tucking away a strand of her hair that refused to stay behind her ear. She smelled of the sea. I know I shouldn't have stayed. Should have been making my escape and getting as far away from Newcastle as possible. Hard to regret the decision, though, when she was the first thing I got to look at.

Watching her get up, I swung my legs over the edge of the bed and searched for my clothes. Angling my head down like that did something to my stomach that sent me crashing into the walls as I ran for the bathroom. Hand clamped over my mouth, I only just made it. I shut my eyes as I heaved into the porcelain and let the cold of the tiles seep into my body.

'You alright?' Karen called from the other side of the door.

'Just give me a moment.'

'You got a bug?' she asked as I staggered into the bedroom. Maybe it was a bug. It felt like a hangover. My whole body was mud, brain sludgy from what felt like the tightest of elastic bands squeezing around my temples. Most likely stress.

Karen placed a wet cloth on my neck. 'Is it a migraine?'

Migraine? I'd never had a migraine before in my life. More evidence I needed to get those drugs off my hands.

'Feels like a hangover. I'm gonna head home. Sleep it off.'

At the front door, the bright morning light set me squinting. From the look of the sky, it was going to be hot.

'Should I come with you? You going to be alright?'

Checking I had the essentials – wallet, keys and phone – I assured her I'd be okay.

'I'll call you later. See how you're feeling,' she said.

I wasn't going to argue.

If this had been a hangover it would have needed a half-dozen dim sims and about two litres of Coke: the black doctor. The idea of the dim sims and Coke grew until it was all I could think about. Despite the harsh light burning into my brain with a rhythmic throb, my journey home was going to involve the nearest fish and chippie. Doing something, anything, might distract me from how crap I was feeling. The breeze had stiffened. It was perfect beach weather. If my brain didn't leak from my ears soon, maybe a dip would help too.

It was then that I noticed a white Mercedes delivery van crawling in the gutter not even twenty metres behind me. Thinking of Karen and where to find some deep-fried medicine, I'd missed it. Seeing it trailing me meant one thing: trouble. So I did all I could think of doing. I bolted.

Banging head, rising heat, the glare, they all combined to thwart me. Instead of doing a Ferris Bueller, leaping over fences and dashing through backyards to safety, I tripped at the first driveway and went sprawling onto the concrete. Chin grazed, I spat out grit as a hand on the back of my head held me down and another pair of hands frisked me, taking my wallet, keys and phone. They picked me up and carried me to the van. The side door slid open and I was tossed in. Literally. I flew into the opposite side of the van and lay dazed on the floor as the door slammed and the space went dark.

As least the darkness was good for my head.

45
FORTY EIGHT HOURS

There was no way of telling where the van was going. Maybe freaks who spend too much time with homing pigeons might have been able to sense the direction, but not me. I just lay there as the van accelerated and took every turn, speed bump and pothole hard. There were moments when I was airborne and came crashing back to the van floor in a skidding thud. I was desperate to find a way to brace myself before I was sent skywards again, but I failed. I could already feel the bruises forming.

Then the van stopped. The world went silent, bar the faint ticking of the cooling motor. Interestingly, all traces of my headache had gone. Sitting up, I tried to hear something, to pick up a clue or hint of what was happening, to work out where I was. Nothing. Then the side door violently slid back and hands reached into the van to pull me out. I blinked, the faces starting to shift into clarity. Standing before me were Damo and Tiny. Behind them was the Fishy Man, hands on hips, chin jutting forwards. He didn't look happy to see me.

'Lachlan Munro. Did not expect to see you again.'

I lifted a hand to shield my eyes, desperate to catch some clue as to where I was. I made out a tractor and some road-building equipment, piles of scree, sand and dirt. A road construction lay-by somewhere in the pastoral north between Fern Bay and Williamtown was the best I could manage.

'You got anythin' to say to me, Munro? Anythin' to share about where my man is?'

'I think he's dead.'

The Fishy Man looked at me and spat on the ground. 'I guessed as much, you simpleton. Think I don't watch the news? So what happened? Cos I sure as fuck don't believe you had the balls to pull any trigger.'

I tried to explain how Greasy and I had met and then I had headed off, leaving the brick as arranged.

'Wait. You were walkin' about with a whole brick of brown down your pants? As a sample?' He looked like he would hit me right there and then. 'You are a fuckin' idiot. A fuckin' idiot.'

'Your man told me you wanted a brick. I was following his instructions. He wanted a brick. I took him a brick.'

'I'd never ask for a whole brick. All we wanted was a sample. A small amount to test the quality, an amount that is nowhere near a commercial quantity. Why the fuck would we risk gettin' picked up in the open with somethin' that carries a twenty-five-year sentence?' he hissed, but his words slowed with realisation. Furious, the Fishy Man turned to glare at Damo and Tiny, who looked equally terrified as they shrugged and shook their heads.

'What happened then?' the Fishy Man said.

Was I protecting him? I don't know. But instinct told me not to mention Gary cornering me in the toilet or my suspicions he had shot Greasy – I might have been wrong. All I told the Fishy Man was that I walked out of the toilet block, reasonably assuming that the package would be picked up by Greasy and all would be right with the world. Instead, on the way home, I heard the sound of sirens and news of a shooting filtering through the neighbourhood. I left out the stuff with

Karen. Let no man say I am not a gentleman.

The Fishy Man did not like the sound of any of this. It must have been difficult to hear that his lieutenant had been trying to do him over. As he paced the dust, I turned to Damo.

'You never sent Roxy that message like you said you would, Damo.'

The Fishy Man looked at me like he was about to have a stroke. Tiny looked at Damo, who shuffled his feet in discomfort. It was then that my phone started to ring. Dave and his impeccable timing.

'Should I answer it?'

'Sure. Go ahead. Make sure you say hi from me,' said the Fishy Man.

I took the call.

'Mate, it's Dave. Where you be?'

'Just catching up with some people,' I said, as those people stared at me in disbelief and the Fishy Man went even redder in the face.

'Right. I'm doing the same here. Gary is with me.'

'Dave, you need to be careful. I think —'

'I'm trying to be careful. His gun pointing at me is making me feel extra careful, Lachie. Some would go so far as to say the experience is very sobering.'

Down the line came the sound of rustling before Gary's voice was loud and clear in my ear.

'Lachlan, you know what I want. Now you know I have Dave. I think a trade's in order.'

The other three faces staring at me while I took the call helped me play along.

'I'll give you an hour to collect what I'm after and then

I'll call back, arrange a pick up.'

The line went dead as I looked at the screen for an answer. The Fishy Man wanted me to fill in the gaps.

'Um, I think we might have a problem,' I said.

Negotiating was not one of my strong points. It wasn't made any easier standing on the side of a road, my voice wavering as my stomach clenched and unclenched, trying to decide which way it wanted to empty as I desperately tried to think of some plan, any plan, that would help keep me alive.

'You bet your fuckin' dollar we have a problem, Lachlan. Who is this clown Gary?'

There was no way I was going to get away with avoiding filling in the biographical details on Gary. It was time to share all I knew about him. Which was not a lot.

'So you're telling me this joker appears back in town about the same time you find the package. Seems to consistently appear in the same areas that you are and you don't get suspicious? Not once?'

'I was suspicious he was dodgy. Now I know.'

Tired of being pushed around, I had an idea forming. At this point, backstory, history and the benefit of hindsight really seemed surprisingly unimportant. This was business and I needed to protect my end of the deal. The impediment was not one of my making. Deep down, my instinct might have been to simply get out of town and forget all about this whole damn affair, but it was time to make a stand.

The Fishy Man was looking at me curiously. I realised my lips had been moving again. He looked at Tiny, who was as communicative as a brick wall. Glancing at the heavens with a sigh, the Fishy Man seemed to be attempting to come up with a solution. I beat him to it.

'We both want the same thing. You also want to know what your man was up to.'

'How can you help with that?'

'Leave all this to me and I'll find you some answers.'

The Fishy Man clearly had never heard someone pitch such a bold and arresting idea as this, because his jaw dropped and his eyes blinked quickly, trying to understand what his ears had just heard.

'What d'you mean, leave it with *you*?'

Tiny and Damo looked at each other, not sure what to do either.

'Give me forty-eight hours to make this right. I'll deliver both the drugs and the guy I think killed your man. It's a win-win for you.'

Damo and Tiny shuffled ever so slightly away from me as their boss processed my offer.

'The best bit is, though, whatever happens, your hands are clean. I'll be the one doing all the work.'

'And if you don't deliver?'

'You have forty-eight hours to think up what you'll do.'

That part, the Fishy Man really liked. 'You got twenty-four hours. Then I want the packages and this guy Gary,' he said with an unblinking stare before nodding his head in the direction of the van. 'Boys.'

He walked away. I followed, collecting my keys, wallet and phone. Climbing in the back, I looked for things to hang on to as I heard the Fishy Man say he admired my balls. Judging by the long string of missed calls from Karen on my mobile, he'd have to line up behind her to claim them.

46
HEROES

What balls have to do with bravery, I've no idea. Women have the good sense to hide all their plumbing internally; the weakest part of a man's anatomy is out there dangling in the breeze. Which was exactly how I was starting to feel. Maybe that's where the bravery comes in: brave is the man marching into battle with his balls on display. How very *Braveheart*.

Swallowing, I stood in the middle of my lounge and dialled.

'Lachie, what you calling for? Gary is gonna call you.'

'I'm getting in first. Want to know where to meet.'

The sound of the phone being snatched away, then Gary huffed down the line, 'You don't get to call the shots, Lachlan.'

'Okay, so how about I be at Dave's in forty-five minutes with the stuff you want.'

Judging from the silence, I was going to be allowed to call the shots.

'Don't be late.'

I didn't have long. Collecting an old backpack that was threatening to grow a nice layer of mould thanks to the flood, I threw it and myself over the back fence. I looked around to see if anyone was about but really that was the least of my concerns. From the closed windows, it seemed that the neighbours weren't home, which was some comfort. The sight of Horace in full health trotting up to me with her mouth full of bedding gave me even more.

Crawling through the undergrowth to get to the hiding

spot in the cubby house, my mind flipped through options. I didn't really have a master plan for delivering Gary to the Fishy Man in twenty-four hours. What I did have was a healthy instinct for survival and total belief in my ability to wing it.

Unpacking the seventeen bricks from the stove, I shoved them straight into the backpack. I experienced an amazing sense of calm. At any other time you could have described it as an almost Zen-like clarity. It was energising. Or maybe that was just the fear.

With the backpack bulging, I jumped back over the fence again, praying no one was indulging in a spot of Neighbourhood Watch. A guy leaping over a back fence with a bulging backpack was never a good look. With that thought in mind, I realised I needed some insurance to prevent me turning up a headless torso on a surf beach. So I rang Karen. By this stage it was no surprise she was not answering so I left a message.

'Hey, I'm really sorry. Sorry I made you mad and … sorry for the whole mess. I know this looks bad but —' I didn't know what else to say so I stopped. How could I say any of it without raising an alarm or sounding like a madman? So I finished with a simple, 'Hope I can explain soon and apologise properly in person.'

Heading down the driveway, I knew it would be a miracle if I ever got to do either. My banging on his back door got Harry up from his television. Seeing me through the screen, I could tell he knew this was not a call to borrow a cup of sugar.

'Son? Off somewhere?'

'Harry, your offer to help? If I got in over my head?'

He nodded.

'I'm there. In over my head. That guy who got shot in the park? I think I know who the shooter was. I think a mate might be involved.'

Harry started waving his hand with a very serious, some would say cross, look on his face. 'I don't want to know. No specifics. Just tell me what ya want, how ya think I can help.'

'Insurance. If you don't hear from me by this evening, I've got myself in a spot of bother. Go to the police and speak to Detective Sergeant Baxter. Tell him – you got a bit a paper?'

Harry studied me without comment before going inside for an old envelope and pen that was on its last legs. He watched as I wrote down Dave's address, Gary's name and the Fishy Man's address in Marrickville.

'He'll understand what this all means.' I folded the envelope in half and held it out to him. 'Can you do that for me, Harry?'

With a nod, Harry took the paper and shoved it, without looking, in his pocket. 'Change yer mind on the rosco?'

I shook my head. As he'd said, if I took his gun, I had to be prepared to use it.

'Then you keep yer head down, lad. Heroes are what they use to fill cemeteries, y'hear?'

Did I ever.

47
SEVENTEEN BRICKS

When I arrived at Dave's ramshackle mess of a house, it took an effort to physically step onto the property. Squinting in the afternoon glare at the long grass and dead pot plants in the front yard, I tried to imagine what was going to happen next. Each scenario played out in full Tarantino-esque glory no matter which I imagined. There was no escaping it, I just had to do it.

Shifting the weight of the backpack, instead of walking down the side to the backyard as I'd normally do, this time I made a big show of going to the front door. I banged on the door, calling out to Dave. Then I peered through his windows, cupping my hands and yelling for a bit more emphasis. Neighbours in Dave's street didn't tend to pay much attention to loud noises and things that go bump, but thanks to the ruckus I was making, I saw some curtains flick open and the glimmered flash of venetians being pushed aside to see what was happening in the world. If I never walked out of there again, I knew that one of the neighbours would have seen me and be able to give a description to the police of an average-looking guy banging on the front door with an old backpack over his shoulders.

Despite my efforts, Dave didn't come to the front door so I had to walk down the driveway to the backyard anyway.

Dave was at the barbecue and Gary was perched in one of the camp chairs. Both looked in my direction as Dave pointed at me with his tongs. 'About time, Lachie, snags almost done.

Chops are over there, getting cold.'

So much for a gun being held to his head.

'Don't just stand there looking like a nong, Lachlan. That the gear?' asked Gary, pushing himself up as he held out his other hand for the backpack. Still trying to work out what the hell was going on, I handed it over without question. Game over.

'Good boy. All there?'

Nodding, I looked at Dave, who was grinning at me as he sucked on a stubby, tongs pointing to the sky like a rabbit-ear TV antenna.

'Sausage? Or chop?'

The sausage decision seemed easier so I took the snag and onions in bread that Dave held out.

'Sauce? Full range of con-die-mints as per sir's plea-zure,' said Dave. Hostage or not, he was clearly enjoying the experience.

I looked at the table where the sauces stood at greasy, dribbling attention. Crouching beside it, Gary had the backpack open and was pulling out the bricks, stacking them like pavers as if he was preparing to do the edges of the garden bed.

When I turned back to see the look on Dave's face, it all kind of made sense.

'So you and ...'

Dave nodded.

'All along?'

Dave shook his head as he sucked on the beer. 'Nah. Just recently. He made me an offer. Couldn't refuse.'

Biting into my sausage, I chewed in silence as that sank in. Then I got annoyed.

'For fuck's sake, Dave!'

My tone took him by surprise and he backed away, hands up.

'All this time, I've been dealing with fucking Lloyd, meeting with those Sydney thugs … The police are sniffing about me. And you do this? Now?'

'Don't get hoity on me now, Lachie. Way you were pointing the finger at me, you gave me no choice. Think I want to stay in this shithole? Think I'm gonna let that bitch of an ex-wife keep sucking me dry? This is gonna let me get out. Set me kids' future up properly.'

'But you waited till now? You could have done this days ago and saved me all the grief.'

'Some bricks are missing,' said Gary from behind me.

I turned to see him pointing a brick accusingly at me.

'Should be twenty. Only seventeen,' he said, scowling.

'Lachie? Where are the missing bricks, mate?' Dave turned to me, menacing with the tongs.

'When you flooded my place, a few went missing. For a spell I thought the neighbours' dog ate one –'

'Dog ate one? What is this? Your fucking homework? How did a dog eat one? You don't have a dog!' Gary vented.

I filled them in on the tale of the neighbours' hapless labrador who eventually had a happy ending that thankfully didn't involve heroin. 'She's alright though. Stomach got pumped by the vet.'

'A dog eating any of this wouldn't make it to the vet's in time to have its guts pumped. And if that did happen, the vet would have told the cops and the cops would be swarming all over the place looking for how the dog got to eat a bellyful of hammer.'

'True. Turned out to be a bowel obstruction from eating

a sock. Labradors!'

Gary stepped towards me, pointing a very ugly snub-nosed Smith and Wesson revolver.

'Really?' was all I could muster as I seriously regretted not taking Harry's gun. Not that I'd have been able to pull it out at this point.

'Gaz, mate, what you want that for? If Lachie's got some stashed at home, we'll just go and take another look.'

From the look on Gary's face, he was not interested in doing anything of the sort. 'I knew you were amateurs, but Christ! Shoulda fuckin' yanked your chain days ago. Doesn't make any sense. I didn't take anything from your place. Public dunny? Yes. Yours? There was nothing worth taking. Whole thing's pear-shaped.'

'My buyers don't care who they deal with, Gary. They just want to make the deal. I can take you there now.'

Smiling in the way I imagine a white pointer smiles as it approaches a surfer, Gary shook his head, picked up a cushion from the outdoor setting and placed it over the hand that held the gun.

'We're past that. Got me own connections anyway. All's left is the loose ends.' Then he paused. 'You gave them a whole brick to test? You like getting ripped off or what?'

My attention was on the gun, which was a blessing. It gave Dave a chance to come good as he slammed his beer into Gary's head, sending him down to his knees, where Dave swung the barbie's gas bottle underarm into his head.

I didn't really see that last bit. Unfortunately, when Dave hit Gary with his beer, Gary's reflex was to pull the trigger on the revolver. The one pointed at me.

48
WINGED

If you've never been shot before, the feeling is much like a good punch. No real pain at first. That came later.

Lying flat on my back on the concrete path, staring at the sky, panting, I was too dazed to do anything – especially not exploring how badly I'd been shot. My mind preferred to create images of me bleeding out on the concrete, camera pulling back into the heavens for the clichéd God shot.

The next thing I saw was Dave looking down at me. If he was an angel, I was totally screwed.

'You right? Give us a look.' He pulled my shirt up and checked the wound. Sat back on his heels. Not a good sign.

'Winged ya. Seen worse from a skateboard fall. Bleeding a bit but … fuck. Check that out.'

I refused to move.

'Bloody ripper! Fuckin' bullet grazed your side and passed under your arm. Hole in your shirt to prove it. Better keep that as a souvenir.'

I was still wearing the shirt but that didn't stop Dave worming a finger through the hole. Impressive as my near miss was, the large bloom of bright red blood had more of my attention.

'Ya gotta get up, Lachie. I was serious, mate. This is my ticket to happiness. You understand. This is for me kids. You've got nothing and no one, Lachie. So, I need this more than you. You'll land on your feet.'

Without any warning, he pulled me upright with my left

arm, causing me to spontaneously vomit. Guts purged, I felt lightheaded as I looked into Dave's face. Had to say, he looked more alive than I'd seen him in years. A drop of my blood landed on the concrete and Dave winced.

'Take what you need out of the house. Don't need any of it any more. I'm outta here.'

'You've thought of everything, haven't you, Dave?'

'Nah, completely winging it.'

Clasping my good shoulder, he shook it gently, the closest to a manly hug he was capable of before he packed the bricks into my backpack and slung it over his shoulder.

On the ground Gary rolled slightly and groaned. Although not yet fully conscious, he wasn't far from it.

Dave bent down and picked up Gary's revolver, shoving it in the back of his pants like every TV show and movie has taught us to do. Standing up, he aimed a savage kick at Gary's scone, sending him back into the land of nod with a sickening smack.

'You up to helping me tie him up?' Looking at me, he answered his own question, and tied Gary up with what he could find.

With Gary hogtied, Dave made his exit. As I slowly hobbled towards the house, I saw the gun slip out of his pants and clatter on the drive.

'Fuck. Need a belt. How the blazes do they do this in the movies?' With a grin, Dave waved cheerily with the gun and left.

Inside the house, I went to the bathroom mirror, still not brave enough to look at my wound. Somewhere in the back of my brain, I was sure Dave had lied and that when I took off my shirt, my guts would tumble free like raw sausages. So be it.

Dave hadn't lied.

It was a bit more than a graze, but I told myself it was just a bit bloody. Nothing some Dettol and a bandage wouldn't fix. Dabbing on the Dettol, the pain became searing, reducing my vision to white-hot nothing.

I must have blacked out for a minute or so. Coming to, I carefully stripped off before doing my best to clean myself up with my shirt. Clumsily, I wrapped a bandage about my middle. My shirt was beyond saving and when I looked down I saw my pants had blood on them too. Everything went in the bin. Unfortunately, that meant I had to make a selection from Dave's hideous collection of casual wear.

Rummaging through the wardrobe, I found a black short-sleeved shirt with the least hectic print – almost conservative for Dave. I pulled on a pair of his baggy khaki cargo shorts. As I lifted my arm to put on the shirt, I nearly blacked out again. I bit back the bellow of pain as tears flowed into my eyes, blinding me, and I dropped to my knees. The jolt caused the wound to open a little and fresh blood blossomed through the bandage. I closed my eyes and took shallow breaths until I felt I could move again. I had to keep moving. I had to pull myself together. Standing, I wavered on the spot for a moment, fearful that any movement would start me bleeding again. Focusing on my pain, I took the journey that began like every other, with one foot in front of the other, praying I was going to make it back home without fainting and bleeding out on the street dressed like a suburban dad.

49
PAIN LiKE A BASTARD

My world was unravelling. I have no idea how I got home, but I woke the next morning in my underwear on the floor spooning a cushion, my side in agony. Attempting to sit up to get my body and my mind back in sync, I had to catch my breath while the pain shifted to something manageable.

Being shot was bad enough but my twenty-four-hour deadline was closing fast. My plan to stay one step ahead of the Fishy Man had misfired as only a plan with little to no planning can do. As much as it would have been all warm and fuzzy to think my hands were now clean, that I was in the clear, I had made a promise to the Fishy Man, a promise I needed to keep if I wanted to stay alive.

To save myself, I had to get the drugs back. There was no alternative. If I could deliver them to the Fishy Man maybe I could sweet talk him and his goons into accepting that the definition of me fulfilling all the conditions of the deal was simply telling them that Greasy's killer was Gary Newman and sending them to Dave's place, where I hoped Gary was still tied up and unconscious. It wouldn't fly but it might buy me more time for a better solution. *If* I delivered the drugs. That I first had to get back from Dave. Once I found him. Sounded so easy in my head.

As I sat on the floor stewing over my next move, Harry's arrival was a welcome surprise.

'Lachie. Just checking in,' he called softly as he came through the front door. He stopped when he saw the bloody bandage on my side. 'Jesus!'

'Just a flesh wound, Harry.'

But the old man wasn't having it. In an instant, he was pulling the bandage off to take a look. Muttering and clucking, he shook his head and muttered some more. 'You got a first aid kit? This don't look clean.'

I shook my head and started to protest but Harry wasn't interested. He went off to his place to fetch his first aid kit and ordered me to the bathroom.

Leaning on the bathroom basin, I caught a glimpse in the mirror of my pale skin and the dark circles under my eyes. I looked rough, and not in a good way. The tufts of hair standing on end and the stubble weren't helping. Everything that had happened in the past week suddenly caught up with me and I was on the verge of tears by the time Harry returned with his little green first aid kit. Plonking the kit on the basin next to me, Harry came over surprisingly tender.

'This is gonna hurt like a bastard, but it's got to be cleaned up. You'll get yourself blood poisoning or worse if it ain't.'

I nodded permission and let him minister my wounds. He was right – it did hurt like a bastard. But in a good way, in a way you knew was healing.

With my wound clean and properly bandaged, I followed Harry back to the lounge and slumped down onto one of my milk crates, back against the wall, and closed my eyes.

'So, there anything else out there that needs … cleaning?'

I opened one eye to see what he meant before realising he was asking if I'd killed someone.

'No. God, no. He might have a sore head. But I was definitely the loser.'

'Good. Not sure what I'd have done if you'd said yes. I might have come up with something but … I'm long retired.' Patting my thigh, he headed to the kitchen to put on the kettle.

While it boiled, there was a knock at the door. Harry went into high alert, positioning himself defensively, fists clenched, ready to king hit whoever came through the front door.

'You expecting anyone?'

I shook my head as my panic rose, only for it to dissolve as I heard Karen call my name.

'Lachie? It's me. You there?'

I opened the door and made a grab for her, pulling her close with relief. Except for the pain from my wound that had me buckling at the knees. But it was worth it. True to form, Harry made his excuses and slipped past.

'Be back at mine, lad. If y'need me.'

Karen registered my sharp intake of breath and the pain in my face as she helped me back to the milk crates. Her face was a mix of completely bamboozled, angry, confused and concerned. Who could blame her?

'What's going on?'

Ashamed, I shrugged. I wiped my brow and ran a hand through my hair, trying to work out where to start. None of it helped. As she stood before me, hands on hips, I thought that even if I could come up with a plausible excuse for what happened, she deserved the truth.

'I'm in a bit of trouble.'

'No shit. You spend the night with me and then disappear. You refuse to answer any of my calls and then leave me a weird message. Finally, when I decide I need to have it out with you so I can tell you to fuck off, you're like some invalid, buckled over in pain, with an old man boiling your kettle. So, yeah, you better to tell me what is going on.'

I took a breath. 'I got shot.'

Thankfully, that stopped her questions. After a brief silence, she rallied and calmly asked where I'd been shot and whether I was alright. I told her and assured her I was okay as she opened my shirt to see the damage for herself.

'What did the doctors say?'

'It was just a graze. Harry took care of it.'

'Are you a dickhead? What about infection? You might need stitches. Tetanus shot.'

'All of that attracts cops. How do I explain all this to them?'

I pushed myself up off the milk crate and retreated to the kitchen to boil the kettle again. I didn't want coffee or tea but my hands needed something to do so I made her one. Karen looked stunned as she took the hot drink.

'Forget the cops. How are you going to explain this to *me*? The only people who get shot are crooks and soldiers. I know you're not one of those.'

She had a point.

And I had no answer.

'Tell me what's going on or I'll call the cops right now,' she said.

Seems I didn't have a choice. Confession is always an unburdening and I realised I was more than ready to share my burden. Telling a secret, no matter how convoluted and complicated and twisted and downright bad, should bring some sort of relief. Looking at Karen's face, I saw that, as much as she needed to know, she probably wasn't all that keen to hear my tale. But I shared it with her regardless. Shared every bit of it with her. Apart from the abalone poaching. And Billy Wong. I kind of left out Lloyd too, just called him a bikie mate of Dave's. Seemed safer that way. Also left out the bit where I thought I'd poisoned Horace, even though it had a happy ending. Why share everything? My survival instinct probably was the only thing I hadn't lost at this point. And mystery is the spice of romance.

When I had finished my story, Karen drained her now cold coffee in one long hit. Holding the mug out to me without a word, she looked as though she was calculating, working out her next move.

Standing there helplessly holding the mug, I waited to hear her verdict.

'You're a drug dealer?'

'What? No. It's all a mistake.'

Before I could say anything more, Karen held up her hand and shook her head. 'I'm not ready to hear any more. Just, a whisky would be good. Or whatever you have.'

Thankfully, I did have some whisky left. Also some gin but that was probably the wrong thing for the moment. Splashing whisky into a glass, I took a swig from the bottle before re-corking it and taking Karen her drink. She sipped it then slung it back in a stinging mouthful that I felt the burn of just watching.

'So now you've made me an accomplice in your drug dealing, what's your plan?'

I stood staring at her, but she must have thought I was waiting for permission.

'You can talk now.'

'I was thinking.'

The way Karen scowled, I needed to think quicker.

'I was thinking maybe some backup would be good. Then I've been trying to think like Dave. Trying to work out where he would go.'

'Why?'

'Because he's a mate –'

'How's that going for you?'

'– a mate who's in over his head,' I finished, realising that I was also describing myself to a T.

Karen looked away and paced to the kitchen window. 'Do you think Dave is the sort to skip town or stick around?'

I would have skipped but Dave – Dave loved Newcastle.

'Stick around. For a bit at least.'

'Okay. Getting somewhere. Does he have any friends? Someone he might go to?'

That would have been me. With me out of the picture, Dave was all alone.

'What about his wife? Where's she in all of this? Could they be working together?'

Dave turning to his despised ex in his time of need was highly unlikely. My guess was that he would be in his car somewhere, unsure what to do. But then it occurred to me that I didn't really know Dave half as well as I'd thought.

'Okay. He might not have gone to see her, but would he have called her?'

It was the lightbulb moment. Beaming, I grabbed Karen and kissed her briefly on the mouth, ignoring the bolt of pain in my side. For a moment, holding her made me feel that it was all going to be okay, that equilibrium could be restored. Forehead to forehead, I heard her sigh.

'Easy, tiger. I'm not sure yet. Let's just get through this and see where we're at.'

I guess the universe had other plans after all. Nodding, I signalled that this was okay. Inside, I felt far from it. Yet a small piece of me clung to that 'we'.

'Should really drive you straight to the police station. That's what I should be doing.'

I smiled sheepishly at her and her face went blank. I could see she was struggling with her decision and it was not going to go my way.

'No. I can't do this. I know that's what I should be doing. I should be taking you to the police station,' she repeated, panic rising in her voice.

'No … Karen, you –'

'You've made me an accomplice!' she said, pulling away from me. Shock was ramming the reality of my actions home hard.

'Do you understand what you've done to me? You've fucked me. You've ruined me. My career. Compromised. An accessory, an accomplice. What have you done? I'm screwed.'

'No, you're not. I'm gonna sort it. Give me twenty-four hours. I will make it right, I promise.'

She didn't believe me. She couldn't see how I could possibly make any of this better and she wasn't the only one. But I wanted to try. I wanted to fix this for her as well as for me.

It took a lot of convincing but she finally, reluctantly, agreed to the reprieve. I could see the struggle on her face but in the end she gave in. Then left without another word.

As she drove away, I took out my phone to call the one person left in my arsenal.

50
VEE-DuB

'Hey ho, Lachie Munro!'

Standing in the doorway to my place was my pint-sized former apprentice, Maxie. It was odd seeing my old workmate in clothes that weren't white. But I was very happy to see him.

'Crap, man, you redecorating or is this some Buddhist monk thing? I had a mate who did this retreat, two weeks without talking. Nearly drove him deadset mad. I picked him up and he was like, natter, natter, natter. My God, he did not stop talking for like a day, day and a half. Did my head in.'

Maybe bringing Maxie on board wasn't the best idea I'd ever had.

Plonking himself down on one of my milk crates, he finally stopped talking long enough to hear what I needed help with.

'So your mate has gone missing? We can put the word out. Use the old network, see who's seen him. Must be somewhere. Maybe a new girlfriend? Big bender?'

'I want to go to his place and take a look. See if there isn't something there to tell me he's okay or where he's gone.'

Maxie accepted this as his eyes roamed about my small shack, taking it all in.

'No problems, man. You have to direct me. But I can do that.'

As I led Maxie down the drive, I spotted Harry peering out his window. He saw me and simply raised his eyebrows before he dropped his net curtain. When we reached the street, I was surprised to find Maxie had an old Volkswagen Beetle. I then made the mistake of asking why.

'Pride and joy, man. Classic 1970 original, last model before the Super Beetle. I don't drive my baby to work. Rebuilt the engine, full strip-down and rebore. I –'

I had to stop him there. Nothing is more boring than a car geek telling you all about the minutiae that makes their car unique. Any other time and I'd have let Maxie share it all but not today.

'You asked, Lachie.'

Now my apprentice and personal chauffeur was sulking. At least it meant that the drive to Stockton was silent apart from my directions. Which allowed me to think about how I was going to handle what happened next.

Maxie peered over the steering wheel at Dave's house. 'Your mate not believe in gardens?'

Looking at the expanse of dull, overgrown turf and broken concrete that passed for the pathway and drive, I had to agree. It was a long way from the home Dave had when he was married, the home he'd described to me in loving detail more times than I cared to remember. That place had sounded like pure McMansion, with an immaculate manicured lawn and a garden that flowered on cue just like the automated watering system he'd installed.

'Wait here, okay? If I'm not back in ten, call the cops. Hear any loud noise, call the cops.'

'Wait, wait, wait. I thought you knew this guy, that he was a mate. Missing like.'

'He is. But the less you know, Maxie, the better.'

Before he could interject again I was closing the car door

behind me and sneaking up the drive, trying desperately to be quiet. My heart was beating so fast I thought I could hear it. When your heart beats at a hundred kilometres an hour, you feel your pulse in strange places. My neck was pulsing; my thumb. Who has a pulse in their thumb?

Reaching the corner of the house, I paused to listen for any sound to indicate that anyone was inside or out. Nothing.

I saw a documentary once about how Native American hunters are able to silently walk through the forest when stalking their prey. The host was shown how to do it – stepping on the side of the foot and rolling in with each step. Apparently it muffled the sound of twigs and sticks, kept the imprint on the earth to a minimum. It's complete crap. Or at least, no Native American ever tried to step silently on an old wooden deck. It creaked and cracked under my weight. If anyone was inside, they would have been alerted to my presence immediately.

Giving up, I flattened my feet out and walked normally to the back door. It wasn't locked. I was unsure if this was a good sign or a bad one – did the unlocked door mean Dave had returned?

'Hello?' Calling out seemed like the natural thing to do. You walk into a friend's house through an open door, you say hello. No one answered.

Stepping over the usual mess, I came to the phone mounted on the wall by the kitchen bench. Sorting through the takeaway pamphlets and scraps of paper, I found what I was after: the old green address book with the slide down the middle that opened at the right letter. I slid to 'Mc' and popped the spring-loaded button. Up flipped the lid and my finger tracked down the names until it landed on Tina McGilvray, Dave's ex-wife. It was then that I heard a noise.

'Hey, dickwad!'

Ducking behind the kitchen counter, I peeked carefully over the top, hoping to see who it was before they saw me, praying hard it wasn't Gary. A figure hopped into view and I breathed a sigh of relief.

'Lloyd! You scared the crap out of me.'

Seeing how Lloyd jumped, even with his leg in plaster and supported by crutches, I reckon I'd repaid the favour. Hand on his heart as he regained his breath, Lloyd glared at me.

'What you doin' here? Where's Dave?'

Before I could start filling him in, Maxie burst in swinging his arms like a kung-fu movie star.

'It's been ten minutes, Lachie. And then I saw this guy walk up the driveway,' said Maxie as his hands whizzed blade-like through the air, eyes never leaving Lloyd.

Confused, Lloyd looked at me with a face that said it all as he held up one crutch to keep kung-fu Maxie at bay.

'Maxie. Relax. This is Lloyd. He's on our side.'

Dropping the kung-fu chop, Maxie's lethal hand of fury instantly transformed into a welcoming hand of greeting. Not that Lloyd took it, instead choosing to ignore Maxie totally and focus on me.

'You *are* on our side aren't you, Lloyd?' I asked.

He didn't bother answering, just curled his lip and shook his head dismissively. It was then that I noticed he was still wearing his hospital bracelet.

'Yeah. Got out this mornin'. Got home. Felt lonely. So I came here. Thinkin' of keeping the bracelet for a bit. Fuck with people's heads. Like I'm some escaped mental patient.'

'But what're you doing here, Lloyd?'

'Could ask you the same. Dave rang and left me a message yesterday to come. I only got out this mornin' and as Dave wasn't answerin', decided to come and check what me cuz wanted. What's your story?'

I shrugged. My explanation could wait until Maxie was not in the room. Turning to Dave's phone, I dialled the number I had for Tina. Both Maxie and Lloyd wanted to know who I was calling. Holding up a finger for them to be silent, I listened to the phone ringing. With a click, the other end picked up and the voice was not a happy one.

'Dave, you fucking arsehole. Why weren't you here to pick up the boys? I've got a good mind to go to my lawyers and have you hauled over the coals. You knew I had stuff to do today. And you didn't even call to give me a heads-up. They'd have missed their game if Tayla Prakesh hadn't offered to take them to Myers Park.'

'Hi Tina. It's Lach? Lachie Munro?'

The voice changed in an instant, becoming much more warm and friendly. 'Lach? Sorry. Thought it was Dave. It's his number ...'

'That's why I'm calling. You haven't seen Dave then?'

Tina calmed down a little as she filled me in. I explained that I hadn't been able to track him down so I'd called her.

'You say he's missing? You're at his place?' she asked, her voice sharp. She sounded genuinely worried.

'Look, don't worry. I'm sure he's fine. He might just have wanted some time to himself. He's had a bit on his mind of late. You got any ideas where he might be?'

She didn't. After reassuring her that I'd let her know when I found him, I hung up. I looked at Lloyd and Maxie.

'Either of you got any ideas?'

'Done a runner. Must've. What I'd have done if I had them packages,' said Lloyd. As if to emphasise his point, he gingerly made himself at home on the couch and rested his plaster cast on the coffee table.

'Why? What packages? What's he done?' asked Maxie. He didn't get any explanation from either Lloyd or myself.

A runner didn't seem like something Dave would do. Ironic I should think that, after what he'd just pulled on me. More to the point, I knew he wouldn't shoot through without seeing his kids. He would need time to make his plans, not because he was methodical or careful but because he was the opposite. Hardly the arch criminal, Dave was perfectly suited to driving a large truck down to the bottom of an open-cut mine, turning it around and heading back to the top. No decisions required. Which was great for someone who flip-flopped on nearly every decision he made. Then again, Dave had outwitted me on this one. So where the hell was he?

'Does he have a friend? A girlfriend?' Maxie was running through the hypotheticals. All of them dead ends. I was pretty much Dave's only friend, or at least I was sure that had been the case until Gary had shown up in his backyard. Maybe Dave did have a secret life I didn't know about. As for a girlfriend, if he had one of those, Dave would have been a lot easier to be around.

'Nah. All he ever talks about are me nephews and the goals they've kicked. Real chick magnet stuff,' said Lloyd.

Myers Park. That was it. That was all I had.

'How'd you get here, Lloyd? You come on your bike?' The

idea of perching on the back of his hog was not appealing.

'What d'you reckon, Goldie-Lach? Not match-fit for me Harley. Still in the shop anyways.'

'What's wrong with my car?' asked Maxie.

I really wanted to keep him out of this. 'You've been a great help, Maxie, but we can take it from here.'

Bundling them out of Dave's place, Maxie grumbling all the way about being left out just when things were getting interesting, Lloyd's clapped-out old Laser caught me by surprise.

'When are the wreckers coming to collect that piece of shit?' asked Maxie. He had a point. Every panel on that car was a different colour while underneath it, a small oil pool formed that should already have been attracting the attention of Greenpeace.

'It's me mum's, arsehole. Needed an automatic because of me leg and that's the only one in the family.'

'Maxie, you get your wish.'

With Maxie grinning widely, I clambered into his VW.

'I need the front.'

I hesitated. Since we weren't going to use his car, Lloyd didn't need to come. With his injuries he'd be as much use as, well, a one-legged bikie.

'Think I'm missing this? C'mon, Lachie. I've been bored shitless in hospital. Get in the back.'

Reluctantly, I got out again and squeezed into the back seat before two crutches speared for my head.

Glancing at me as he started the ignition, Maxie was as unsure as I was cramped. But before any of us could complain any more we were off to find Dave as fast as the car's exhaust could fill the street with its distinctive *flaffa-flaffa-flaffa*.

51

BAD GUYS SWING

'You gonna tell me what your plan is?' Lloyd asked. Which was tricky as 'plan' was such a generous term.

'Turn here and head down the Pacific Highway, Maxie.'

'Well?' Lloyd wasn't giving up.

'He was supposed to be with his kids at a park. Dave likes to watch his kids play soccer. They're playing at Myers Park.'

Lloyd rolled his eyes. He didn't think it was likely. He was sticking with his theory that his cousin had done a runner. Maxie didn't care, along for the ride and the adventure and the chance to show off his pride and joy, cheerfully ignoring Lloyd's offers to help make the vee-dub go faster by sticking out one of his crutches and paddling.

Pulling into Myers Park, I scanned the area for Dave. There were kids kicking a footy and tackling each other on the sidelines of the oval where a series of under-twelve soccer games were taking place. With all the kids, parents and supporters milling about the space, trying to spot Dave was like looking for the proverbial needle in a haystack.

Just as I was about to give up, I spotted him on the other side of the playground on the swings.

Beaming, I waited to be let out of the car as Lloyd grumbled that we should have taken his mum's Laser. The contortions of exiting the back seat made my bullet wound throb but I ignored the pain and took off across the oval as speedily as I could manage. Maxie was on my heels, auditioning for the role of my faithful hound. Much further back, Lloyd and his crutches kept up a cracking pace.

I approached Dave as he listlessly pushed himself back and forth, the creak of the swing's metal chains beating a steady tempo. He didn't look good. Like he was dazed, not really there.

'Dave?'

He saw me, then Maxie, standing on the edge of the wood chips. He went to say something then saw Lloyd approaching. He waved at his cousin.

'Lachie, I couldn't do it.'

He made me feel like a priest, about to hear his confession.

'I thought it was the solution to all me problems. But then all I could see was the road and a mirror.'

I knew exactly what he meant. The promise of freedom in the road stretching ahead was tempting but the reality is always having to look over your shoulder to see who was following you.

'Practically a poet, mate. I get it completely.'

Dave sadly nodded at that, still swinging, his heels on the ground. 'It was me kids. Couldn't do it to them.'

His eyes never left the group of youngsters playing on the field – I realised that two of them must have been his kids, the ones he was supposed to have brought to the park.

'Tina is worried about you too.'

'Hardly. She's only worried because me not showing up messes with whatever Zumba, Pilates, latte-sipping session she had planned. Nah, me kids. The thought of never seeing them again. Even if I did work out some way to stay in touch, I'd never be able to ... Someone would come after me or, worse still, do something to them to make me come back. Every way

I looked, I was just putting them in danger.'

By the side of the swing's frame was the backpack, still bulky with the bricks.

'That the gear, Dave?'

He nodded but as I stepped to collect it, he leaped off the swing and made a grab for it. 'What d'ya reckon you're doing?'

'Taking it back. Gonna get rid of it like we should have in the first place,' I said.

'But I've taken care of it. Someone's coming. It's all sorted. Life will be back to normal in about half an hour. Me boys will kick the winning goal. We'll go get some Macca's on the way home. Normal.'

Panic started to rise. Who had he contacted? 'They coming here?'

'Mate, don't worry. It's sorted. I tried Lloyd but he never called me back so Gary is coming to take it off my hands.' Holding the backpack to his chest, Dave settled back onto the swing and started rocking again.

On the oval, an umpire blew his whistle for the next game. The crowd of parents standing around the field to watch their kids play had doubled. I knew we had to get out of there, away from Dave, but with the drugs.

'It's time to leave,' I said to Maxie.

Standing at the edge of the playground, Lloyd looked very pained to hear we were leaving. He hadn't even caught his breath.

But it was too late anyway. Over Lloyd's shoulder I saw Gary, his head sporting a wide bandage, ambling along in his bright orange crocs, smiling and adding his encouragement to the soccer players as he went. Maybe it was the sight of Gary or the forlorn performance Dave had just put on, but a wave of anger took me over. Dave had stolen the drugs from me. He'd schemed ever since I'd found them to get more than his share and had been a general pain in the bum. The thought of him simply handing the package over to Gary after all his betrayals and what he'd put me through was too much. So I strode over and pushed him off the swing.

Dave landed on his back with a loud *oof*, winded, legs tangled in the swing's seat, arms above his head. I grabbed at the backpack and bolted for the car.

'Keep up. Head for the crowd,' I yelled to Maxie and Lloyd.

I think they were as dazed as Dave, although Lloyd was smiling, enjoying the sight of Dave flat on his back. Maxie was a pace behind me and Lloyd hopped along a few behind him. I urged them to keep moving.

'Dude! What's happening?' puffed Maxie.

'Putting things square. But if you don't hurry up, there won't be any need to. The bad guys will win.'

'Bad guys? Who are you, Lachie? Fucking James Bond?'

Looking over my shoulder, I saw Gary had been momentarily distracted by the soccer game. A small kid had booted the ball too hard, sending it sailing over the goal bar. The crowd, and Gary, roared at the effort that was good but not good enough. With a shake of his head, Gary turned back and continued on his way to the swings, where Dave was now dusting himself off.

'Hey, that's Gaz! Didn't know he was back. Haven't seen him in ages.' Maxie slowed as we hit the edge of the crowd.

'Yes. That's Gary. Except he's actually the bad guy, Maxie.

And a killer. With a gun. So keep moving.'

'That is so *cool*!'

Urging him on, I paused to let Lloyd catch up. He was struggling.

'Brother, I gotta bail.'

This was not good news. Self-preservation screamed we had to stick together.

'It's me leg. Weighs a tonne. You try swinging it around this park.'

'Lloyd, you have to keep going. Get to the car and we can drop you somewhere.'

Lloyd shook his head and waved me away. He lifted his shirt and undid his belt, which was actually a length of chain.

'Got to get to the clubhouse anyway. Need to see the lads. Show off me scars. Supposed to be a bit of a floorshow this afternoon with pole dancers! Missed the last few.'

At the swings, Dave and Gary seemed to be having words. Gary looked back to the soccer field before pulling on his spectacles for a better look. I could see the stupid nanna chain around his neck. Ducking slightly, I dropped the backpack from my shoulder to my hands in a vain attempt to hide behind the forest of legs and bodies. I clapped Lloyd on the shoulder.

'You really gonna use that?'

Having dropped one of his crutches, Lloyd had the chain wrapped a few times about his hand, the rest dangling loose. 'Only if he gets close enough. Most don't.'

By the time I was at Maxie's car, he had it unlocked and was trying to get it started. Tossing the backpack into the passenger-side footwell, I looked back to see Gary running up the grass towards us with Dave in tow. They split up and swung wide around Lloyd and his chain.

Reaching behind my back, I pretended to go for a gun hidden in my belt as I stared Gary down. Seeing me with one hand behind my back, the other outstretched, placating, Gary stopped. He raised both his hands and lowered his eyes to the ground in submission. Behind him, Dave was arguing with Lloyd, just out of range of the chain.

As I clambered into the passenger seat, Maxie didn't need me to tell him twice to get us out of there.

52
GETAWAY

We drove away fast enough to get us to safety but not get us pulled over by every police officer in the city. Sensible when you have a backpack with a hell of a lot of heroin sitting at your feet.

'What's the plan? Is there a plan?'

'I don't have a plan. All I know is that we have to go somewhere no one will look for us until I can get this to someone who wants it.'

'That's your plan? *Jesus.*'

'That's it.'

'What's in the backpack?'

'Drugs. Smack.'

'You *what*? You ... in my car? Are you crazy? That shit kills people.'

'I didn't import it. I just found it. And if I don't deliver it now, I'll be the one killed. So keep driving.'

'Nah. You got to get out.'

Seeing there was no way to reason with Maxie, I reassured him that all I needed was for him to drive me a bit further so I could slip out at a set of traffic lights. Calming down a little, he slowed even more, inching along like a grandma on her way to church.

'Maxie? Drive faster, okay? This is Newcastle. Going slow attracts more attention than breaking the speed limit,' I said as another car blared past doing twice the speed of the Volkswagen.

'Lachie, I hear you, but I have to be honest with you. There's a bag of weed in the glovebox. If we get pulled over, that's the first place the cops will look.'

To say I was dumbstruck was an understatement. But I wisely kept my comments to myself and adjusted my backpack with its fortune of narcotics at my feet, letting Maxie worry about his small bag of herbs.

Nibbling nervously at his lip, Maxie drove on silently, randomly turning through the city centre, down by the waterfront, up around the docks then back into the CBD. It was more a case of having no idea where to go than a brilliant escape technique. Stopped at a set of traffic lights, Maxie stared into the rear-vision mirror.

'You notice the red Subaru?'

I checked the side mirror and saw the Subaru in question three cars behind us.

'I think it's following us.' His voice was soft and had a waver to it. 'I can't get arrested. Way I look? In prison?'

Sitting in silence, my attention was split between him and the red Subaru. Not for the first time, I realised that I'd messed everything up.

'How long has it been there?'

Seems the Subaru had followed us through two sets of lights, always a couple of cars back. Maxie had to lose him.

'Turn left at the next intersection.'

When the lights went green Maxie impressed me with his clutch technique, leaving a texting P-plater in his hotted-up Nissan Soarer sitting in our wake. I kept an eye on the mirrors. Sure enough, the Subaru followed a few seconds after.

'How fast does this thing go?'

'Pray for a set of traffic lights.'

We followed the road up and down and around, the red Subaru still on our tail. Then finally a set of traffic lights shone their green welcome. Maxie slowed into the traffic around us as the lights went amber. Just as he approached the intersection, he floored it and sailed through the red, leaving the Subaru stuck at the lights.

'Should do it,' said Maxie.

'Where'd you learn that trick?'

'Ever played *Grand Theft Auto*?'

'Take the next right.'

Pulling into the side street, Maxie drove away deep into the maze of suburban homes. Once we were far enough away, I got him to pull over.

'Now I'm getting out. You were right. Shouldn't have got you involved in this. But thanks.'

He sat in silence. I couldn't tell if it was annoyance, acceptance or fear. Probably all three. All my energy had been focused on just getting rid of the package and avoiding getting hurt but the reality was that along the way I'd dragged innocent people like Maxie and Karen, even Harry, into my mess. Having been involved with or known several colourful characters of dubious backgrounds, become a person of interest in a murder investigation, and now in possession of a backpack full of drugs, if I was arrested the conviction would destroy any future ideas I might have except how to decorate a prison cell on ten dollars a week. Then there was the abalone poaching. I was well and truly in a jam. The only solution was to make sure I didn't get arrested while trying to minimise the fallout for anybody else.

'Can't wait to hear the whole story, dude.' I realised that Maxie was far too excited to be scared. 'Don't get caught,' he said, grinning as he gave me a weird rock-and-roll hand signal.

'Maxie, best not tell anyone about this.'

'Lachie, you know what's in my glovebox. I know what's in your bag. I think we have enough on each other to know we can trust each other.' He held out his fist for a friendly bump.

Watching him drive away, I threw the backpack over my shoulder again without thinking. It slammed into my injured side, making my eyes water. Taking some deep breaths, I was ready to face what came next alone.

53
GREEN DRAGON AND HEAVENLY WINDS

They say a day is a long time in politics. I say, try doing a drug deal. Taking a deliberately complicated backstreet route to avoid being seen, I made my way to a familiar alleyway that ran parallel to the main shopping strip.

In the daylight, Billy Wong's looked a bit worse for wear. The paint was faded, the bins overflowing, the ground blotchy with indeterminate stains. But it was a relief to make it. As odd as it may seem, this place was my only haven.

Walking through the back entrance, I nodded at the cooks and kitchen hands, who eyed me warily. Stepping into the restaurant, I saw Billy sitting at one of the large tables having his customary pre-evening work meal with his staff. They were laughing and chatting away until Billy glanced up and saw me. His mouth full of noodles, he looked puzzled but waved me upstairs with his hand.

Upstairs was silent and empty. Which was surprising. I'd always been told the games never ended. I guess even illegal gambling dens have to shut down occasionally. The back blind was up and sun streamed through the small window that had been opened to air the place out, upsetting the dust motes in the process. It felt soothing to sit and just watch for a bit before Billy came up the stairs with some jasmine tea and a couple of Tsingtao beers.

'Didn't know what you wanted, but I know you want something, Lachie.'

I accepted the beer and took a big slug. It reminded

me how little I'd had to drink that day. Dehydration, fear, adrenaline. None of that was good news.

'If you are after that shooter you asked me to find, have it in the safe. Sadly, price bit more than quoted.'

I shook my head.

Pulling out a chair, Billy sat down and stared at me, waiting for me to tell him what was going on. Where to start?

'Life's been a bit crazy lately, Billy. Just needed a place to catch my breath for a bit. Lay low for a few hours.'

Leaning back, Billy squinted slightly.

'See ...' Words were not on my side. Taking another long draught of the beer didn't help. 'Remember when I told you about a mate who was causing problems?'

Billy remembered.

'I was right. He was trying to do me over.'

At the bottom of the stairs, the first step creaked. I killed my story. The last thing I needed was anyone eavesdropping on my tale. I waited for the head to appear so I could shoo the waiter away.

Slowly, a floppy khaki hat perched on white bandages emerged at the top of the stairs, followed by a familiar faded Hawaiian shirt. Gary stopped and stared, apparently genuinely surprised to see me sitting there with Billy. With a look that can only be described as bemused, Gary lifted his glasses from where they dangled on his chest. With them on, he looked even more the genial hippy uncle.

'Lachie, this is Gary. Been helping me with a few problems I ...' Billy's words trailed off as he twisted back in his chair and saw my face. Probably something to do with my wide-eyed terror.

By now, Gary had joined us at the table and pulled out a chair, his nasty revolver in his hand.

'Lachlan, of all the places! Who would've guessed you'd be sitting here, drinking a beer. You still carrying?'

Not trusting me when I said no, Gary decided not to give me the benefit of the doubt and made me stand as he did a one-handed pat-down, eyes never leaving my face. Satisfied, he put his own gun away, took the second Tsingtao and drained it in two pulls. Then he spotted the backpack.

'You brought it. Whacko! Very smart.'

Puzzled, Billy looked from Gary to me and then at the backpack. He sat upright, suddenly much more focused and alert. I was getting the business Billy.

'Right, you two Aussie bozos better tell me what the fuck's going on.'

'Why don't you go first, Lachlan? Tell us what you're doing here?'

He wasn't getting off that easily. 'How the hell did you follow me here? I lost your Subaru at the lights.'

Now Gary was looking puzzled. 'What are you talking about? I'm in me LandCruiser. I didn't follow you. Either way, you have something in that bag that doesn't belong to you. It belongs to a friend of Billy's here.'

With a sinking feeling as to who was in the red Subaru, I reached down to hand the backpack across to him. Thoughts of throwing it into Billy's or Gary's face and making a dash for it flitted for the briefest of moments before I realised it was futile. There was nowhere for me to run to. The time and opportunity for running was over.

'It all here?'

'All except the sample I left for the others and the two you took from my place,' I said, a weight lifting from me.

Gary was just looked at me. 'I told you – I never took any bricks from yours, Lachlan. Didn't find a sausage.'

'Guess someone got lucky then, *Gaz*.' I drained my beer to show how little I cared. It was over. Watching Gary unpack the bricks to stack them on the table made it even more so.

'Well, I'll keep an eye on things at street level. Some junkie tries to use this, spike in ODs will soon show us the culprit. Stuff's practically pure. Pure as you can get. Like my heart.' Gary sniggered.

But Billy pointed a finger accusingly at me. 'You had this? All along you had this? I've been sending people everywhere looking for it. Keeping tabs on what's on the street, chasing around to see if someone had picked it up and was selling it. And all the time, you had it?' He laughed. 'Lachie, Lachie, Lachie. We need to work better on our communications.'

Despite how jovial he seemed, I had a bad feeling. The food started to arrive as Billy walked to the window with his mobile and started talking loudly in Mandarin. This left Gary and me sitting at the table, eyeing each other over the spring rolls.

'So we were on the same side. Who'd 'a thunk?' Gary's tone made it clear he didn't accept it for one second.

'You really not driving that Subaru? Didn't borrow one for the day?'

Hot spring roll clenched between his teeth, Gary shook his head and blew air over the fried pastry.

'Dave know?' I asked.

'Why should Dave know? He was the obstacle stopping me

from returning the property to its rightful owner. He's just a nuisance – like you, mate.'

While I dug into the noodles, greens and sauce-laden meat, Gary's words were not filling me with a sense of calm. But my appetite wasn't suffering. The food, as always, was good. I can think of worse last meals.

Coming back to the table, Billy grinned and cupped his hand over my ear, shaking my head the same way you'd greet a favourite dog.

'Lachie, all this time, you – you came to me for advice and I gave it to you. I could not make this up.' He started laughing again.

All I could feel was exhaustion.

Downstairs, someone dropped something in the kitchen. Then we heard the sound of loud voices before the heavy, measured thud of footsteps on the stairs.

54
BUSINESS

The enormous bulk of Tiny bounded into the room with a pistol in his hand. The three of us sat stunned. Maybe I was a little less stunned.

'Clear, boss!' yelled Tiny after scanning the room.

From down below two more sets of boots clomped up before the heads of the Fishy Man and Damo appeared.

'Lachlan Munro. Mate, keeping well?' The Fishy Man strolled into the room like he owned it. With his two heavies alongside him, I guess he did.

Billy looked daggers at me. 'You know these guys? You bring them here?'

'Bloody knew you weren't working solo,' Gary hissed.

The Fishy Man answered for me. 'Don't worry about him, Lachlan is the innocent party here. We've been followin' him for days. Since we made our little deal.' For emphasis, the Fishy Man plucked one of the remaining spring rolls up and bit into it with great relish as I sat there, mouth dry, unable to make a sound.

'And who are you?' The Fishy Man double dipped his spring roll in Gary's sauce. By chance, I'd delivered on my promise to the Fishy Man but I didn't think he was going to be seeing it that way, even if I could do more than squeak.

'Just a guy looking for some good Chinese,' Gary said.

'Nah. Don't think so. I think you're much more than that, Gary Newman,' said the Fishy Man, grinning at Gary's filthy look as he nodded to his men to collect the pile of bricks. Tiny shoved Damo in the shoulder, pushing him forwards to do it while he kept his gun on us.

Billy Wong looked so angry I expected him to be frothing at the mouth rather than cursing in Mandarin. The Fishy Man just watched as his men quickly and efficiently packed up the bricks.

'How did you find me?'

'Damo followed you. He lost you but I had other eyes and ears about town. In the end, I knew you'd struggle to deliver. This game isn't in your nature. But deal or no deal, I didn't care who I did business with so long as I got the product. Dig?'

'The red Subaru,' muttered Gary, scowling at me.

The Fishy Man looked about the room, licking spring roll off his fingers. 'Sweet setup. What is it? Poker? Blackjack? Baccarat?'

Billy Wong just glared at the Fishy Man, who found that amusing.

'See, Mr Munro? People always behave as you expect them to.' He pointed at Billy. 'Your man here is angry because he thinks he's being ripped off. When, really, this is just finders keepers. He should've put the product somewhere safe as soon as he got his paws on it instead of sittin' down to have a meal.'

The tension in Billy's jaw could crush rocks. Gary just sat in his chair, head bowed, chin on his chest.

'What's your problem, Surfer Joe? Very quiet there.'

'Just staying out of the way.'

'For the best. We'll get to you soon enough.'

Behind the Fishy Man, having finished stashing the drugs in the backpack, Damo was struggling to balance the bag on his shoulder at the top of the stairs.

'Help him,' said the Fishy Man.

As Tiny turned to help, Gary sprang up and pulled two guns. Where they came from, I've no idea. Time slowed as I watched Gary fire with both hands, taking out Tiny with a shot to the chest. The Fishy Man fell to the floor with a shot in the gut as another bullet drilled a hole through the skull of poor old Damo, decorating the red stairwell walls with grey.

Tiny clawed at the carpet, trying to move. In two strides, Gary was standing over him, discharging an execution shot into his skull. The Fishy Man clamped his fingers to his stomach, his skin clammy and very pale, watching. He looked up at Gary, resigned to what was about to happen.

'You,' the Fishy Man said.

'It's just business,' said Gary.

The Fishy Man opened his mouth to say something but Gary shot him before any sounds were formed.

What was I doing when all of this was happening? Sitting open-mouthed, feeling like I was screaming but shock and hyperventilation preventing me making a sound. As Gary returned to his chair, he looked at Billy Wong and then me.

'Shut your mouth, Lachlan. Fucking flies'll zoom in there and make themselves a new home.' It was said casually, as he placed a pistol on the table.

I could smell the hot oil and cordite. I did as I was told.

Billy pushed his chair away from the table and stomped over to the bodies. It was clear he was not happy. But my attention stayed on the gun, sitting right there in front of me.

'Gary, why you do that? Why you shoot them? In my place? This is a bloody big problem. Lots to clean up.'

'I did what needed doing. You want someone to just sit

here and let them walk all over you, Lachlan's your man.'

'I knew who they were. We could have taken care of it later. Fuck.'

Gary stood and went to survey the bodies. Then he bent down and calmly wrapped each one in tablecloths, forming red-stained mummies. He hefted the first over his shoulder and carried it out of sight.

'What is the world coming to, eh, Lachie?' Billy said, so matter-of-fact he could've been bemoaning a teenager tagging graffiti on his back fence. He turned from the two remaining bodies and stared intently at me.

My life was seriously rushing by before my eyes, a demented flip book of regrets and things that seemed like good ideas at the time.

'You good? You need a drink?' He was already at one of the cabinets where the gambling pieces were kept, pulling out a red bottle of Chinese rice wine and what looked like a pair of thimbles. Pouring wine into each thimble, he handed me one. 'It'll help.'

He downed his, watching me to make sure I was going to drink mine.

'Bad luck to drink alone, Lachie. To the ancestors or whatever the bloody hell you want.'

The liquid was smooth, like water, until I finished the mouthful – then it burned. In a good way. My expression must have tickled Billy, because he chuckled before handing me the bottle.

'Only the best.'

Holding the bottle out for him to take back, he shook his head and told me to have some more. With a smile, he looked at the gun and then at me. He picked it up, feeling the weight in his hand.

'So much power in these small pieces of metal.'

Uncomfortable barely covered how his behaviour made me feel. Then Billy began wiping the weapon down with one of the napkins, methodical, rhythmical and thorough; like polishing silver. Once he was satisfied, he dropped both the napkin and the weapon back onto the table with a heavy thunk.

Sighing, he relieved me of the bottle of rice wine. Taking it back to the cabinet, he asked me to bring over the gun. For safety.

Like an automaton, I reached for the gun and carried it across to Billy, who opened a drawer and gestured for me to put it inside. Once it was lying in the drawer, Billy quickly shut and locked it. It was then that I noticed that he was carrying the rice wine bottle by a finger shoved down the neck. With a shrug, Billy looked at me with a sad smile.

'Business, Lachie. I like you. But I need insurance. Your prints on both those, we're good. Without them, I'd have to add you to the spring rolls as well.'

I must have blanched. His laugh didn't do much to clear the image of 'long pork' spring rolls being on the menu for the next month.

'Lachie! Only joking. The spring rolls are fine.' Then with a deadly serious face, he added, 'But maybe order vegetarian for a few weeks, okay?'

'What now, Billy? You got the gear. Your rivals are taken care of. What happens now?'

'Nothing. It's all over. You go home. Have a rest. We're

square. Your gambling debt gone. All debts gone. Apart from the guns. You owe me for the one you didn't take. And Gary's. He'll need replacements. You pay for them too.'

He was sincere but I knew we were never going to be square. I didn't wait to be told twice. As I went to flee, Gary blocked the stairwell again. As I passed him, he grunted before softly humming a few bars of 'Hotel California' in my ear.

Looking him in the eye, I told him the last person to mention that song ended up dead in a toilet block.

I walked out through the restaurant kitchen. Gary followed.

As I reached the door, he called, 'He said you were all square. What was that about?'

I didn't turn around. Through the door I could see the sky and a seagull drifting on the wind. 'Business, Gary. Just business.'

Taking a step outside, I fully expected it to be my last. But the bullet never came. Instead, the kitchen door slammed its metallic thud behind me and I was alone. And alive.

55
FAREWELL

I slept for twenty-four hours. When I woke up, I tried to reassure myself I didn't have to worry about anything as I attempted to stir sugar into my morning coffee without shaking.

The bitter black brew hit my stomach, and another sort of bitterness chewed at my mind.

Who was I kidding?

There was no way I was going to be able to stick around in Newcastle. I was done, spent, and the clock was ticking for me to get out. I'd up and left places before so I knew the drill. I needed to find a new place, somewhere safer where no one knew my name. I had to put a hell of a lot of kilometres between me and anything associated with the events of the past week. *Hasta la vista*, Newie. It's been nice knowing ya.

Pouring the rest of the coffee out, determination drove me through the flat, grabbing what I could, what I thought I'd need, and leaving what I could do without. Thanks to the flood, there wasn't much I wanted to keep.

Job done, I headed for the door. Standing in the doorway was Harry, with a longneck of Carlton Draught.

'Hot one today. Figured the sun's over the yardarm somewhere in the world.'

Seeing the bag slung over my shoulder, he casually asked if I was going somewhere. He popped the top on the beer. 'Want me to look after the keys? Or this a more permanent thing?'

All I could do was hand the keys over.

'Sorry to lose you, son. Been a good neighbour. I could see something was up. Even before the flood. But don't worry. Won't breathe a word. I know nothing, I've seen nothing. That philosophy got me through some bad times, reckon it'll still work now.'

He handed me the longneck for a swig.

'Old times' sake.'

So we drank in silence, passing the bottle, me more quickly than Harry, until it was all done. Then we shook hands.

The problem with leaving a place is how to do it. The decision needs to be quick, sudden, like ripping off a bandaid. Do it slow and there are all sorts of things to drag you back or change your mind. That said, there were a couple of goodbyes I had to make without making it seem like it was goodbye.

There was no way I was going to see Dave. That headcase wasn't going to get so much as a Christmas card from me ever again. Lloyd, well, someone like that, if I saw him I'd say something. If not, no biggie. There was Muzz and Maxie. Those two and Karen. How was it that after all my time in Newcastle, my farewells were reduced to so few?

I found Maxie sitting in the front bar of the Great Northern, king of all he surveyed as he worked on developing his beer belly.

'Lach, legend! Knew you'd be sweet.'

Sitting down, I gave him a tight-lipped smile before asking him if he needed another drink. Returning with his preferred beer and a packet of nuts, I handed them both across.

'Good call with the nuts, Lach.'

Clinking our glasses, we sat in silence and stared out at the darkening waters of the channel as a storm built up, threatening much but guaranteed never to deliver. As the beer level in my glass went out with the tide, I listened as Maxie updated me on what was happening in his life, both of us ignoring the elephant that was yesterday. Seemed that our old boss Muzz was coming around to forgiving us. Maxie got the call from him late the day before, which meant that I would be destined for one too. Accidents happen on the job and we were a good team. Muzz had probably worked out he needed us. Having made us do a spot of penance, he was now ready to welcome us back. I didn't let on that I wouldn't be joining Maxie.

Beer gone, he offered me another but I had to keep moving.

'Y'know, Maxie, about yesterday. Best you don't share any of it. With anyone. Ever.'

Theatrically, his hand mimed padlocking his lips together. 'And then,' he murmured, adding a further sewing mime, sealing his lips good and tight.

'Nice blanket stitch, Maxie. Or is it running stitch?'

Outside, a bright flash of lightning was followed by the low rumbling of thunder a long way away.

'You ever find your car, Lach?'

I shook my head. 'Police did nothing – it's just an old bomb to them. Had some mates take a look for it. Nothing. Car's gone to a better place.'

'Burnt somewhere out bush, more likely. Fuck, woulda loved to seen that. All that paint and stuff. Woulda made a toasty little explosion.'

I nodded in agreement and, with a wave, headed off. It was a nice place to leave Maxie, face alight with the thought of my old car going up in flames.

Proactive was not just the new twenty-four-hour gym that had opened up around the corner, it was also my mission for the day. Taking out my phone, I dialled Muzz. Better to get in first. He answered on the second ring and sounded like he was happy to hear from me. In the background, I could hear a TV playing and kids fighting.

Casually, I asked how he was going, making sure to ask about the family as well. It was good to hear his voice. Like Maxie had said, Muzz wanted me back.

'Mate, got a big job on. Need my best dickhead.'

It was easy to sound like I was interested and enthusiastic. If nothing else had happened in my life, I'd be there in a shot. The work suited me, the guys were great. But I was bailing on Newcastle.

'You got a car yet? My brother-in-law's looking to sell his. Good price.'

I fudged and said I'd have a think about it.

Standing on the top of the hill, Newcastle spread out in front of me, the storm to the north giving way to clear blue sky again, it was a beautiful place to be. If I hadn't messed it all up by finding a box of drugs floating in the water, it could be the best place on earth.

The next conversation was going to be harder.

56
AIN'T OVER TILL IT'S OVER

'You can't be here.'

It wasn't exactly the response I imagined when I knocked on her door.

'Seriously. You have to leave.'

My expression must have been interpreted as 'let me in' because she barred the door with her foot.

'You have no idea what you've done.'

Now I was surprised and confused. 'Do you mean the –' Where did I start?

The next thing Karen was pulling me into her house with a quick look up and down the street. I was still no wiser as she paced before me, gnawing the side of her thumbnail. With a deep breath, she began.

'Lach, I've known it was you all along. From day one. Then it got complicated before I came to my senses and ... I could lose my job. You've compromised me. I compromised myself.'

'Karen, I have no idea what you're talking about.'

She started pacing again. Then she whirled around to face me, crossed her arms and blurted it all out. 'I know it was you. You. You're an abalone poacher. The DPI have been monitoring the waters around here for six months. We have you on tape in the act. My plan was to keep you under surveillance to find out who you were supplying. But then I had a big night and you woke up in my bed. The pressure for a result from my bosses caused me to have the brain fart to go undercover, unauthorised, get everything I could on you and your operation. Make a name for myself in the department. Then it got complicated. But we have all the evidence. You're done.'

I sat down. I'm not sure if I was shocked or if I found the whole thing hilarious. Until I saw that she was crying.

'Are you kidding? You were ... But we ... Isn't that entrapment?'

'All the evidence is from before we got together.' She buried her face in her hands. 'I'm a bad person. I feel awful. I thought I was doing my job. I had a lock-tight case. Then it got complicated ... I liked you,' she said through tears.

'I'm screwed.'

Here I was, having dealt with drug dealers, witnessed several murders and become privy to what had happened to some other colourful individuals, and now Karen was telling me I was about to be taken down for stealing some slimy, waterlogged leather called abalone? It was too much. I started laughing. She took it to be hysterics and went to fetch me some water. I drank it in one gulp as she wiped away her tears.

'That's why I told you. I really liked you. Thought we had a shot at something. So you need to leave. You've got till the end of the day.'

I handed back the empty tumbler. 'I think I'm in a lot of trouble.'

She nodded, believing she knew what I was talking about. As I went to the door, she gave me a farewell hug and the sort of kiss I'd expect from an auntie.

'Whatever you do, don't come back here.' She meant her

place. I took it to mean Newcastle.

'I won't tell them anything about you. I'll keep you out of it,' I offered.

She gave my upper arm a quick, reassuring rub and closed the door in my face.

Standing on the street, I could see she was still there behind the frosted glass. Then it hit me. This was it. There was nothing keeping me in Newie any more. I was well and truly done with the town.

Realising that was one thing. Actually stepping away was another. Having just experienced the most bizarre break-up in history, I wasn't really able to do anything. So I walked over the hill and down towards the channel. I saw the city and yet didn't see a thing. Karen had really done a number on me. Like so many times before, just when I was about to make a decision, the universe stepped in to force my hand.

Standing at the corner waiting for the pedestrian light to go green, I looked up from my mental chatter and saw an unmarked police car sitting at the lights. In the driver's seat was Detective Sergeant Jon Baxter. Next to him slumped his partner, Detective Shannae O'Keefe.

'Lach, heading somewhere?' Baxter called. 'Mind coming with us down to the station?' He reached behind him and popped the rear door.

My options were exhausted. There was no getting out of this one. I could have tried to run, done the Harold Holt, but where would I have gone?

Without a word, I dutifully climbed into the back of the car. It was a womb, a warm, protective shield from what was going on in Newcastle that the people walking the streets in the late afternoon sun were completely oblivious to.

Maybe it was an epiphany. That here, in the city known for surfing and shipping, underneath all the effort to clean itself up, the underworld was alive and well. Scratch the surface and if you knew where to look, there it was. Much like an abalone. You'd never spot one just swimming through the water, but once you were shown where to look, you'd see them easily. Crime, and the organisations behind it, were exactly the same.

'What you smiling at, Lach? You find the back of a police car humorous?'

'Exhaustion. Nothing more, detective.'

The two detectives shared a quick bemused glance as we approached the police station. I watched the boom gate to the carpark open and we drove inside. No escaping now until it spat me back out again. When that would be was anyone's guess. I was resigned to my fate.

At least, that was what I told myself as I sat in the interview room watching the two detectives set up the recorders and video camera. I'll defy anyone not to feel guilty sitting in an interview room as all that takes place.

Sure, I had been involved in a few things, but I was the aggrieved party, the one who was in trouble, the one who needed help.

Tapes and cameras ready to log it all, I decided to play my last card.

57
RETURN OF THE BEAST

'I want to do a deal.'

Detective Sergeant Baxter stopped and stared at me.

'That deal you offered me. I want to take it.'

He looked at his colleague, who raised her eyebrow. He straightened his paperwork in front of him. Without looking at me, he said, 'You tell us what you know and we'll make the assessment on how useful that is, yeah?'

'That wasn't what you said.' The offer had been made and I was standing on a burning building ready to leap. They knew it, I knew it. So I wanted all the mucking about to stop.

'Detective Sergeant Baxter, you offered to make me safe, to use me as an informant to share whatever I could find to back up your theory about the bikies and the drug trade. And you want a big collar to get yourself out of this town as much as I want all of this to be done. So let's just cut the crap so we can both get what we want.'

Baxter shifted uncomfortably and I realised then that when he'd made his offer, he had done so without authority. I'd just made it official.

'So what are you offering, Lach? Not that I'm in any position to promise anything,' he said.

So I told him. I went right back to the beginning and spilled my guts on everything I knew. How it had been going on for ages, who was involved, how it worked. I shared breakdowns on pricing, where the stuff came from, where it went. Even went so far as to tell him how I got started.

When I was done, I looked up at the two silent detectives.

'Lach, abalone poaching was not what I was interested in.'

'It's what I've been doing.'

'Right.' Baxter sat seething, arms crossed, eyes locked on me before he terminated the interview and his partner took over.

'Mr Lachlan Munro, this interview has now concluded. Has any threat, promise, or inducement been given to you either before or during your statement?' She wasn't looking at me. Her annoyance was directed at Baxter as she asked me if I had any complaints about how the interview had been conducted.

I said no and she excused herself from the room, leaving me alone with Baxter. Fury was not even close to what he was giving off. 'I don't know what you're playing at but we both know abalone poaching is not what I'm interested in. It's not even my jurisdiction. You've thrown me in a bucket of shit, paperwork and interdepartmental bureaucracy. So help me, I'm gonna come down on you like a ton of bricks, yeah?'

'You and I both know if you had something, anything that would stand up in court, you'd charge me.'

Without another word, Baxter left. Alone, I sat and wondered what my revelations might mean for any evidence they might have had, now that his promises and inducements were in the mix.

It took some time before O'Keefe returned with my record of interview. Dutifully, I did as instructed and read it through, initialling each page.

'Don't leave Newcastle, Mr Munro. Someone from the Department of Primary Industries will be in touch,' O'Keefe said, handing me a copy of the transcript.

Nodding, I took the material and shoved it under my arm, ready to leave.

'By the way. Highway Patrol picked up your car abandoned on the F3,' O'Keefe added.

The day suddenly looked brighter as I was ushered out into the corridor where Baxter stood, stewing.

'They think it was used in several petrol thefts from local petrol stations. They'll want to talk to you as well. You'll find them down the corridor, left, left, then right,' added O'Keefe.

'Like we give a shit,' Baxter snarled.

I stood there watching as the two detectives left to do whatever it is detectives do when they've completed an interview. The thought of all the follow-up paperwork they would now have to wade through was my only consolation.

Turning on my heel, I followed the directions to Traffic and Highway Patrol. How long my car had been there, I had no idea. Dutifully, I spent the next couple of hours answering questions and demonstrating that my car had been stolen before all of the dates it had been used for the petrol thefts. Finally, I was shown the door.

The Beast sat waiting in the parking lot. I looked it over: everything seemed to be there. Happy to be reunited, I climbed in behind the wheel. After having the accelerator pumped a couple of times, the Beast started first go, clearly happy to be going home. A cloud of blue exhaust smoke filled the yard and I took heart that it would somehow seep into the police station air conditioning and cause a stink right over Baxter. Some days, the simple pleasures are all you've got.

As I drove out over the speed humps, the temptation to point the bonnet towards the Pacific Highway was almost irresistible. But the reality of a life on the run stopped me. I was now busted and on record, two things I had worked so hard to avoid. Run and all of that would follow me, catching up at some point in the future and causing a whole lot more pain. When a break in the traffic appeared, I turned the Beast towards home to await my day in court.

58
SOMETHING FOR NOTHING

Court was no picnic.

No doubt assisted by the good Detective Sergeant Jon Baxter, they threw the book at me. They had no evidence that linked me with Billy Wong, funnily enough, but they had Dave's setup in his shed and the tanks in his boat, so they'd established that we'd been involved in poaching. Dave was seen as more of a low-level accomplice. His 'good' record meant he got to keep his job in the mines. I, on the other hand, had to endure my entire record being dug up and aired to all and sundry, making it seem like I was the ringleader. I guess Detective Sergeant Baxter had to get something right even if it did mean my mother was rolling in her grave.

In the end, I copped a crippling fine and a ban on all diving. I had to surrender all my scuba equipment. Dave lost his boat. And every day of the trial, I had to watch Karen sit with the prosecution.

It was a bit of a coup for the locals. Luckily, the good people of Newcastle embraced the trial as thoroughly entertaining – an old-fashioned example of sticking it to the man. While the papers painted me as the big bad poacher, locals would buy me a beer and deliver it with a quiet word of encouragement. Even Mario and Jess surprised me by leaving casseroles on my doorstep.

Having my name in the papers didn't help too much with the painting but Muzz kept me on the team and let me take time off for court when I needed to, which was a lot. For most of the trial he put me solo on a large new development that the project manager was in no rush to see done. I had about twenty apartments to slowly work my way through, prepping them for the all off-white and cream finishes that were to come, every apartment a version of the other, just oriented slightly differently to avoid peering neighbours and to maximise the views. The monotony was healing. By the time the trial was done, I was halfway through and grateful for the solitude.

About a month after the trial, during one of the more monotonous work days, my phone rang. Happy for the excuse to down tools, I answered without looking at who the caller was.

'Feel like a drink?'

Karen. Despite the elation that she'd called, my wounded pride forced me to play it cool.

'Stop being a dickhead, Lachie. Tonight at the pub on the headland.' She rang off.

The chance to see her again had me working double time to get the day's work done just that little bit earlier.

Home, showered and freshened up, I headed to the pub where I'd taken Karen months before on our first 'date'.

She was already there, waiting. As I walked up, she smiled. 'Been painting?' She pointed to just below her elbow.

I looked at my arm and saw the smudge of paint. There's always one that escapes detection. 'Busted.'

'So you're back at work then. Good to see you're keeping busy.'

I just nodded. Karen already had a beer waiting for me so she couldn't have been there long. It was great to see her like this again. We didn't talk that much, just idle chatter. Then she dropped the biggie.

'I wanted to apologise. Say I'm sorry.'

'Why?'

'I'm leaving Newie. Got a new job with CSIRO down in Sydney. That's why I called. Really have no one else here to say goodbye to.'

'Congratulations. On the move, not the no-friends thing.'

'The change will be good. This town has been getting to me. Once you see the underbelly of a place, it no longer seems all happy and sunny.'

I knew exactly what she meant. We talked some more about her new job, when she was leaving. She was moving out of her place that weekend. It was all happening too quickly. Not much of the rest of the conversation really went in. I did the polite nods and smiles but my head was ringing with how the entire episode had been one giant cock-up.

'Do you have a plan? Or are you still just going where the tides take you?' she asked.

Lost for words, I shook my head. I didn't have an answer. What was I going to do? Everything in Newcastle was kind of tapped out. I wasn't doing anything specifically Novacastrian and had no special loyalty to the town. What was keeping me here?

'I did like you. But you were breaking the law on my patch,' she said.

'Shame you're leaving. We could have had another shot.'

'Not a chance.'

Saying our goodbyes at the front of the pub, we were both caught by the view of the purpling sky and darkening grey of the sea.

'What is it about horizons? They don't really offer anything to look at other than …' Karen had her hands up like a fisherman indicating how big the fish that got away was.

'I guess they just give you something to aim for.'

The answer earned me a farewell kiss before I got to watch her walk away.

Melancholy is too strong a word for what I felt. But it took me some time to get home after that. By the time the first street lights were flickering to life against the evening sky, I was walking up my driveway. Which was when I realised that the place was unusually silent. The lights were off in Harry's, his radio wasn't playing. Harry always had a light on and the radio playing.

Puzzled, I let myself into my flat and knew straightaway that someone had been inside, even though everything seemed in its place. Then I saw it: an envelope with my name on it, leaning on the kitchen counter. My heart decided to relocate into my throat as I mentally ran through who could have left it.

It was a relief to discover it was from Harry.

Lad,

It's been weighing on my heart, but now it's done I felt you were owed an explanation. Especially since things have gone quiet and you've kept your nose clean. I found something of yours a while back under your sink. Not sure why I took it, but I did. And I felt bad about it ever since. In the end, worked out for the best. Hope you see it that way. I've left instructions with a mate, you can stay as long as you want – rent free. I'm gonna see the world. Spent too much of my life looking after boats that travelled and not travelling at all myself.

If our paths cross again, I'll shout you a beer.

Yours sincerely,
Harry Kinniburgh
P.S. Look in the freezer. I'd be hating you to think this was all something for nothing.

Doing as I was told, I opened the freezer with Harry's letter still in my hand. Sitting in front of my two-litre tub of neapolitan was a neat stack of fifty dollar bills, bundled up into lots of twenty. Reaching for the cold notes, I flicked them like a deck of cards. Twenty-five thousand.

Pulling up one of my milk-crate lounge chairs, I sat stunned, staring at the money. Twenty-five thousand. After everything I'd been through. Twenty-five grand?

Old Bloody Harry. *Harry* had done me over?

Fury raged through me. I scooped up all the bundles of money and threw them at the wall. They fluttered around me as if I was in a snow dome. Bloody Old Harry. He kept those cards close to his chest. As I started to pick up the thawing money, I shook my head and smiled. At least one of us had got something for nothing.

ABOUT THE AUTHOR

Andy Muir is a television screenwriter with credits ranging from *Neighbours* and *Home and Away* to comedy series *Thank God You're Here*. As a member of the writing team for the hit franchise *Underbelly*, crime stole his heart. Nominated for an Australian Writers Guild Award for *Underbelly Squizzy*, he also adapted that TV series for the novelisation *Underbelly Squizzy: The Story of Australia's First Celebrity Gangster*. Originally from Melbourne, he lives in Sydney. *Something for Nothing* is his first novel.

ACKNOWLEDGEMENTS

This is a work of fiction. Any resemblance to persons or events is pure coincidence. Newcastle is real, my story is not.

But I do need to thank all the cops and crooks who've shared their tales, along with everyone else living somewhere in between those two who have done the same. The world is an amazing place if you keep your eyes and ears open.

Thanks to the team at Affirm Press for their excitement and enthusiasm when they met Lachie Munro, especially Fiona Henderson who introduced me to her red pen along with Kylie Mason and her gentle queries. Special thanks also to those who answered research queries and general questions about Newcastle along the way. All errors, though, are my own.

I also want to thank those who read drafts when I was secretly wondering if I was simply lost in the backstreets of Newcastle with a guy called Lachie - Nick Price and Caroline van de Pol. Hearing you liked my world and characters was a huge boost and reassurance.

To all my family and friends who have been interested in where the book was at, here it is. I'm sad some of you are no longer here to see it.

To my agent Fran Moore, without whom this book would still be in the drawer, you are worth your weight in gold.

Lastly, and most importantly, thanks must go to Pip. None of my words would be possible without you.

Lachie Munro will return.